Vanity and Vexation

Vanity and Vexation

A Novel of Pride and Prejudice

KATE FENTON

Thomas Dunne Books
St. Martin's Press ≉ New York

THOMAS DUNNE BOOKS.
An imprint of St. Martin's Press.

www.stmartins.com

Library of Congress Cataloging-in-Publication Data

Fenton, Kate.
   [Lions and liquorice]
   Vanity and vexation : a novel of pride and prejudice / Kate Fenton.—
1st U.S. ed.
      p. cm.
   ISBN 0-312-32801-X
   EAN 978-0312-32801-6
   1. Austen, Jane, 1775–1817—Film and video adaptations—
Fiction. 2. Women television producers and directors—Fiction.
3. Television actors and actresses—Fiction. 4. York (England)—
Fiction. 5. Novelists—Fiction. I. Title.

PR6056.E54L56 2004
823'.914—dc22   2004041880

First published in Great Britain by Michael Joseph, Ltd.,
under the title *Lions and Liquorice*

First U.S. Edition: July 2004

10 9 8 7 6 5 4 3 2 1

With love to Sallie, Keith, Sam and my new godchild

Vanity and Vexation

Prologue

'Fairy tales?' shouted Nicholas Llewellyn Bevan into the telephone. 'You cannot in all seriousness be suggesting that what I write are –'

'Wish-fulfilment fantasies for superannuated schoolboys?' suggested his ex-wife.

'Spare me the girlie agit-prop.'

'Big prick, big gun, big busty broad?'

'Have you actually read any of my books?'

'I was speaking generally.' Her yawn gusted out of the receiver. 'Or do I mean generically? After all, a thriller is a thriller is a –'

'You're only speaking,' he hissed, tilting back in his chair and grabbing a book from the shelf above his head, 'to – to *one of the wittiest and most stylish exponents of the genre to emerge in recent years* . . . Just reading from my dustjacket, you understand. *Times Literary Supplement.*'

'I don't read the Murdoch press either.'

'*Playing on* . . . *Guardian*, this is, *playing on his readers' innermost fears with the skilful subtlety of a virtuoso.*'

'And earning less than if you were sawing a fiddle outside Brixton Tube.'

He glared at the telephone. 'Were you ringing for anything in particular, Caro? Or just to abuse me?'

'Well, someone's got to make you face economic facts, old friend, because –'

Nicholas Llewellyn Bevan slammed down the receiver so

hard it bounced out of its socket again. His word-processor screen blinked, the office geranium coughed pink petals over his hand, but Caroline's voice was still buzzing away.

'. . . not saying money's everything, but –' She broke off. 'Are you still there?'

He picked up the telephone again. 'No. I mean, possibly, but I'm not listening.'

'Did you ever? And don't grind your teeth. You won't get those crowns replaced on the National Health nowadays.'

'*What?*' But his roar fractured reluctantly into a laugh. 'Caro, you poison-fanged hag, I swear if you were two hundred miles closer I'd overcome the liberal scruples of a lifetime and throttle you.'

'Too late.' Her answering laugh was blithely unoffended. 'You've missed your chance of penning true confessions of a wife-strangler. Shame. Probably sell a million in these blood-lusty times. Are you writing now?'

'Course,' he snapped with the reflexive speed of an author chronically short of a plot.

'That bad, eh?' said his ex-wife equally promptly.

'I'm tossing several ideas round.' Tossing them into the cupboard under the geranium. The door gaped under the pressure of rotting manuscripts, stories which had sprouted swift as beansprouts, only to wither and die after a dozen or so chapters of labour-intensive, sweat-irrigated cultivation. Over coffee this morning, Nicholas Llewellyn Bevan had actually found himself wondering how, after a silence of many years, God would feel about a call from this inky sinner for a spot of editorial guidance.

Whereupon, on cue, the phone had trilled. Not the Almighty on the line, but Caroline. Who was now sighing. 'And you used to be such a good journalist.'

'Stick to insults, would you? Less wounding than your idea of a compliment.'

'Look, are you OK? Financially I mean?'

He automatically twitched a sheaf of bills out of sight. 'Fine. Anyway – anyway, the new book's out soon and George's got great hopes for it. Thinks this might be the big one.'

Caroline's voice sharpened. 'Has he interested anyone in telly? Film? I tell you, dramatization's your only hope of cracking the bestseller lists these days.'

'Give the guy a chance. The thing's not published until –'

'I thought not.'

'Besides, the publicity machine's only just cranking up.' So far he had been underwhelmed by a single invitation to appear on local radio. At nine o'clock on a Thursday night when, as he well knew, they'd be lucky if the listenership throughout North Yorkshire reached double figures. 'I'm doing a BBC arts show next week,' he declared, cunningly generous with the truth. He rummaged through his in-tray and, before Caroline could ask any pertinent questions, continued: 'Alongside Lavinia Stacey. Best-selling . . .' He winced. The very words 'best-selling' were as silver paper on the fillings of 'interesting newcomer' Nicholas Llewellyn Bevan. 'Best-selling author of –'

'I know who Lavinia Stacey is, prat. Plugging her latest searing saga?'

'Actually no. This one's called *Love Letters*.' Tracing the gold embossed title with an envious finger, he read: '*A practical guide to the writing of romantic fiction*. Seems she's sharing the secrets of her success with aspiring authors. The producer sent me a copy to gen up.'

There was a rude chuckle from the telephone. 'Looking for a few tips, are we?'

'Do me a favour,' said Nicholas Llewellyn (sophisticated master of suspense) Bevan loftily. 'Any old hack could churn out her brand of tosh.'

'Well, considering the money it makes,' replied his ex-wife with asperity, 'I'm amazed they bloody don't.'

Episode One

From *Love Letters* by Lavinia Stacey:

It is often said that Jane Austen created for us in *Pride and Prejudice* a timeless model of the perfect romantic novel. The heroine Lizzy, without being especially beautiful (her sister Jane is recognized as the beauty of the Bennet family) is lively, witty and thoroughly likeable. The hero, Mr Darcy, is not merely tall, dark and handsome, he is everything that a hero should be: strong, wise and high-principled. Older than Lizzy, naturally, he is also wiser in the ways of the world and of superior wealth and social standing. If his pride makes him a little daunting that can only add to his fatal allure. We stray from Miss Austen's recipe at our peril . . .

Scrawled in margin by N.L.B.: *Bollocks*

I

It is a truth universally acknowledged – at least according to certain shiny magazines – that a single actress in possession of fortune, fame and more work than she can handle, must be in want of *something*. Otherwise life wouldn't be fair, would it? And when that actress has reached the age of twenty-nine, it seems reasonable to assume she might be in want of a husband. Babies even. In fact, it would be nice to think she's secretly yearning for some plain, routine domesticity of the kind experienced by us ordinary mortals who read such magazines.

As it happens, this is pretty much what the celebrated and beautiful Ms Candia Bingham confessed. 'I long to be a mother,' she told Our Correspondent. While sitting on her elegant suede sofa in cashmere leggings and a luxury apartment overlooking the Thames. In London's fashionable Chelsea. 'I want to settle down and bake bread and make curtains and everything. I absolutely adore children. But, so far, I'm afraid Mr Right hasn't walked into my life.'

Mr Bernard Nuttall was studying this article during the quiet hour before noon in maroon polyester slacks and the saloon bar of his establishment, the Red Lion. Overlooking the green, in North Yorkshire's picturesque, but not noticeably fashionable, Maltstone. He was reflecting that he wouldn't mind assisting the nubile Ms Bingham along the road to motherhood. Were he twenty years younger. He blew the froth off his morning glass and drank deep before reapplying his finger to the print.

7

The magazine in which Candia Bingham was exclusively opening her heart and her wardrobe was not Bernard's regular journal. It had been shoved into his hands by Mavis from the post office. With a smug pursing of the lips, she had suggested Bernard study page seven, if he knew what was good for him. Interfering old know-all.

Bernard laboured down page seven – and eight and nine – even though he soon wearied of Ms Bingham's extensive career and couture. Finally, however, he hit gold.

'Sarah,' he roared, heaving his bulk up from the bar. 'Sarah, where are you? Shift your arse through here, you daft cow.'

It was some minutes before Mrs Nuttall consented to appear in the doorway from the kitchen. She was as thin as her husband was stout, with the wiry muscles and red hands of one who has laboured thirty years in the subterranean caverns of catering. Nevertheless, even in chef's trousers with her greying hair scraped up into a rubber band, she was a handsome woman with well-turned cheekbones and intelligent hazel eyes. She was wiping her hands on her apron as she glanced round the bar. Her brow wrinkled when she saw the stub-filled dish at Bernard's elbow.

'Finished your breakfast?' she enquired, plucking the ashtray away.

'Get a load of this.' Bernard was brandishing the magazine in front of her. 'It's here. Us.'

'I'd have a better chance of reading it if you put it down. Anyway, I've not got my specs.'

'I'm telling you. By, I nearly fell off my chair. This here Bingham bird – you remember her, pet, she were in that programme, hell, name's on the tip of my tongue, you were dead keen on it, all peacocks and nancy boys . . .' Bernard tossed the magazine aside. 'Doesn't matter, any rate. She's doing a new telly series now. And guess where they're filming?'

8

'This the dramatization of *Pride and Prejudice*, is it?' said his wife.

Bernard's blue eyes bulged. 'You knew?'

'They were talking about it in the butcher's yesterday. Llew was saying he hopes they're doing a decent job, because it's not the BBC. Some independent company.'

'Well, bugger me. Thanks for letting us know.'

Sarah Nuttall patted her husband's plump shoulder. 'You'll be seeing them down Haygate any day, from what I've heard. All the aerials and wires and what have you are coming down tomorrow. They're out top end of the valley now, turning the Pilkingtons' garden upside down with their cameras. Mind, they're paying old Colonel Pilkington a packet. *Supposedly*. One thing I know for a fact is that they're staying up at the Hall. Booked every room and Dorothy's in seventh heaven. I should think so too, with trade the way it's been.' This was said with feeling.

'Why didn't you tell me?' demanded her husband.

'What's it to us?'

'What's it to us? We're talking mega-media invasion of the village; this is the only pub with grub worth mentioning and you're asking me –'

'I do not,' interrupted Sarah frostily, 'serve *grub*. I run a restaurant. You, however, run a pub and it's opening time in ten minutes.' She wiped out the ashtray and, after replacing it on the bar, gazed at it thoughtfully for a moment. 'Then again, I suppose it might be nice for Llew. Bit of interesting company could be just what he needs.' She sighed. 'Though you can never tell.'

'Llewellyn Bevan? What's he got to do with anything?'

'I like Llew,' said Sarah flatly. 'And not just because when I give him *crêpes framboises* he doesn't say he'd sooner have lemon on his pancakes. Unlike some I could name. Poor boy's been looking miserable as sin recently. I reckon he's lonely.'

'Comes from locking himself away with a typewriter,' said Bernard. 'Not natural, is it? Anyway, there's always company down here.'

'Llew's clever,' stated Sarah as if this explained everything, adding rather wistfully: 'and he makes me laugh.'

'Bloody awful batsman.' Bernard emptied his glass down his throat in one well-practised gulp and let out a fruity belch. 'By gum though, this'll put some heart into the rest of the lads. Stand by Maltstone Lions for a boarding party of actresses.' He gave a throaty chuckle. 'Yo ho ho and all hands on dicks.'

'Bernard!'

'Mind, we mustn't let this put us off our stroke for the Valleys Cup.'

'Come again?'

Bernard rinsed his glass and began polishing it vigorously. 'Well-known fact: women and cricket don't mix. Saps the vital energies.'

'Then presumably your team's been working their way through the *Kama Sutra*,' said Sarah tartly. 'If their performance on the field's anything to go by.'

'Leave the gags to me, sunshine,' retorted Bernard. 'I'll bet our Chris is champing at the bit already. Where is he?'

'School, where else? Half-term doesn't start till Friday.' Sarah gathered up the magazine. 'Thank the Lord.'

'Where're you going?'

'I've two dozen steak and kidneys waiting for pastry, and the dairy orders to phone through.'

'I want you to get on to this television company,' he protested. 'Drop them a few brochures.'

'We've run out of brochures,' said Sarah. 'I told you last week there was only a handful left, but you forgot to order any new ones, didn't you?'

And, with a sweet smile, she retired to her kitchen.

2

The committee meeting of the Maltstone Lions Cricket Club was held, as always, on the last Thursday of the month in the pub from which the team took its name. Not surprisingly, given their recent playing record, the members soon abandoned cricketing business in the back room and adjourned to the Red Lion's public bar. Here, they fell to discussing the interesting new arrivals in the area.

There were hearsay reports of live thespians being sighted but no one present could offer eye-witness testimony. The wicket keeper, however, had personally spotted a convoy of vehicles lumbering along the top road at sparrow fart this morning – including a large grey lorry indisputably labelled British Broadcasting Corporation.

His scoop was spoiled by someone else pointing out that this bunch wasn't supposed to be the BBC.

'Independent company, co-production job, using BBC crews and facilities,' said Llew. 'I expect.'

Llewellyn Bevan – author, cricketer and regular – was hunched on a stool in the corner of the bar like a vulture on its favourite crag. A certain swarthiness in his colouring had, in his childhood, prompted mutterings from his Dad about Italian milkmen. Only for Mam to retort that her little prince with his sooty hair ('and eyes the colour of treacle, my lovely') was every inch a Valleys boy. And, to this day, his voice had not quite shed the accent of his coal-cutting fore-bears. Actually, strictly speaking, his father had worked in the

Co-op, but Llew was not a man to let mere facts muddy a poetic tradition. Stood to reason that if you were born and bred in South Wales there must be a few miners burrowing round the roots of the family tree.

A rangy, beak-nosed man, he was looking this evening both disgruntled (which was unusual) and disreputable (which was not). After all, a guy didn't quit the rat-racing city for rural North Yorkshire in order to sport tie and pinstripes, did he? And never mind if the cricketing farmers grouped round the bar were clad, to a man, in nattily monogrammed sports shirts. Llew fancied his shapeless, straw-tattered sweater was the epitome of bucolic suitability.

Since his city job had been in newspapers and he was even now a writer of sorts (although of what precise sort no one in the bar was entirely clear), his team mates evidently expected him to be well informed about television companies and suchlike exotica. But after that brief burst of erudition he disappointed them. No, he knew no one involved in the production. No, sorry, but he hadn't a clue if there were any famous names taking part – well, apart from Candia Bingham if Bernie was to be believed. And no, of course he didn't know if she herself was actually up here yet.. How should he?

'You're a fat lot of good, Llew,' said young Christopher Nuttall, pulling an expert pint and plonking it on the bar in front of him. 'Hey, I wonder if they're looking for extras?'

There was a chorus of whistling from the assembled cricketers.

'What's so funny?' protested Christopher, flushing.

'It's not children's television,' advised a voice from across the bar.

'I'm not a child,' he retorted. 'I'm seventeen and I can pass for twenty-one.'

This, thought Llew, was probably true. The boy, Bernard and Sarah's youngest son by many years, was already six feet tall and smoothly muscled as a panther. His fair hair flopped with fashionable decadence over one eye and his voice rumbled deep as a train in a tunnel. Only his face, which was almost girlishly pretty, showed his youth. He had inherited his mother's splendid cheekbones and (so she claimed) his father's stupendous bone-headedness. 'A guy at school got taken on in crowd scenes for an episode of *Country Doctor*. Sixty quid a day, can you believe it.'

Llew frowned. 'Correct me if my senile memory falters, lovely boy, but when you hogged my word-processor last holiday, wasn't this on the understanding that your towering talents were destined for the world of journalism?'

'So? This is television, isn't it? Contacts are everything in this business.'

'Thanks for the tip.'

'That's an idea, though,' continued Christopher, thrusting his hair out of his eye and leaning forward over the bar. 'Maybe I should try and line up an interview with Candia what's-her-name. What do you reckon, Llew?'

'What about?'

'Feature profile job. No, better, see if I can get her on tape. I mean, print media's dead, isn't it?'

'Along with grammar?' enquired Llew.

Christopher naturally disregarded this. 'You haven't got a decent tape-recorder I suppose? I'm meant to be starting my media project this half-term and I fancy the old steam wireless. Bit of a buzz getting a film star, eh?'

'Media project,' echoed Llew, wincing. 'Whatever happened to good old-fashioned A-levels?'

'They're not till next year,' said Christopher impatiently. 'Anyhow, where are they going to get me?'

'University?'

'What's the point?'

'The working world is a mean and *crew-ell* jungle,' Llew declared, rolling his words with a very Welsh relish. 'Qualifications are by way of being the mosquito net of the middle classes.' The sonority of this turn of phrase pleased him. He repeated it, smiling to himself.

'Huh,' said Christopher, unimpressed. He was prepared to argue the point, but Llew had turned towards the door.

'John! And about time too, you backslider. Well, don't hover on the doorstep, man. You're safe: all the trivial business is concluded and we're into the serious drinking. What're you having?'

The man who walked into the bar possessed what Llew had once defined, with barely a shimmer of malice, as knitting-pattern looks. John Hapgood was handsome in a broad-shouldered, square-jawed, fresh-complexioned, solidly English style which – unlike the haggard elegance of modern male models – might have been invented to display to advantage a cable-knit cardigan. What's more, his crinkled hair was the colour of hay and his eyes as blue as a postcard sea. That a certain elusive sadness shadowed his smile, and a few lines were chiselled in the noble brow and manly jaw, only added (in the view of most of the women of Maltstone) to his very considerable allure. He was also a useful spin-bowler and universally acknowledged Good Bloke. Such a Good Bloke was he that his cricketing colleagues were prepared to overlook his poncey public-school accent and his effect on their wives. He earned his living by restoring, designing and making furniture. His friend Llew spoke of him, with a respect bordering on reverence, as an artist in wood. He called himself a joiner.

'What've I missed?' he said, accepting a half-pint of cider and dragging up a stool besides Llew's.

'Sod all squared.' Llew lapsed back into ill humour. 'I've been mug enough to let them elect me secretary again, *pro tem* – which might not have happened if you'd turned up on time.'

'You're the writer,' said John tranquilly.

'Did the neighbours ask Picasso to touch up chips on their skirting boards?'

John grinned over the edge of his glass. 'And?'

'We've sorted the cock-up over the music for the hop, confirmed the friendly against Hopewell for Saturday, weather permitting – and that's about it. Far as I can see, our worthy captain's more interested in securing home fixtures in the pub with a visiting television company than cricket matches.'

'Aye, that's something to put the sparkle back in your eye, Johnny boy,' chipped in Bernard, non-playing Captain of the Lions, who was leaning on the bar beyond Llew. Bernard preferred, when possible, to run his establishment from the customer's side of the bar and regarded it as the prerogative (if not the bounden duty) of a genial host to intrude upon everyone else's conversations. He thrust himself between them, offering his cigarette packet to John, who waved it away, and then to Llew, who, with a guilty grimace, drew one out. 'By heck,' said Bernard, 'I'd give my right arm to be a young bachelor like you two now, with all these dolly-birds flocking in.'

Neither of the men was, in fact, a bachelor. Nor were they particularly young. John Hapgood, at thirty-five, was a widower of nearly three years' standing, and Llew Bevan a thirty-four-year-old divorcee. They exchanged glances, and Llew lit his cigarette from the stub of Bernard's before enquiring: 'Where are they then? All these gorgeous women?' He glanced round. 'Looks like the same old butch faces to me.'

Bernard's face fell. 'Where d'you think, Taff? Up Maltstone bloody Hall, paying through the nose for gold bath taps and raspberry vinegar on their lettuce. I tell you, if we could just get 'em down here for a few dinners on their fancy expense accounts . . .' He sighed longingly, 'I reckon Her in the kitchen and yours truly'd be booking for Florida come July.'

'That'll be the day,' remarked his wife who, unobserved, had emerged from the dining room and was standing at her husband's elbow. 'Thirty-two years of marriage and the nearest we've got to America is a paddle off Penzance.'

'Fancy Florida, do you, Sarah?' enquired Llew.

She considered the question. 'Sooner have Florence. But I'd go anywhere someone else is cooking.'

Bernard squeezed her shoulders. 'Did you get on to them printers?'

Sarah shook her head.

'Blimey, woman. How'll they know where to come if we don't tell 'em?'

'They'll find their own way. The whole county knows about Sarah's cooking,' said Llew, smiling at her.

His slightly crooked smile always had just such a conspiratorial air, like an invitation to share a private joke, and Sarah returned it warmly. 'Are you coming in tomorrow night, love?' she enquired.

'Course not,' grunted Bernard. 'He's over the village hall. Can't have the cricket club disco without the secretary making sure everyone's present and incorrect.'

She frowned. 'Damn, I'd forgotten.'

'What about you, Johnno?' said Bernard.

'Tomorrow?' John glanced up warily. 'Lord knows. I don't want to be anti-social but I've a stack of work and –'

'Rubbish. A good bop's what you need. Tek you out of yourself a bit.'

'A *bop*?' echoed Christopher from behind the bar. 'How sad can you get. Let's twist again like we did last century . . . Well, you can count me out for one.'

'There are times,' said Llew soulfully, 'when I feel very old. Very old and very alone in this modern world.'

'Give over moaning,' said Sarah. 'Next you'll be telling me all you need is the love of a good woman.'

'Ah, *cariad*. If only you'd have me . . .'

'Bad woman more like,' said Bernard. 'And you can keep your lonely mitts off my missus.'

'Llew and I have an understanding,' said Sarah. 'I'm his mother-confessor figure.'

'And I'm fighting my Oedipus complex,' agreed Llew. 'I'll turn up at the disco if you'll dance with me, darling.'

'The last waltz – if you're lucky. I've a busy dining room tomorrow.' There was a lilt in her voice which made Llew eye her curiously.

'Rubbish,' said Bernard. 'One lousy four and a pair of twos last time I looked in the book.'

'Didn't I mention it?' Sarah's air of innocence was profoundly unconvincing. 'I dropped in at the Hall this afternoon to lend Charlie my big fish kettle. Although why Dorothy won't buy him a decent one of his own, with the number of salmon he has to cook is –'

'Bugger the fish,' cried her husband. 'You called in at the Hall. And?'

'Oh, there were a few people drinking out on the terrace. From the television company, I guessed. Well, obviously they were because I recognized that Candia Bingham.'

'The girl who was in the film about Cambridge spies?' exclaimed John. 'I say, she's terrifically good.'

Bernard waved him to silence, his eyes fixed on Sarah. 'So?'

'Well,' she said with maddening slowness. 'Someone did happen to ask what I was doing with a damn great fish kettle under my arm . . .' She stretched out her fingers on the bar and smiled down at them. 'And, one way and another, there's a party booked in for dinner tomorrow. Four, possibly more. I said not to worry about exact numbers.'

'Tomorrow?' wailed Bernard, dashed. 'But I've got to be over at the dance.'

'No, have you? What a shame. Ah well . . .' Sarah's smile broadened contentedly. 'We'll just have to struggle along without you, won't we?'

3

Maltstone, bigger than many villages but by no means a town, trickles haphazardly along a green valley between hazy, moor-topped hillsides. Once, beyond even the longest living memory, its broad principal thoroughfare housed a bustling weekly market. Now the settlement can boast only a post office, a general stores, a butcher and three gift shops, the largest of which is housed in the handsome old Fire Station – Devon fudge and Irish tea towels being more vital to a local economy these days than anti-incendiary appliances.

At the heart of the village, stone villas flank a chestnut-fringed green. On Friday, as golden afternoon softens into blue evening, Bernard Nuttall can be seen crossing and recrossing the shaggy grass at an anxious trot. On one side of the green the mullioned windows of the Red Lion tranquilly mirror the glow of the sky. On the other, the gabled wooden hut which serves as the village hall flickers and twangs fitfully with the testing of discothèque equipment.

Follow the River Malt upstream, beyond the churches – squat stone Anglican and soaring brick Catholic nose-to-nose across the road – and continue round the village school whose windows are presently festooned with crêpe-paper sunflowers. Then turn sharp left at the cattle grid, climb the hill for half a mile or so, and you will reach Cote Green Farm.

It is evident this jumble of lichened stone buildings no longer functions as a farm. Too tidy. Besides, there are chintz curtains behind windows in what must once have been the cowshed and potted plants line the stone steps up to a former hayloft. This loft, tastefully sky-lighted, rough-plastered and open beamed, is Llew Bevan's office.

No light shone in the office that evening however. Llew's angular face could be seen contorting itself behind a lower window as he shaved. The telephone rang, the razor slipped and he cursed loudly before thumping into his kitchen.

'Oh George, hi. No – no, fine. Just cutting my throat.'

'My dear boy.' The voice of Llew's literary agent was as portly as his person. If a voice can be imagined sporting a jauntily knotted, maroon-spotted silk bow tie, then this was such a voice.

'I was shaving. Mind,' added Llew, 'that's not to say I won't be applying the carving knife to my jugular any day now.'

There was a cough of Jeevesian delicacy from the telephone receiver. 'Woman?'

'Chance'd be a fine thing. D'you call for anything in particular?'

'Just to enquire . . .' his agent's voice paused tactfully, 'how the new masterpiece was coming along.'

Llew scowled at the phone. 'Consigned to the rejects cupboard last week. Along with its brothers.'

'Oh dear.'

'George, I've got a writer's block the – the size of a Henry Moore.'

'Not, if you'll forgive me, one of your more striking metaphors.'

'Thanks.'

'Chin up. It's like riding a bicycle.'

'I don't think I've exactly forgotten the knack.'

'No, no. After a fall, essential to get straight back on.'

'Isn't that horses?'

'Otherwise,' continued George, ignoring him, 'one can

lose one's nerve. You must get back to that machine and write. Anything, just to keep the creative juices flowing.'

Llew grinned evilly. 'Poetry?'

George made a rude retort forgivable in a literary agent with one present and two former wives to maintain.

'How about a letter to the bank manager then?' enquired Llew. 'Reassuring him that your selfless labour of lunching every executive producer in the English-speaking world has finally borne fruit – and that film and television rights will be pouring in to plug the leaking overdraft?'

'That's my boy,' said George comfortably. 'Stick to fiction.'

Across a tidy, tub-strewn expanse of gravel which had once been a muddy farmyard stands Cote Green Barn, now the home of John Hapgood. A similarity of style inside barn and farmhouse arises from John having been responsible for the renovation of both. He had first lavished labour, paint-stripper and rolled steel joists on the farmhouse. This he inhabited with his wife, until she cycled into the path of a careless lorry driver. Unable to bear a house empty of her but full of memories, he had thrown his energies into converting the barn. Llew, divorcing, and with neither the will nor the skill to wield his own Black and Decker, was looking for just such a ready-made writer's retreat. They had been neighbours – and friends – ever since.

This was in spite of having little in common. John, young-est son of a family of Surrey stockbrokers, had followed public school with a short and wretched stint in the City. This, he said, might have been more successful had he been able to add up. Having, among other un-glittering career moves, sold ice-creams on Brighton Pier and chicken dung in Scotland, he eventually found serenity in Cote Green Farm and a potter wife, and his vocation – in wood.

Llew, by contrast, had hurried from grammar school

through Manchester University to a local newspaper in that city. By his late twenties, bets were being placed by his *Manchester Evening News* colleagues on how young he'd make editor of a national daily. Whereupon, with a perversity which enraged his equally high-flying wife, he had quit papers to try his hand at writing novels. At least now, he said loftily, he could legitimately recognize what he penned as fiction. His two published thrillers, however, had earned more acclaim than money. His income, he had recently calculated, was comparable to that of a bus conductor. Minus sickness, pension and holiday benefits. This he reluctantly supplemented when necessary (which was often) with freelance features for the local press. His agent George maintained a sturdy faith in his prospects. His wife did not. The marriage had dissolved and Caro was now in London, editing a well-known women's magazine.

Single heterosexual men over the age of thirty being (as is well known) rare as diamonds in a coal mine, neither John nor Llew was bereft of female friends. And, while John was undeniably the handsomer of the two, some women had been known to claim they preferred Llew. The short-sighted ones, he assumed. They were charmed not so much by his treacly Celtic eyes, nor even by his neatly sculpted bottom (though this had attracted admiration in its time) as by his wayward sense of humour. Or so he liked to think. Neither man, however, had a regular partner. Nor even, as Llew complained, an irregular one.

In fact, Llew, in his bleaker moments, had been known to grumble that the pair of them were bedding down into middle age together with the cosy incompatibility of Mr and Mrs Jack Sprat. John rose with the birds, Llew worked bat hours. John played folk guitar, privately, soulfully, and rather well; Llew, jazz clarinet, noisily, publicly, and on the whole badly. John was a gardener. It was he who tended the pots and flowertubs round the yard. Llew had few practical skills beyond cooking, on which he prided himself, whereas John filled himself with food as unenthusiastically as he fuelled his car with petrol. Fair and dark; a stoical, reserved Anglo-Saxon and a volatile, gregarious Welshman; they were bound as much as anything, perhaps, by a passion for their own work, and a considerable admiration for each other's.

As Llew returned to his shaving mirror, he could see John in the open door of his workshop across the yard. He was kneading a waxy rag into the dull surface of a refectory table he'd picked up in a sale. His huge hands caressed the wood with the tender passion of a lover, thought Llew, not for the first time. The man took a visible – dammit, almost an erotic – pleasure in his labours. Pity there wasn't a woman in John's life to soak up some of that same tender loving care, he thought. Not for the first time.

'Couldn't Llew take you, then?' John said, not raising his eyes from his task. He was talking to Christopher Nuttall who, in jeans and seriously black sunglasses, was leaning against a bench at the back of the workshop chewing gum.

'Jazz Club,' retorted Christopher with disgust. 'He says. And Dad can't leave the bar. And there are no rotten buses Saturday night.'

John continued waxing, blowing a wisp of sawdust out of his path, tracing the grain with strong careful strokes. 'Why is it so vital you get into Ebcaster anyway?'

'I *told* you. This bloke from Radio Dales is having a party at Uncle Ernie's pub.'

'You're under age,' said John mildly, smiling down as golden life began to shimmer under his hands.

'I work in Dad's bar, don't I?' said Christopher exasperatedly. 'Anyway, I'll drink Ribena if it makes you happy. This is business, OK? It's a chance to meet some of these guys, chat them up. See if they'll let me hang around the station a bit this week. Uncle Ernie reckons they take on a stream of kids from the DSS. I mean, it's only *local* radio, sure,' he added, with unconvincing cool, 'but a guy has to start somewhere. It's really important, John. Look, do you want a hand?'

'Not like that,' said John, appalled, as the boy picked up a rag and started scrubbing. 'You have to coax the shine up.'

'You've shown me often enough,' muttered Christopher. But he discarded gum and sunglasses, rolled up the sleeves of his sweatshirt and, when he resumed, measured his strokes more carefully to John's.

John watched him for a few moments. 'That's more like it.' He stretched and yawned. 'Thing is, Chris, I'd like to help, honestly, but I've so much work on. A set of chairs, a garden bench, your mother's been waiting ages for her bookcase –'

'She won't mind waiting a bit longer then.'

'And,' continued John firmly, 'I can't even finish this table tonight because I feel I've got to show my face, at least, at the hop.'

'Tell you what,' said Christopher cunningly, 'why not let me finish the polishing for you now, while you go off to the wrinklies' rave? Llew's waiting for you, look.'

'Well . . .' said John.

'Then you can run me into town tomorrow. Deal?'

At that moment Llew's voice floated across the yard, asking whether they were going to this bloody do or not. And if so, who was driving.

'We can walk, can't we?' bellowed John.

'I hate health freaks,' shouted Llew.

'Give me ten minutes. Quick shower.'

'Deal?' repeated Christopher hopefully.

'What?' John hesitated. Christopher, peering up from the table leg, looked all at once very young. Eager as a fledgling for a scrap of worm. 'Oh, OK. Drop the latch when you're through. Mind, I want that table looking like a mirror when I get back.' He wiped his hands on his trousers as he strode across to his kitchen door. 'With you in a minute, Llew.'

'Just call me Cinders,' said Christopher cheerfully as the two men strolled out of the yard a little later in a fragrant miasma of shampoo and shaving soap. 'Home not a second after midnight, mind. And I hope you've left some beer in the fridge.'

4

Bernard stomped through the louvred swing doors into the kitchen of the Red Lion. 'They're not coming,' he moaned.

The party from Penhaligon Television had booked their table for eight o'clock, and might thus have been expected to be swigging aperitifs in the bar long since. Bernard had produced bowls of black olives and Japanese crackers in their honour. It was now half past eight, however, this was his third foray back from the dance, and the bar was as empty as the cracker bowls. Empty of strangers, at any rate. A handful of regulars lingered, claiming they were waiting for the disco to warm up before they decamped across the green. They were waxing witty about Bernard's much-advertised celebrity guests: 'What're they filming then – *T'Invisible* bloody *Man?*'

'They'll be along in their own good time,' said his wife, imperturbably. She tasted a sauce, pursing her lips. Aproned girls with salad bowls and bread baskets bustled round her. 'Get back over to the hall, for goodness' sake, Bernie, see to your disco and –' She broke off, cocking her head to one side. There was a murmur of laughter, the distant slamming of car doors.

'Bingo,' said Bernard. He hitched up his trousers and prepared to enter the restaurant.

'Not in those muddy shoes, you don't.' Sarah was barring the door like St Peter at the Pearly Gate. 'Besides, I've umpteen starters going out and I don't want you under the girls' feet. On your bike.'

Bernard's mouth sagged open. 'Sarah, love?'

'You heard me.'

There were times when his wife was not to be argued with. The Rock of Gibraltar was as putty in comparison. Bernard, indignantly promising himself that *nothing* would keep him from his rightful post next time this lot dined, trudged back to the village hall and soon forgot his disappointment riffling through the records imported by the hapless disc jockey (way-out load of rubbish) in search of some proper party music.

'Water, water every where Nor any drop to drink,' sighed Llew, eyeing the heaving dance floor.

'Since when did you drink water?' enquired John.

'I was speaking meta-bloody-phorically, wasn't I?' He twirled lukewarm lager round a plastic beaker. 'What am I doing here, that's what I want to know. What's the point?'

'Village events and all that. Got to do our bit.'

Llew scowled. 'Tell me, sonny boy, were any of your illustrious ancestors missionaries?'

'Matter of fact, I believe Great-uncle . . .' John broke off. 'Why on earth do you ask?'

'I have a vision of a nineteenth-century version of you in moustache and solar topee, leading the cannibals in a quick chorus of *Cwm Rhondda* even as you stewed in the pot. "Just supporting native customs, old chap . . ."'

'Balls. Everyone's having fun, aren't they?'

'I dare say,' retorted Llew. 'And, were I eighteen, I too might be tripping the light fantastic with a gladsome heart. And why? Because at that age you know damn well what a Friday night hop's for: getting pissed or getting laid. Preferably both. At my advanced age, the options have narrowed to one. And I can't afford to drink.'

'That's no way to talk.' Julie, barmaid for the evening, leaned between them. 'Do us a favour, John love, and take this Campari over to our Cheryl. Her old man's buggered off and she's a lost soul.'

'The redhead?' John, naturally, was picking up the glass with a polite smile.

'There goes the original boy who can't say no,' murmured Llew, watching his friend shoulder a path across to the abandoned Cheryl, who stubbed out her fag and patted the bench beside her with quite un-lost alacrity. 'And never says yes, either.' He raised his voice. 'You shouldn't do it, Julie. Cruelty to innocent females.'

'If she's innocent, I'm Queen of Siam,' she said. 'And they're both looking for a bit of company, aren't they?'

'Aren't we all?'

'So quit griping and get out there, kid.'

Llew grinned but shook his head. The blessing of village life is that you know everyone and everyone knows you. The curse of village life is exactly the same. The teensiest, tipsiest peccadillo guarantees celebrity status in the local soap opera. Women, women everywhere – and every last one somebody's daughter, neighbour, mother, wife . . .

That is not to say that when his marriage had cracked Llew had not boozed and screwed a truly Hogarthian path through the dark days. But that had been in a city. Moving here had restored him to sense and (relative) sobriety.

He glanced at John, who was chatting to pretty Cheryl on the bench. The guy looked for all the world like a visiting vicar about his parochial duties. No, on second thoughts, make that a priest. If ever a man was vocationally celibate . . .

Well, Llew dared say the death of a wife couldn't be compared with mere divorce. Unlike him, John hadn't ranted and rampaged. According to all accounts he hadn't even wept, and to this day he never uttered Sally's name. It seemed he had shut a door on that part of his life. His stoicism had been admired locally at the time, but was all too soon taken for granted as evidence of recovery. And yet, that he was still bleeding – as devastated by his loss as any man could be – Llew was certain. His instincts screamed it. A sense for other people's feelings, uncomfortably acute as an emotional geiger-counter, had made Llew both a good journalist and a reluctant one. He never again intended to ask the frozen-eyed mother of a dead child how she felt.

As for John, well, he might have retreated inside the precision-mannered armour of your middle-class Englishman, but Llew, for one, was not fooled. Possibly the only one, however.

John strolled back to the bar, oblivious of Cheryl's hungry gaze following him.

'You could've asked her for a dance,' said Julie, disappointed.

The alarm in John's face was comical. 'Haven't danced in years. Anyway – anyway, it's not the most brilliant music, is it?'

'You're not kidding.' Llew drained his beaker. 'And I've had enough of this pigswill. Having done our bit for village life – God bless her and all who sail in her – can we call it a night? My soul thirsts for civilized music and fine whisky.'

John raised an eyebrow. 'Your idea of civilized music, or mine?'

'Folk isn't music,' retorted Llew. 'It's noisy anthropology. But I'd put up with a whole orchestra of Peruvian nose-flutes for a decent malt, if you have such a thing. My own drinks cupboard is quite unaccountably bare.'

John smiled faintly. 'Never.'

'And I suspect Bernie's about to hi-jack the turntable and then Heaven help us.'

'I'll finish this lager and we'll push off, OK?'

'Now then, ladies and gents . . .' Bernard had indeed scrambled on to the stage and was elbowing the disc jockey away from the microphone. With an ear-torturing screech he whizzed the needle off the record. 'Testing, testing,

ONETWOTHREEFOUR. There's this Englishman, Irishman and Scotsman . . . No, seriously. The time has come, the walrus said, to get things going with a swing. Ladies, this is your big chance. All girls on the floor please, and that includes you, Tracey Bullock. Now, gents, shut your eyes. No peeping. Ready? Girls, take three paces forward. Turn to your right. Two paces, then –' Bernard broke off, peering at the back of the hall. 'Hey-up, do I see strangers?'

John, silly prat, was frozen with his eyes closed. Llew naturally skewed round to look at the door. And caught his breath. Dammit, how often had he gazed at that face ten feet tall on a cinema screen? Even in the flickering disco light there was no mistaking Candia Bingham. It wasn't that she was startlingly beautiful. Pretty, certainly, with a froth of fair curls, a forehead high as a medieval Madonna's and an absurd button of a nose. What made her so lusciously and irresistibly watchable, though, was the animation in those less-than-perfect features. Llew had rarely seen a face more alive – at this moment with curiosity. She was beckoning into the hall after her two youngish guys, both of whom exuded so much metropolitan chic Llew could almost smell their leather jackets. One of their sharply carved profiles, at least, looked familiar from the box. Finally, lagging several reluctant yards behind, they were followed by a veritable Amazon. Llew was quite sure he didn't recognize her. Toweringly tall and Roman-nosed, streaming yards of dark, poker-straight hair, she wasn't the sort you'd forget in a hurry. She froze in the doorway, eyeing the rustic revels with all the enthusiasm of a vegan visiting a battery farm.

'Well hello, hello. You've arrived just in time for the Ladies' Excuse Me. Come right on down,' bellowed Bernard with relish. 'Gents, keep your eyes shut. Girls, grab the nearest fella. Go on,' he roared, pointing straight at Candia Bingham. 'Get in there, girl.'

Llew pulled a face, half amused, half embarrassed. But to

her credit the actress only grinned, chucked her bag and jacket on to a bench and turned to her companions. The men promptly backed away, miming horror. She thrust two fingers up at them, shook back her curls and looked round. Before Llew had the wit to compose his most winning smile, however, she had strolled over to John and tapped him on the shoulder.

'May I?' she enquired. Even in two words, that honey-soaked croak of a voice was unmistakable. And John's face, as he opened his eyes and found himself gazing down into Candia Bingham's famously delicious smile, was a picture. Llew nearly laughed aloud. For a moment, the lad could only gape, stupid as a landed fish. Then he flushed purple.

'I should jolly well think so,' he said, seizing her arm and steering her on to the dance floor.

Llew shrugged and turned back to the bar. About to order another lager, he decided he deserved a consolation prize and asked for a large Scotch instead. With a packet of crisps.

'Whoever's that with our John?' demanded Julie, indignation warring with maternal fondness. 'He told me he weren't dancing.'

'Swept off his feet. By an invading film star.'

'Never.' She peered over his shoulder. 'He is and all.' After a few moments she added wonderingly: 'He's a grand little mover too.'

Watching the dancers, whisky in hand, Llew acknowledged with surprise and not a little envy that John was indeed – for a large man – nifty on his feet. No bashful shuffling for him and the vivacious Miss Bingham, they were already jiving. Soon John was chucking her to and fro with the easy assurance of a lumberjack wielding an axe.

'Fantastic,' she panted when the music slackened briefly and they swirled up beside Llew, shiny-faced and jubilant.

'Drink?' gasped John, but she shook her head.

'Let's get back out there,' she said, locking her arm into

his. 'You're the best partner I've had in years. Can we get him to play some more Elvis? Mary, *Mary!*'

Her long-nosed, long-haired friend was chatting in a desultory way to the two men at the far end of the bar. Neither drinking nor dancing, the glum-faced trio had glanced occasionally towards the floor with the air of adults at a chimpanzees' tea party, prepared to be indulgent provided it didn't go on too long. Llew didn't hold this against them. While he was obliged to be glad for John, he felt much the same.

'. . . should have introduced you,' John was saying now. 'This is Llew. Llew, Candia.'

She dazzled him with a quick smile before renewing the assault on her friends. 'Get on to the floor, you miserable sods. That's it, you make them.' This encouragement was aimed at a pair of blushing, mini-skirted girls who, with beermats and biros in hand, were elbowing each other forward. The two men, exchanging wry glances, nevertheless scribbled their autographs as requested and then allowed themselves to be peeled off the wall to dance. 'And you, Mary.'

The tall woman turned towards them very slowly, raising her eyebrows. A llama, thought Llew, that was it. She had exactly that animal's air of leisurely superiority. 'I'm too old for this sort of thing,' she said. Her accent wasn't English. American maybe? 'Anyway, it's too late. Roddy and Patrick have dumped me.'

'So?' Candia Bingham grinned at Llew. 'Sorry, what did you say your name was? You'd like a dance, wouldn't you?'

'I feel pretty old too,' he replied, raising his voice to reach the tall woman called Mary. 'And I'm more a jazz man than a rock and roller, but . . .' This time he was prepared. He was beaming his Friday-night-best, knock-'em-dead, two-hundred-watter, straight across at her. De Niro moody, he flattered himself, with just an endearing twinkle of Dudley Moore.

The llama didn't actually spit. She stared at him measuringly for a minute, then turned her back.

'You do talk rot,' began John but the speakers were twanging and he was yanked away by a whooping Candia.

Llew resigned himself to a long wait for the Glenmorangie.

5

A chill early morning sun glinted on the River Malt, a young pheasant skittered balletically along his garden wall – but Llew Bevan did not notice. A tidal wave and a platoon of tap-dancing ostriches would have passed the hayloft unremarked. Amidst a rubble of books, magazines and old newspapers, he was cross-legged on the floor, thumbing through, of all unlikely publications, a tattered paperback of *Pride and Prejudice*.

He was unshaven and a touch bleary-eyed. At the advertised closing hour of eleven-thirty, the disco had still been roaring. By then, however, Llew had forgotten the whisky bottle at home and was actually hoping Bernard would keep the joint buzzing for a few dances more.

This change of heart had nothing to do with John, although no friend could fail to be touched by his antics last night. Touched and amazed. Frankly, Llew could hardly have been more astonished if Sir Osbert Ramsbottom had tripped in from his plinth in the churchyard to shake a marble leg. Maybe this was what John had needed all along: a woman bold enough to storm those impenetrably polite defences – hell, Candia Bingham hadn't even noticed 'em. She'd just swooped down and closed her pearly talons round his wrist. And, as the evening progressed, she showed no sign of letting go. Well, good luck to him, Llew had thought at the time. Jammy bugger.

Nevertheless, his friend's interests had not been uppermost

in his mind as he combed the dance floor. He had been searching for the llama. Whose name, he had learned, was Mary Dance.

'Dunno what she's done, though,' his informant remarked, going on to describe in detail a role played by the male actor jigging nearby in a recent episode of *Casualty*.

But Llew did know what Mary Dance had done. The name made him choke on his crisp. If it was *that* Mary Dance, and he didn't suppose there were two in the industry. Her accent was surprising, though, because he'd always assumed Ms Dance was a home-grown phenomenon.

Llew, it should be said, had been a movie-buff since his mother force-fed him aniseed balls through three consecutive nights of *The Sound of Music*. These days, living far from the multi-screen complexes of big cities, he saw more crits than movies and he had read plenty about Mary Dance. Didn't a film she directed for Channel Four a few years back take the American box office by storm? And surely he recalled other triumphs? Mary Dance was a name to conjure with. This morning, he'd begun by rummaging fruitlessly through reference books and the film press in search of her, but the books were too old, the selection of newsprint too random. Nevertheless, the very fact that this latest so-called saviour of British cinema was here in Maltstone, shooting *Pride and Prejudice*, was inspiring him to renew his acquaintance with Jane Austen.

Last night, dazed by the discovery of her identity, he had plunged into the crowd to find her with enough alcohol washing round his veins to obliterate any qualms about what he might actually say to this six-foot wunderkind. Fortunately, perhaps, he could not locate her. Candia Bingham was twirling under John's arm and her actor chums were mooching round the perimeter in an admiring gaggle of girls. But Mary Dance?

'Looking for a partner?' Llew had glanced round to find Sarah at his elbow.

'No,' he murmured distractedly. 'I'm –'

'Good,' she said. 'Julie wants to pack the bar up and if we don't give her a hand . . .' She nodded at the stage where Bernie was flapping his elbows, urging everyone on to the floor for the Birdie Dance, 'the old bugger'll be here all night.'

So it was that Llew was on his knees behind the bar, stacking goblets into boxes when he overheard Candia's distinctive voice cry: 'Mary! Where on earth have you been?'

'Walking round the green to get the smoke out of my goddamn hair.' (Definitely American: anglicized East Coast.) 'Can we go now?'

Llew, his fists bristling with glasses, glanced up helplessly.

'Don't be such a misery guts,' said Candia. 'Join in and dance, can't you?'

Llew promptly shed the glasses and prepared to rise.

'For Chrissake, Candia,' he heard Mary Dance retort. 'I've been working my balls off since five this morning. Roddy and Patrick might enjoy having their egos massaged by the local jail bait but I've better things to do than be groped by some beer-bellied yob flashing his bum crack.'

Llew ducked and twitched his waistband.

'The one I'm dancing with hasn't got a beer belly,' protested Candia, outraged. 'He's edibly bloody gorgeous. And –'

'OK, OK, your little friend's Adonis in Blue Jeans. So go have your ball and leave me in peace, will you?'

'That guy who was with him: dark, Italianish. Where's he got to?' Llew, who had surfaced from behind the bar, now cleared his throat. But the women had their backs to him and didn't respond. 'I thought he looked quite interesting,' said Candia.

'Halfway presentable,' yawned Mary Dance. 'If you like that kind of thing, and frankly –'

''Scuse me,' said Sarah, bustling up with a tray of glasses

and the two women moved away without a backward glance. 'Don't stand there gawping, you great lummock,' she told Llew fondly. 'Take these, can't you?' The disc jockey, having wrested control of the microphone from Bernard, was announcing the last dance. 'Thank the Lord,' murmured Sarah, hurrying off again.

The lights dimmed and out of the corner of his eye Llew saw Candia nudging John into the shadow of a barricade of stacked chairs. Her head was snuggled into his broad shoulder and her hands locked behind his neck. Next thing, she had lifted her face with unmistakable intent, pulled his head down and they were kissing. *Kissing?* Llew whistled softly. He could almost see lightning snapping blue across the smoky gloom of the floor. He was surprised nearby dancers weren't stunned by stray voltage.

'Where is he then?' Bernard puffed up beside him. 'Prancing round all night with that lass like Torvill and bloody Dean.'

Llew blinked. 'Sorry?'

'Our John. Someone wants to tell him he shouldn't be wasting his time dancing, not with an armful of –'

'Gone,' said Llew, recovering his wits smartly. Mary Dance was not to be seen, but the duty of a friend was only too evident. 'How about a last one for the road over at your place before I, um, follow him home?'

'Fine,' responded Bernard, but he was still scouring the room.

'Did you see the vicar's wife then?' said Llew, edging him determinedly towards the door. 'Tangoing with Larry the milk?' And by way of diversionary tactics he was giving a spirited impersonation when he stumbled into a black-booted foot, staggered, grabbed wildly – and found he was clasping Mary Dance's tall, thin figure. She said nothing as, mumbling apologies, he released her. Just eyed him with faint, chilly astonishment and stepped back to let them pass through the door.

'Who's that snotty piece?' enquired Bernard in a resonant *sotto voce* as they quit the hall.

Llew groaned. 'Only the answer to a starving writer's prayers.'

'Blimey, you don't fancy her, do you?'

'I didn't mean that,' he retorted impatiently. 'She's . . . Oh, never mind. And no, I damn well don't fancy her.' He gave a bark of laughter. 'Wouldn't matter if I did.' And, as they strolled across the green, he repeated Mary Dance's verdict on him.

'Halfway presentable? She's no room to talk,' roared Bernard. 'Miserable bloody maypole. It isn't like she was even *famous* or owt.'

What the hell, thought Llew now in the sober light of morning. Even if I hadn't happened to stamp on her foot, just what was I intending to say to the woman? Can I buy you a drink – and flog you a novel? Come up and see my manuscripts some time? Grinning, he tossed aside the copy of *Pride and Prejudice* and was steeling himself to face the word-processor when a faint whistling percolated through the open window.

He scrambled to his feet. A familiar, fair-headed figure was striding up the lane. No, not exactly striding. The silly clot was giving a skip every now and then and whipping the tops off blameless dandelions with a twig.

Llew waited until the walker had reached the gate before sticking his head out of the window. 'Morning! Been down to pick up the papers, have we?'

The whistling stopped. John Hapgood looked up, shading his eyes from the sun. 'Papers?' he echoed. As though he'd never heard the word before. As though one or the other of them didn't collect the newspapers from Mavis every morning. 'No, 'fraid not.'

'Surprise, sur-bloody-prise,' murmured Llew before yelling

that the back door was open and a kettle recently boiled if John wanted to brew the coffee. He shovelled books and magazines under the sofa, loped down the stone steps three at a time and kicked open the door to the kitchen. 'Review section's in Saturday's paper,' he said reproachfully. 'Sure, the book's not out just yet, but you never know your luck.'

'Didn't think. Sorry.' Rarely had a man sounded less sorrowful. Such cavalier behaviour in one of Llew's most reliable fans was unprecedented. He was squatting in front of the open fridge. 'Anything to eat, Llew? I'm famished.'

Llew flourished a hand round the kitchen. '*Do* help yourself. Please.'

John straightened, a lump of cheese in his hand. 'You weren't waiting for me last night? You seemed to have quit, so I thought I might as well go up to the hotel. For a nightcap.'

'You amaze me.'

'With, um, Roddy and Patrick, you know.'

Llew's eyebrows shot up. 'With Roddy and Patrick, eh? Now you really do amaze me.' But irony was wasted.

'Why? They're nice chaps. Actors, but not at all luvvieish. I say, is this all the bread you've got?'

'Gives a man one hell of an appetite, doesn't it?' agreed Llew suavely – adding, as John's head swivelled towards him: '*Walking*, I mean. And it must be a good four miles back here. From the Maltstone Hall Country House Hotel.'

John hesitated a minute, then grinned sheepishly. 'How'd you guess?'

'You were wearing that shirt last night. Your shoes are thick with clay off the spinney path, and it doesn't take Sherlock Holmes to decipher the look on your face, mate.' He watched, with relish, his friend flush to crimson before taking pity on him. 'Go on. Make the toast, you lucky bastard.'

'She is – pretty amazing. Don't you think?'

The words were banal, and John spoke offhandedly. But Llew heard emotion so raw it made the hairs on the back of his neck twitch. Hell's teeth, he felt downright embarrassed. 'I'll take your word for it.'

'To be honest, I still can't quite believe it.'

'Oh, I can,' said Llew cheerfully. 'Coffee?'

'No I meant, well, the incredible luck that out of all the villages in . . .'

'All the gin joints, in all the towns, in all the world, Candia Bingham walks into –'

'Look, I just meant –'

Llew, sighing a tune, was fingering an imaginary keyboard along the kitchen table. 'Play it again, Sam,' he crooned.

John laughed. 'Sod off. No one ever said that in the film anyway. And I was talking about them choosing Maltstone for their location.'

Llew broke off. 'Matter of fact I've been wondering about that myself. It is pretty surprising they should be filming in North Yorkshire when I happen to know the book was set in cosy, Home-Counties Hertfordshire.'

'Is it?' said John, without interest. 'Where've you hidden the toaster?'

'Slap bang in front of you. Do you suppose,' he said, handing over a breadboard and knife, 'that any of them have actually read *Pride and Prejudice*? After all, the director's a Yank, and I don't know why it is, but I got the impression the reading tastes of your chums, um, Roddy and Patrick, wouldn't extend much beyond the labels on their jackets.'

'They're OK, I tell you,' said John. 'Good company. Anyway, I should've thought you'd be delighted they've come to Maltstone. Lord knows, you complain often enough how dull this place can be.'

'Purely for effect. I actually *like* being dull. There's no excuse not to buckle down and write. And with my present overdraft I should be at it twenty-five hours a day.' He cleared his throat before asking casually: 'D'you talk to, um, the Dance female at all?'

'Mary, you mean?'

'That's the one.'

'She's the director.'

'And Elizabeth's Queen of England. I know that, you idiot. And?'

'They go back a long way, she and Candia,' offered John, his voice softening in boyish pride as he uttered the name.

'Actually,' said Llew, with asperity, 'I was wondering if she'd happened to mention to you she was looking for new ideas for her next mega-bucks project?' He grinned. 'Specifically, for an authentically British thriller, hot off the press, new to the screen . . .'

'Sorry? Did you say the kettle was boiled?'

This was, thought Llew, like conversing with a drunk. John's mouth might be working, but the brain was palpably disengaged. He was gazing out of the window now with the mugs dangling from his fingers like castanets. 'It can only be good for all of us,' he said dreamily. 'New faces round the place. Stirring things up for a bit.'

'If you say so,' agreed Llew, relieving him of the mugs and spooning coffee into them. 'I mean, don't get me wrong, I can see it's heaven on wheels as far as you're concerned. But village life,' he declared with gloomy gusto, 'is like village ponds. Plenty of mud at the bottom, and better not stirred too hard.'

John blinked. 'You really think that?'

'No,' said Llew. 'But I wrote it in a novel and I like the sound of it.'

'Frankly,' said John, with a smile so soppy it made Llew's teeth ache, 'since the moment Candia tapped me on my shoulder, I've felt like I'm living in a novel myself . . . Llew? What's so damn funny?'

6

The choice of Maltstone as a location had come about more by luck than research. Several villages in the topographically authentic county of Hertfordshire had been offered by scouts, only to be tossed out by the director as too prettified, too suburbanized and, above all, too goddamn crowded.

'England was a much emptier place in those days,' Mary Dance had declared. 'This was peasant country, not commuterland. I want dirt tracks and hawthorn banks, not Leyland conifers with pylons screwing half the camera angles. I want a Netherfield Park I can seriously believe is a muddy three-mile walk from its neighbours. I want green and pleasant village sodding England.'

What Mary Dance wanted she generally got.

Nevertheless, it was accident led her to Maltstone – accident and a script for a movie which thus far had excited no one but herself and the writer. Back in October, insisting that *The Liquorice Fields* was the richest idea to come her way in years, she had dragged one of her partners in Penhaligon Productions away from his desk for a weekend in Yorkshire. Andrew, she declared, would be convinced, once he'd seen the area where the story was set, breathed the landscape, tasted the atmosphere . . .

Andrew, sceptical, tired and damp (the weather was unremittingly foul), had trudged across fields, glowered down terraced alleys and announced he felt a cold on the way. By Saturday lunchtime he was leafing through glossy hotel guides. By mid-afternoon, he was demanding five-coursed, preferably Michelin-rosetted, consolation. Thus, after a further hour's drive in teeming rain and tight-lipped silence, they had rolled up at the Maltstone Hall Hotel. Whereupon they had drowned the quarrel and Andrew's cold so comprehensively that, over a final Armagnac, he was persuaded to admit there might be something in the lishquor . . . liquer . . . the bloody fields script after all. Once *Pride and Prejudice* was in the can.

As it happened, a hungover ramble next morning led them past a manor house whose gentle tree-studded grounds were, he remarked, the very image for him of Jane Austen's England. He would not be surprised, he said yawning, to see Lizzy Bennet tripping across the lawn in bonnet and parasol any minute. Mary had muttered that in her condition she wouldn't be surprised by a troupe of pink elephants. Nevertheless, she found herself staring thoughtfully at the house. It was not the honey-gold stone mullions caught her eye, still less the lop-sided topiary, it was something less tangible. There was a quality in the light up here, a pearly haze which softened the kitschiest of calendar-shots into a watercolour landscape. Even the sky managed to look aqua-tinted. Once they had discovered Maltstone's sleepily unimproved cobbled streets, she telephoned the location scout.

Driving up here again to film, she had been obscurely pleased by the notion that today's four-and-a-half-hour car journey must surely be comparable in time with a horse and carriage trip from London to rural Hertfordshire a couple of centuries earlier. The feeling of remoteness from the metropolis – if anywhere could be said to be remote in today's world – was absolutely right. Although darned inconvenient.

Mary Dance was thirty-eight and, contrary to Llew Bevan's assumptions, would not have described herself as American. Born in New York, she was the only child of an English father and Bostonian mother. The latter was dead and, although her father still lived in the States, she had won a scholarship to Oxford and stayed on. Seven years on the BBC staff were followed by a stint as a freelance director. Now, as one of the founding partners in the company commissioned to make this four-part classic serial, she was sharply aware that she must deliver the product on time and profitably inside budget. Also aware that yesterday's darling of the arts pages was today's chip-wrapping and tomorrow's garbage, she intended to achieve this without compromising the standards on which she prided herself. Television commissions might be Penhaligon's bread and butter, financing (to her mind) more desirable and (to her partners' minds) more risky cinematic ventures, but that did not mean she lavished less sweat, not to say blood, on their making. Tears, Mary Dance expended sparingly.

They were recording the Hertfordshire exterior scenes only up here. The greater part of the drama was safely in the can, shot amid spindly-legged chairs and harpsichords in penurious stately homes conveniently close to the M25. One of these houses had diversified into location work so whole-heartedly that the butler's pantry had been transformed into a permanent make-up suite. At this moment, Mary was feeling sorry to have swapped those sweetly controllable conditions for the capricious air of a Yorkshire early summer.

Striding round the honey-stoned manor house – now giving a talented performance as Longbourn, home of the Bennet family – she glanced up at the sky and prayed for consistency in the light.

Sweat-shirted technicians were adjusting cables across the drive, watched by Roderick Chadderton and Patrick Mather, the latter magnificently booted and caped for his role as Mr Bingley. Mr Darcy not being required in this short scene, Roddy was swathed in his usual leather jacket and yards of scarf. His distinguished larynx required protection in all weathers. He offered a throat lozenge to Mary, which she waved away.

'Where's Candia? She's supposed ·to be behind that window.'

The two men exchanged glances. 'She might possibly have retired to the Winnebago,' offered Roddy in a voice as richly reverberant as cello strings, 'while you were setting up the shot. Catching up on lost sleep, I shouldn't wonder.'

'Terrific,' hissed Mary.

But at that moment Candia rounded the corner of the house at a fast hobble in long straight gown and satin slippers, ringlets dancing round a face exquisitely made-up to look exquisitely un-made-up. Twenty-nine, she could pass for the required nineteen with enviable ease.

'I'm fucking freezing,' she announced. 'Aren't you bastards ready yet?'

'There speaks your authentic Elizabeth Bennet,' said Patrick.

'It's all right for you in your ten layers of coat,' she retorted. 'I'd swear it's colder inside that damned barracks than out.'

'I thought you'd have your lust to keep you warm,' said Roderick, and smiled slyly at Mary. 'You shouldn't have rushed up to bed last night, my love. You missed the most hysterical cabaret in the hotel lounge.'

'What?' Mary twisted round to hear what the Second Assistant was shouting and accepted a polystyrene cup from a passing PA before turning back. 'By the time I finally escaped from that lousy barn dance, a one-man show by William Shakespeare couldn't have kept me from my bed.'

'Nor me,' murmured Candia, stretching and yawning with the smugness of a well-fed cat.

Roderick laughed. 'We noticed.' He turned to Mary. 'Sprawled on the sofa like Cleopatra she was, hungrily eyeing the stairs while her hunky chum felt obliged to chat about the weather with Patrick and me over the whisky. I didn't dare catch Patrick's eye or I swear I'd have died laughing.'

'Pig,' said Candia, without rancour.

'He's got wonderful manners, I grant you that.'

'He's wonderful, period,' she said grinning. 'Take my word for it, Roddy. I've never met anyone like him.'

'Since last week.'

'Ever. Even you've got to admit he's amazingly good-looking.'

'Not my type, treasure . . .'

'Very funny.'

'Candia, love, after all these years I thought I was past being surprised by your antics.' He shrugged. 'But I suppose if that's what turns you on . . .'

'He'd turn any woman on,' she said hotly. 'Come on, Mary. Back me up.'

'Sorry?'

'Mary prefers her men more sophisticated,' said Roderick swiftly. 'Don't you, darling?'

Mary Dance, frowning at a script, barely glanced up. 'I prefer men who don't bug me when I'm working.'

Roddy laughed uncertainly, but Candia – with the confidence of one who had shared a flat with her in the days when Mary Dance was churning out afternoon soaps – said: 'But you're always working, Mary. You never stop.'

'Keeps me from getting bored.' She turned aside and waved. 'Look, is there a problem with that branch crossing the shot? Because . . .'

Candia watched as Mary and a gesticulating cameraman studied the offending tree. 'She'll drop dead of a heart attack one day if she doesn't unwind once in a while. I tried to get her to have a dance last night but –'

'Darling, she'd have terrified the wits out of the young farmers' club,' protested Roddy, and raised his voice slightly. 'God knows, she even scares me sometimes.'

Mary's head whipped round. 'Since when?'

'I didn't have the nerve to sweep you on to the floor

myself, did I? I thought you might at least have tried to rescue me from the local Mata Haris.'

'You seemed to be having a ball, the pair of you.'

'I'm a married man,' said Patrick huffily. 'Speaking of which, have I time to ring home before we go for another take? She could be going into labour any day now.'

'Not bloody likely,' said Candia. 'I'm hoping we can get through early. I've arranged to watch a cricket match this afternoon.'

'Cricket?' cried Roderick incredulously. 'Did you hear that, Mary? La Bingham is seriously proposing to attend a cricket match. My God, it must be love. Love and a jolly ploughboy.'

'Got it in one,' said Candia, her good humour irritatingly unquenchable. 'And for your information, Roddy, John Hapgood is not a farmer. So you can stuff the horny-handed-son-of-toil gags. And his friend Louis, or whatever he's called, is a writer. You should have talked to him, Mary. I thought he looked just your type.'

'And what type is that?' With just such a smile as he was now fixing on Mary had Roderick recently portrayed the young Casanova. 'I've always wondered.'

'Oh, you know, dark-eyed and brooding,' said Candia, not without an edge of malice. 'And an IQ in four figures.'

'You've a funny idea of my tastes,' said Mary flatly. 'Anyway, he didn't look broody to me. He laughed too much. Now get back in that window and we'll try again, shall we?'

7

'Here, Llew,' exclaimed Charlie Luciano, shouldering through the crowd in the shack that served as Maltstone's cricket pavilion. 'Have you seen who John Hapgood's having his tea with?'

'I can guess,' said Llew. Fielding at long leg a couple of overs before the interval, he'd let a boundary through because he'd spotted a minibus decanting Candia Bingham and unidentified friends.

'Some cake, lads?' enquired Bernard, presiding solicitously over tea and team.

'I'd heard he was drinking up our place last night,' continued Charlie, 'but I never in a million years realized –' He broke off because his foot had been stamped on.

Llew beamed at him. 'Shall we get out of the crush?'

Charlie, no fool, picked up his cup and followed Llew outside where they settled on a splintering, sun-warmed step. At the far end of the field, where the party from Penhaligon Productions sprawled under a splendidly candled clump of chestnut trees, John's white-clad bulk could be seen entwined with a pink-shirted female body.

'Makes you sick, doesn't it?' said Llew cordially.

'And you know I was beginning to fancy my own chances t'other night when she flipped over my *crème brûlée*.' Charlie gave the sigh of one who has spent years perfecting misery as a comic turn. Head chef at the Maltstone Hall Hotel, he was a prematurely balding man with glasses and a gloomy droop to the moustache, made daily gloomier by an employer more interested in curtains than cuisine. 'But I guess I can't compete with old blue eyes there. Where'd I be now if I had John Hapgood's looks? Or maybe,' he added, in a kindly after-thought, 'your brains.'

'Not done me much good.' Llew was hardly listening. He was squinting across the sun-shimmering grass, searching for Mary Dance's tall figure among the group under the chestnut trees.

'You fell over *whose* foot?' George had exclaimed when Llew interrupted his agent's lunchtime aperitif with a tele-phoned request for information. 'Well, I'm not personally acquainted with Ms Dance, no. Word is she's more elusive than Lord Lucan, talented as Visconti, and busier than Jeffrey Archer. Dear boy, if you must force your drunken attentions on –'

'I was not forcing any attentions,' protested Llew, stung. 'The thought never so much as crossed my mind.'

'Well it damn well should've done,' said his agent, changing tack with bewildering suddenness. 'And I urge you to make swift your reparation. Swift and sweet.'

'*Sweet?* George, what are you suggesting? I don't even fancy her. Besides, it'd take a braver man than me to –'

'It may be shooting at the moon,' George had swept on, 'but you have nothing to lose by attempting to cultivate the dear lady. Ooze your boyish Celtic charm, leave no menu card unturned . . .'

. . . and, thought Llew now, grinning as he remembered the final piece of advice: *wrap the red roses in proofs of the new book.* 'Sorry?'

'Don't forget I've met your ex-wife,' Charlie was saying plaintively. 'What a cracker. You must've been off your trolley, ditching her.'

'I didn't,' said Llew, his attention sharply recalled. 'Caro ditched me. Or, at least, it was by mutual agreement. About the only damn thing we did agree on in the last ten years. Talk about a marriage un-made in heaven.'

Charlie drained his teacup. 'Got herself wed again yet, has she?'

'Not as far as I know,' said Llew tightly. 'But I warn you, fifty grand a year's her bottom line.'

'Blimey, Llew. Did you pull that much in?'

'I'm making allowances for inflation and . . .' Llew gave a modest cough, 'promotion.'

'Beats me why you quit then.'

'For my soul's sake. Anyway, I'm probably wronging Caroline. I dare say she's earning that herself these days. She might be able to afford a husband on a bit less to keep her in spares for the Porsche.'

'That's what I need,' said Charlie.

'A Porsche? Take it from me, they're more trouble than –'

'A rich wife.'

'To keep you in the manner to which you'd like to become accustomed?'

'To set me up in a kitchen of my own,' said Charlie flatly. 'With no Dorothy Ludlow trotting in and asking who needs balsamic vinegar when we've plenty of Sarson's best malt.'

'There speaks a true romantic.'

'Romance?' echoed Sarah, appearing with a tottering plate of sandwiches. 'Don't make me laugh.'

'Sells books,' said Llew, with feeling.

'Sex,' declared Bernard, who had followed his wife and was leaning between them to help himself to a sandwich. 'That's where the money is. Bonk every four pages and you're in clover.'

'How about, um, romantic comedy?' said Llew. 'Reckon I could hack it?'

Sarah, who, save for John, was the only inhabitant of Maltstone known to have penetrated beyond the dust jacket of Llew's books, smiled mockingly. 'Your autobiography, is this?'

'Only the comic bits.'

'You want any gags, I'm your man,' said Bernard promptly. 'A walking joke-book I was, in the days when I ran the club.'

'Thanks,' said Llew. 'But I don't think it's jokes I need.'

'Thought you said you was after writing comedy?'

'Comedy isn't jokes,' said Sarah, eyeing her husband. 'It's looking at the real world round you and still being able to laugh.'

'Come again?' But Bernard broke off. He had identified the entwined couple at the far end of the field and a slow, incredulous grin spread across his face. 'Speaking of romance,' he breathed, 'correct me if I'm wrong, but is that or is it not our opening batsman in a twenty-two-carat leg-over situation?'

The opening batsman, in partnership with Christopher Nuttall, scored a respectable sixty-three before he was caught. As he trudged back to the pavilion, stripping off his gloves, Candia scrambled to her feet, clapping and whistling with football terrace stridency.

Mary Dance, lying in the shade of a tree, lifted her sunglasses. 'Shit, Candia, why didn't you go the whole hog and bring bobby socks and a twirl baton?'

'Only making up for the rest of you slobs,' said Candia. It was true that of the dozen or so colleagues she (and a ripe golden sun) had persuaded down to the field, few were taking even a perfunctory interest in the game. The grass was littered with papers, chiller bags, cigarette packets and mobile phones. 'Where's the beer? Poor John must be dying for a drink.'

John, however, although he acknowledged Candia's applause with a sheepish wave, did not immediately walk round to join her. He was waylaid by Alf Briggs, the Maltstone Lions' most faithful fan and fiercest critic, and was told at length, and with much wielding of an invisible bat, exactly how he should have played his last shot – and most of the others too.

'I do not believe this,' said Charlie. He and Llew had not stirred from their step, being respectively eleventh and fifth in the batting order.

'Sorry?' said Llew. He had spotted Mary Dance now and noticed that, far from joining in the banter of her colleagues, she had a newspaper spread across the grass in front of her and what looked like a portable radio beside that. He squinted. Yup, the woman was actually wearing headphones. 'Cheering to have such enraptured spectators,' he murmured. 'Still, what can you expect from a Yank?'

'John,' persisted Charlie. 'Look at him, nattering away to old Alf.'

'Listening, more like.'

'Totally ignoring that gorgeous woman falling out of her T-shirt for him t'other end of the pitch. D'you think he's mad? Or just playing hard to get?'

'Do me a favour. Snap's too sophisticated a game for the likes of Honest John. He's good-deeding for the day, isn't he? Never stops. I wonder how I put up with him sometimes.'

'You're a cynical bugger Llew.'

'No, I'm not. I recognized long since I like people for their vices, not their virtues. Nevertheless . . .' Llew clambered to his feet. 'Maybe I'll go and rescue him.'

'Good deed for the day?'

'Are you kidding? I want to cultivate my acquaintance with, ah, the lovely Candia Bingham.'

'About time too,' said Candia, handing John a bottle of beer. 'And – Louis, isn't it? Nice to see you again. Drink?'

'Llew,' he said, moving a newspaper and sitting down. 'Llew Bevan. No, better not. I'm a bad enough cricketer as it is, without finding myself drunk in charge of a bat.'

Mary Dance, lying under a tree a few feet away with headphones clamped to her eyes, did not so much as glance up from her paper. 'Wouldn't make much difference on that ploughed-up apology for a pitch.' Her flat assumption of authority on such matters was as irritating as it was improbable.

'John had a brilliant innings,' retorted Candia, shooting him a look which, thought Llew enviously, would burn paint off a door.

'I guess he seemed to know what the game's about,' muttered Mary Dance.

'You mean you do too?' enquired Llew loudly.

She shoved back an earphone now, and looked up.

'Llew, this is Mary,' said Candia promptly. 'Mary –'

'We've already run into one another,' she said meaningfully. 'Is that surprise I hear in your voice racist or just plain old sexist?' And she replaced her headphones. So much for boyish Celtic charm. After a minute, however, she cast the radio aside with an exclamation of annoyance. 'Looks like we're rained off.'

Llew glanced in amazement at the cloudless blue sky, and then at her.

'Lord's,' she said impatiently. 'England versus Oz.'

'Shit, Mary,' said Candia. 'A gorgeous day like this, with the real thing happening under your nose, and you're huddled up with a lousy Walkman.'

'What's the score, darling?' The actor Llew had identified as Roderick Chadderton, bulging sleekly out of his designer shorts and singlet, shuffled across and was actually resting his panamaed head on Mary's shoulder. Bold fellow.

'Don't encourage her, Roddy,' said Candia exasperatedly. 'If they're rained off, she can bloody well be sociable for once.'

'Oh, but surely the old buffers chatting their way through a cloudburst is the best bit,' offered Llew, adding with the air of a connoisseur: 'Mind, it hasn't been the same since Brian Johnston passed on, God rest his merry gentlemanly soul.'

'Too right,' said Mary Dance unexpectedly, thawing by half a degree. 'You're a fan?'

He swallowed. 'Of, um, *Test Match Special*?'

Roderick flicked an insect off Mary's bare arm. 'I should warn you, unlikely as it seems, our director is a walking Wisden. Unless you can discuss the last West Indies series in wicket-by-wicket detail, I wouldn't embark on a discussion. I tried, and came seriously adrift.'

'I wouldn't dream of it,' said Llew with an alacrity which provoked a ripple of laughter. 'I know sod-all about cricket,' he admitted. 'And care less.'

'Really?' Roderick tilted back the panama to take a closer look at this eccentric specimen, then let it fall again. 'Of course, I suppose you'd have to be a rugby man.'

Llew cocked a lively eyebrow in Mary Dance's direction and drawled: 'Objection, your Honour, on grounds of *gratooitous* racism.'

She almost smiled. 'That supposed to be an American accent?'

'I'll have you know my Perry Mason impersonation's a legend in Abertillery. You're meant to say "sustained".'

She did smile now. 'What's your game then?'

Llew thought for a minute. 'Scrabble? Although I hate most board games even more than the muddy-field variety. Speaking of which . . .' There was a muted groan from the spectators at the far side of the pitch. 'It seems Christopher's attempted a run too far. I'd better go and pad up. If you like your cricket,' he added kindly to Mary Dance, 'I'd get back to the wireless pronto.'

'Thanks,' said Mary, and raised a lazy hand as he loped off towards the pavilion. He could almost have believed she was laughing.

*

'Funny chap,' said Roderick, nettled by this exchange. He blew away a strand of Mary's hair which had strayed across his face and settled his head more comfortably against her shoulder. 'Working-class chip, I dare say. Probably went to the kind of comprehensive which regards competitive sport as a form of child torture. Maybe, *pace* Candia, our dark and broody writer isn't quite your type after all, Mary.'

She reached for a bottle of beer. 'Oh, I don't know. There's something refreshing about a man who doesn't feel obliged to like boys' games. Move over, Roddy, you're crowding me.'

'What do you suppose he writes?' said Roderick irritably, sitting up and discarding his hat.

'Novels,' said John, overhearing. 'Used to be a journalist.'

'On the *Maltstone Cow Keepers' Weekly*?' There was no reply because John's attention had been reclaimed by Candia so Roderick picked up a tube of sun cream and began to knead it into his shoulders. 'Bit I can't quite reach,' he murmured, turning to Mary, tube in hand.

But she was watching Llew Bevan amble across the pitch, struggling into his gloves. 'If men knew what was good for them,' she said pensively, 'they'd wear cricketing gear more often.'

Candia, draped across John's legs, prodded his groin and chuckled. 'Armour to protect them from predatory females?'

'Whites, dimbo. They're so flattering to a boy, don't you think?' She shook her hair back over her shoulders. 'Or maybe it just stirs memories of long, lusty, sunny afternoons on Christ Church Meadow.'

'Oh God, Oxford,' sighed Roderick. 'It's a shame you and I never met under the dreaming spires.'

'I should think you were still in diapers when I was up,' said Mary. 'Besides, Roddy, I didn't even know you were at Oxford.'

'Poly,' said Candia wickedly.

Roderick's reply was drowned by a roar from John. 'Well played, Llew,' he cried. 'Heavens, did you see his face? He can't believe he actually hit that.'

'I'm not surprised, the way he holds his bat,' muttered Roderick Chadderton.

8

Llew, nevertheless, was still at the crease two hours later, batting for Queen, village and literary agent, when his last partner smashed a cavalier four and thereby the Maltstone Lions' unbroken record of defeat this season. Llew did not flatter himself that his marathon stand had impressed the llama, however, because her party had packed up their chiller bags long before the final ball. He was surprised then, to see Candia in the crowd round the pavilion, along with Mary Dance and Roderick – the latter tapping his foot.

'I've held the whole bus up,' said John, clapping Llew on the shoulder, 'but I couldn't miss your moment of glory.'

'Fluke,' said Llew with careless – boyish – modesty. 'And lousy fielding.'

No one argued. Sod this charm lark, he thought. Mary Dance, looking at her watch, was asking if they needed to wait for John to take a shower in the pavilion.

'The only shower in this place,' said Llew, 'comes through the roof in bad weather.'

At least Candia laughed and, pulling John's sweater from his shoulders, knotted it round her own. 'Never mind, darling, you can have a nice long bath at the hotel.'

Bernard winked and elbowed John in the ribs. 'An offer you can't refuse, old son. And I hope there's someone pretty to scrub your back.'

John reddened and Llew saw Roderick grimace at Mary Dance. Only Candia, linking her arm through John's, was unperturbed. 'If he asked me nicely.' She beamed at Charlie Luciano who gulped like a frightened frog. 'And afterwards I've promised him your drop-dead fabulous *crème brûlée*.'

At such a drop-dead fabulous price, thought Llew, that even George would hesitate to turn the broadsheet pages of the Maltstone Hall menu. There are, however, many less delicious ways of squandering an overdraft . . . He was weighing the *cordon bleu* duty of a writer against a convivial pie and chips at the jazz club when Christopher Nuttall panted out of the pavilion, bag slung over his arm. 'Gone half six, John. Should be on the road by seven. All right if I change at your place?'

'What're you on about?' said his father exasperatedly.

'John's taking me into town,' said Christopher. 'I told you.'

Candia withdrew her arm from John's. 'But you're coming back to dinner with me. We arranged –'

'Course he is,' snapped Bernard, glaring at his son.

'We had a deal,' said Christopher. 'You *promised.*'

John blinked. 'Oh Lord, so I did. It'd absolutely gone out of my head.'

'What had?' demanded Candia.

'It's a party,' said Christopher, blithely unaware of anything beyond his own seventeen-year-old concerns. 'Should be a laugh and a half. Uncle Ernie said the last one made a Roman orgy look tame. You'll have a ball, John, honest. You came down with Llew, didn't you? Where's the car?'

'With you in a sec,' said John distractedly, and turned back to Candia. 'Look, I'm fearfully sorry about this cock-up, but would you mind . . .'

She didn't need to speak. Her face transmitted her feelings with the potency that had transfixed a hundred cameras. John, on the other hand, was frozen as a fish finger. For Pete's sake, man, thought Llew, say *something* . . . Too late: Candia was stripping the sweater from her shoulders. 'It'll just have to be some other time, then, won't it? When you've sorted your busy social diary. Come on, Mary, Roddy. Sorry you've had to hang around for nothing.'

'He's mad,' whispered Charlie in Llew's ear as she flung John's sweater at him and marched off. 'Told you so, didn't I?'

John, however, was already racing after Candia and seized her arm. Llew couldn't hear what passed between them, but it ended in an embrace of Wagnerian length and passion before she climbed aboard the minibus. 'No harm done,' he said philosophically. Except, he thought, to his own prospects of advancing his career across a dinner table. Somehow Mary Dance didn't strike him as a red-roses woman . . .

He pondered alternative strategies as they strolled back to the car. Bernard, in the meanwhile, was growling pithy advice to John about which side his bloomin' bread was buttered. John, with his best boy-scout look, was sticking staunchly to the promises-are-promises tack. 'And speaking of promises, Bernie . . .'

Llew left them to it and climbed into the car. 'I say, what's up with Bernard?' John enquired, when he eventually settled in the passenger seat. 'I just told him I'd be down in the morning to start Sarah's bookcase and he nearly bit my head off.'

Not the least of the crosses borne by Bernard Nuttall was the monstrous injustice of his not actually being the legal owner of the Red Lion Inn. That he enjoyed unassailable tenure as landlord was no consolation. For years he had anticipated inheriting the freehold from his elderly uncle. This gentleman, a widowed and childless former greengrocer, had acquired the pub as an investment and installed the Nuttalls as tenants. He had lunched daily on steak and kidney pie at the corner table of the saloon bar until, in his seventy-third year, he unaccountably remarried. His new wife, whom he had met while attending a funeral in the Cotswolds, was barely half his age. She had entertained the mourners to ham sandwiches and iced fancies in her tastefully appointed guest house.

His own funeral, after a wedding so private as to be almost clandestine, followed predictably swiftly. Not swiftly enough, though, to pre-empt amendments to his will. Bernard had been chagrined to discover that ownership of the Red Lion now passed to the widow, a Mrs Irene Cole. However patiently Sarah (who was herself disappointed) reminded him of the generous terms on which the late Mr Cole had ensured their continuing tenancy, he could not forgive the theft of his rightful inheritance.

This explained (because Bernard was not an ungenerous husband) his distaste for the proposed bookcase. It was Sarah who had insisted on commissioning John Hapgood to fit out the chimney alcove of her sitting room. Bernard was not objecting simply to the cost. A free-standing piece of furniture, no matter how expensive, he might not have begrudged his wife. Building into the alcove, however, equalled adding to the fixtures and fittings and thus, ultimately, enriching the coffers of Mrs Cole. Whom he had never met, but loathed profoundly.

Thus, when John and Christopher returned that night from the party in Ebcaster, he was ready with a fluent string of excuses as to why it would not immediately be convenient for John to begin work. He had reckoned without his wife, who entered halfway through his prepared speech and crisply told John that tomorrow would suit her perfectly.

'It's Bank Holiday blooming Sunday,' wailed Bernard. 'John doesn't want to be wasting his time here, not with his ladyfriend eating her heart out up t'Hall.'

John flushed. 'Candia's working all weekend too,' he said politely. 'So, nine o'clock, Sarah? 'Night, Chris, Bernie.'

Sarah waited until the door shut behind him. 'Just what are you playing at, Bernard Nuttall?'

'Only looking after the boy's best interests,' he protested – adding, with a belated flash of inspiration: 'He should be mixing with her cronies, chatting 'em up. He could pick up a load of commissions from that crowd, ten-piece dining suites for their fancy penthouses. London prices and all.'

'I don't think John needs your help to run his business,' said Sarah with asperity. 'Nor his love life, come to that. Honest to God, Bernie, there are times when I wonder why I married you.'

There were times when many people wondered that. It was not easy to perceive in Bernard today the rudely handsome young club compère who had made her laugh so much on their first date she had spilled gin and French all over her best skirt. Four children and thirty-odd years later, Bernard still made her laugh. Although not quite, perhaps, in the same way.

'What's up love?' said Bernard in surprise. 'Have I done summat wrong?'

'Let me count the ways,' muttered Sarah.

Christopher, exhilarated in equal measure by strong lager and triumph, was deaf to such trivial domestic sniping. 'They said I can go in any time this week and they'll find me something to do,' he announced, adding with only a little disappointment: 'provided I don't expect paying. Still, everyone's got to start somewhere, haven't they? I dare say David Frost answered a few phones for free in his time.'

'What are you rabbiting on about now?' growled Bernard.

'Radio Dales, natch. And before you tell me you're not running me in and out of town all half-term, Uncle Ernie says I can stop over with them whenever I want. So . . .' Christopher beamed upon his mother, 'I'll need my new jeans pressing and a load of clean T-shirts in the morning. Stardom here I come.'

9

'If you're looking for John,' said Sarah Nuttall, without raising her eyes from the *Observer*, 'he's not here.' Feet up on a stool in the public bar, she was sipping thick black coffee from a fine white cup.

'His car's outside,' said Llew.

'He unloaded three planks and a toolbag before love got in the way.' Sarah sometimes gave the impression of viewing love as a species of venereal disease – a hazard of youth, sadly prevalent but curable if treated in time. She sighed. 'How much longer are they going to be out there?'

Llew did not need to ask who 'they' were. If he hadn't known already, the diversion signs and the swarming encampment of film vehicles would have enlightened him. 'Two days, unless the weather makes them overrun,' he said promptly. 'Which, with an army of extras, umpteen horses and, I'm told, more carriages than your average Coronation procession, they're praying won't happen.'

'You're very well informed.' She peered at him over her spectacles. 'Not to mention bright-eyed for this hour of the morning.'

'Thing is, Sarah, I had a brilliant idea at the jam session last night. I got chatting to a mate on the *North Yorkshire News* and –'

'Much as I love you, are you coming or going? There's a wicked draught from that door.'

'Going John is with them in Haygate?'

Sarah raised her paper again. 'Need you ask?'

'I'll go straight round,' said Llew with satisfaction.

'Lord save us, you're not starry-eyed and witless too?'

'You know me, Sarah. Strictly business.'

It so happened that the lead trumpeter of the Drystone Country Stompers doubled as features editor of the *North Yorkshire News*. Llew could not claim Grimesy had jumped at his suggestion of a colour piece on the filming in Maltstone, but then Phil Grimes was an old news man put out to grass in features and he roamed those peaceful pastures like a dyspeptic bear.

'Seven hundred words for the women's pull-out,' he growled. 'And a large Scotch in here. When can you deliver?'

Llew promised to get on to it first thing in the morning, and – press officers being elusive creatures on a Sunday – charmed enough information out of the receptionist of the Maltstone Hall Hotel to convince him that a zealous hack should hasten along to Haygate forthwith. Never mind that this hack had recently sworn that *nothing* – short of starvation – would make him scribble another piece for the lousy *News*. The number of whiskies he'd had to buy for Grimesy, food rationing would seem imminent. More to the point, if there was a finer way of cultivating someone's acquaintance than via a prolonged tête-à-tête interview, then Llew, for one, did not know of it. Women's pull-out, she was a woman director – he would even get paid for it. Piece of cake.

Maltstone's sleepy main street has been magically re-animated into history this weekend ... Llew was insouciantly drafting the scene-setting before he got within a hundred yards of Haygate. *Gone are the telephone wires and television aerials, the Benson and Hedges sign above the post office. In place of cars, the cobbles ring to the neighing of horses, the clatter of carriage wheels* ...

As he reached the crowd of spectators pressing round the barriers at the mouth of Haygate, however, he stopped short.

'Maltstone's sleepy main street has been transported back into history,' he was disconcerted to hear. 'Over the past few days, telephone wires have been crossed – *shit*. Take that again, can we?'

Llew pushed through the spectators and saw, beyond the barriers, a smartly Barboured television reporter, microphone in hand, delivering his piece to camera while behind him swirled a costumed pageant straight off a Christmas card. 'One more time. Maltstone's sleepy main street . . .'

Views North, thought Llew, recognizing the reporter's cheesy grin. Stuff that in your *call-that-a-story?* pipe and smoke it, Phil Grimes. If telly thinks it's worth covering . . .

'Hi, Llew,' said a familiar voice behind him. 'What're you doing here?'

'John,' he cried. 'The very mole I wanted. Can you talk me through the barriers?'

'I vow, I wish I could live in Meryton,' sighed the pretty young actress playing Lydia Bennet.

Mary Dance, a few paces behind the camera, watched with an intensity that had led actors to swear her eyes would bore holes in plate steel. But the girl gave the agreed twirl to her parasol, did not snag her bonnet, did not trip over the doorstep and remembered, as she shut the door, to direct a saucy smile into empty air which would, on screen, be filled with a magnificently mustachioed soldier.

'And . . . cut,' said Mary. 'That was fine. Good, print that.'

'About time too, eh?' murmured the lanky, pony-tailed First Assistant beside her, before raising his voice: 'Thanks everyone. Finished with Lydia for the moment. Moving on then to Ep. One, Scene Nine: yes chaps, it's the big one . . .'

'Hello,' observed Roderick Chadderton, squinting across the street. He and Patrick, as handsome a pair of Regency bucks as ever shared a bag of crisps, were leaning on a displaced litter bin nearby. 'I see Candia's Batman has been joined by his Robin. Or should it be Holmes to our worthy woodsman's Watson? Now there's a piece of type-casting: John Hapgood is surely John Watson to the life.'

He looked to share the joke with Mary, but she was asking the Second Assistant if he had a problem.

The Second Assistant held up his walkie-talkie. 'Reporter bloke's been asking if the soldiers can come down this end of the street. Bit of colour in the background while he spouts his piece.'

'That crew is only here,' said Mary evenly, 'on the basis that I neither see nor hear them.' And, she thought, as a sop to Andrew's mania for publicity. 'I want to get into the tracking shot because, whatever the damn weathermen say, I don't like the look of that sky.'

He twiddled his earring. 'Actually, we can't quite go on rehearsing that yet.'

'The bloody truck's finally arrived, hasn't it?'

'But the police have got to shift the spectators to wheel the carriages through the barriers . . .'

'Ten minutes,' said Mary and turned away.

'. . . not a bad chiseller,' Patrick was saying. 'Candia tells me that big sideboard's his. You know the one, Roddy, in the dining room.'

Roderick's lip curled. 'I suppose it has a certain naïve –'

'Did John Hapgood make that sideboard?' asked Mary in mild surprise. 'It's an impressive piece.'

'Oh very,' said Roddy hastily. 'In . . . in its way.'

'John's a genius,' declared Candia, bustling up to join them, her feathered bonnet nodding incongruously over a vast fluorescent anorak. 'I told you, you should be commissioning him before he's discovered and only sheiks and Japanese boardrooms can afford him. John!' She waved. 'Darling, I'm over here . . .'

Mary's attention was claimed by Mac, a morose genius of a Lighting Cameraman who loped up, chewing his gum ominously fast. She was aware, nevertheless, of John Hapgood and his wise-cracking buddy crossing the camera track, and her mouth tightened. Famous for working with a singleness of purpose which obliterated everything beyond the task in hand, even she could not have failed to notice John padding hither and thither all morning, a docile pet labrador to his demanding mistress. Candia, it must be said, was among the most valued of Mary's few intimate friends. She was talented, lovable, loyal, generous and – thought Mary, as she nodded goodbye to Mac – a prize idiot.

The prize idiot was now unshelling herself from her anorak as the microphone-wielding reporter and his cameraman homed in on her. Mary opened her mouth, saw that the police had barely begun to clear the end of the street, and resolutely shut it again.

'Going well?' She looked round to find John's dark-eyed friend smiling at her side.

'So far,' she said, 'it has taken a dozen attempts to shoot a simple eleven-second scene owing, amongst other things, to an unoiled door hinge and a Nato Strike Force of low-flying jets; two of the Bennet sisters are cross-eyed with hay fever and the low-loader transporting the eighteenth-century carriages couldn't squeeze over the bridge into this Godforsaken village and is thus two hours late. Furthermore, the tracking shot for which I urgently require them has just been described by my Lighting Cameraman as akin to staging the Edinburgh Tattoo in a broom cupboard. Any other questions?'

'Shall I steady the sword so you can throw yourself on it?'

So politely deadpan was his voice, it took a moment for the words to sink in. She gave a reluctant laugh. 'If the weather breaks before this shot's in the can, brother, I may take you up on that.'

'Actually –' he began, but was flapped to silence by John. Candia was still being interviewed.

'. . . adore this part of the world. The view from the

window of my hotel room is utterly ravishing.' She declared this with a fervour which, thought Mary sourly, owed less to the prospect outside her bedroom window than the recent one inside.

'Tree after tree after sodding bloody tree,' muttered Roderick in Mary's ear with the peevishness of an actor who, inexplicably, has not himself been cornered for an interview. 'Well honestly, love,' he continued, raising his voice after the reporter, thanking Candia, put down the mike. 'You couldn't *live* here, could you?'

Candia spun round. 'And why not?'

'God, we walk across that green and we might be creatures from outer space.'

'What do you expect dressed like this?' she said hotly.

'Actors? "Nay lad, bluddy funny way to earn tha living." No love, cross my heart, someone said that to me yesterday.'

'Balls . . .'

Mary let out a small sigh, and Llew Bevan caught her eye. 'Funny,' he said softly, 'but whenever actors talk about filming on location, they always seem to remember the unit as one big happy family.'

She found herself grinning back at him. 'And where, statistically, do most murders take place? Bet your ass it's like a family: quarrelsome, incestuous –' She broke off because Toby was raising his thumb as an elegant, yellow-wheeled carriage bowled past. 'Playtime over,' she announced, gathering up her clipboard.

'. . . can't converse with a view,' Roddy was saying. 'Mary, support me. You're an urban creature too. Wouldn't you shrivel away from loneliness up here after a fortnight?'

About to retort that she didn't give a fuck, Mary was silenced by a mocking laugh from Llew Bevan. 'Lonely? In a place like Maltstone? You'd more likely die of a suffocation of friendliness. Hell, there are times when I think about retreating to a city to get some work done. Give me a solitary garret and silencers on the pigeons and I might just turn out a masterpiece.'

'I was talking about like-minded people,' said Roderick stuffily. 'Kindred spirits.'

'Ah.' Llew shrugged. 'But kindred spirits are surely rare anywhere.' He uttered this with such rich melancholy that an echo of sympathy in Mary was superseded by a suspicion the guy was taking the piss again. Someone tapped her shoulder.

'Mary Dance, isn't it?' The television reporter. 'Look, I was just wondering if –'

'No,' said Mary. And strode off.

Oddly enough, Llew (who generally preferred sharpening his wit to baring his soul) had, for once, spoken from the heart. When plots stuck, his drinking mates up here were sounder on extricating triplets from a labouring ewe than a hostage from a cellar with a gun-toting maniac on the fictional stairs. But it was more than that. He missed, well, maybe not Caroline exactly, but ... dammit, he didn't know what he missed.

Except, in that fatal second of introspection, the chance to fix his interview. The woman was now pacing off down the street like Cardigan on the eve of Balaclava. Still, he thought, not bad so far. He could wait. And, by the look of things, it would be a long wait.

Stumble into a film location in full swing and you'll know how Alice felt in Wonderland, he drafted idly as he watched the scene shift and settle, regroup and animate again. *A gaitered and clogged peasant is chatting into a mobile phone, a Jane Austen lookalike is stubbing out her fag and a troop of redcoated officers, bright as a pack of cards, are passing round a copy of* The Sun. *Instead of a White Rabbit, there are production assistants waving stop-watches and, wherever you are, one of the Red Queen's sidekicks will tell you it's the wrong place . . .*

He and John had been shepherded down to the cordoned-off end of the street where, behind them, a pair of policemen kept an avuncular eye on the encampment of spectators. Candia and her screen sisters, after two interminably interrupted rehearsals, were yawning in their carriage. Roderick Chadderton, looking impressive if a mite nervous, was towering above the crowd on a horse almost as darkly handsome as himself.

'Another rehearsal everyone,' bellowed a pony-tailed guy through a loud-hailer. 'Starting positions.'

'Light brigade, *charge* . . .' murmured Llew, as, once again, the carriages trundled, the costumed pedestrians bustled purposefully and the camera, with Mary Dance riding shotgun, began to glide down its tracks.

'Mary wants to see Darcy across the carriage, *now*!' crackled a walkie-talkie nearby, and its owner pelted forward gesticulating.

'By heck, they waste some time, don't they?' Bernard, prominent among the spectators, was leaning across the barrier.

'Complicated shot,' said Llew fair-mindedly. 'She's following Candia's carriage, except the other two keep getting in the way. I think Darcy was meant to trot up as Candia waved to that blond geezer but his horse hadn't read the script. And whatever the soldiers are supposed to be doing down the far end, they've not got it right yet. Hell, it's like choreographing Strip the Willow on horseback.'

Even as he spoke, Roderick's mount careered towards the camera at a speed which alarmed nearby extras, and by the look of him, Roderick as well. Mary Dance hopped off her perch beside the camera as a handler darted forward to seize the bridle and shove sugar lumps into his charge's mouth.

'Frisky little bugger,' said Bernard. All at once, he looked away and beamed. 'Hey-up, looks like I'm wanted at last. 'Scuse me, constable, if you can just shift this barrier, I'm being summoned . . .'

The summons had come from the television reporter. 'See if we can knock off the vox pops while they're still pissing around,' Llew heard him mutter to his cameraman as he hurried past to clap Bernie on the shoulder. 'Landlord of the local pub, isn't it? Now if –'

'Can we have quiet over there please?' bellowed Pony-tail after a frowning word from Mary.

Bernard and the reporter nodded at one another conspiratorially and prepared to wait.

'. . . different bloody horse for Roddy?' Llew heard Mary ask in the sudden hush.

As Roderick, snatching up the reins, declared the animal was fine, just a bit bored, Llew suddenly felt a raindrop plop wetly on his nose. He wasn't the only one. Pony-tail conferred anxiously with Mary before raising the loud-hailer again. 'We'll go for a take this time, OK? Starting positions.' As the kaleidoscope reshuffled, Pony-tail strode over to the barriers and smiled confidingly at the crowd. 'Look, this is a long and fantastically tricky sequence, so could I ask you, please, to keep absolutely *stumm* until I give the all clear? Thanks.' He hastened back to Mary's side and, after a few fidgeting minutes of silence, said: 'Background action, please. Are we rolling? Then . . .'

Everything, thought Llew, was rolling. The carriages, the camera dolly – and the eyes of Roderick's horse. But the beast trotted forward at exactly the moment Candia lifted her hand, the other carriages trundled round tidily and a mob-capped woman emerged from a doorway with the precision of a figure in a clock. As Roddy wheeled out of shot, mopping his brow, the camera glided smoothly on into the mêlée of soldiers and Llew could swear the crowd behind him was holding its collective breath. He certainly was.

The television reporter, however, now that the action was moving away, nodded to his cameraman and prodded Bernard into a more photogenic position beside Roderick's magnificent horse, which was guzzling a reward of sugar lumps from the fist of its handler. Roderick, though, was not going to appear on the screen even of a tinpot local news programme being led like a child on a seaside donkey, and he gestured the man away. The horse, deprived of his sugar fix, swung his mighty head round and clunked Bernard who yelped.

'Quiet,' hissed Roderick furiously and jerked the reins. A mistake.

The horse gave a trumpeting neigh and began bucking like a rodeo star. Roderick soared balletically upwards and thumped back in the saddle twice (uttering no more than a heroic whimper) before he contrived, with a kick which knocked the handler flying, to slither to the ground. Whereupon the animal, tail and hooves flailing, careered away to share the fun with his equine chums. Llew hadn't even seen John move, just felt a thump to his shoulder, but the guy was already pounding across the cobbles until, with a flying tackle which raised a roar from the crowd worthy of the Arms Park, he contrived to grab the reins. Splayed on the ground, he clung on grimly until the handler tottered to his side.

But it was too late. All hell was exploding down the street. Horses were rearing and twisting, yelling actors were diving for cover, and the camera dolly ground to an unscheduled halt. Only then and with, Llew could not help but think, truly cinematic grandeur, did the storm break. Lightning ripped the sky, thunder smacked like the collision of planets and the hydrants of heaven were opened.

'Roll,' hissed the news reporter gleefully to his cameraman before composing a face of dismay. 'Filming doesn't always go quite to plan. Roderick Chadderton, an actor well known to viewers of the ITV series . . .'

'Jesus,' wailed Roderick, staggering round knees bent.

'John!' shrieked Candia. She had leapt to the ground from her carriage and was pelting up the street. 'Are you all right?'

'Fine,' gasped John, raising himself on one elbow and shaking his head stupidly. 'Trod – on my hand.'

Candia crouched beside him. Llew almost expected her to cry, 'My hero!' and possibly faint. He had been misled by the maidenly costume. 'Get a fucking doctor, will someone?' she yelled.

'What about me?' squawked Roderick, but already actors, policemen and crew were converging on him, followed – with a face marginally blacker than the sky – by Mary Dance.

'Roddy's fine, everybody,' boomed Pony-tail into his megaphone after a few minutes during which giant umbrellas, gaudy as tropical flowers, had blossomed the length of the street. 'Bit shocked that's all. But . . .' He dashed the rain from his eyes, and conferred rapidly with Mary Dance, before continuing with obvious reluctance: 'Looks like we'll have to abandon this shot today, with Roddy out of action. If the weather clears, we'll try for some pick-up shots from the last scene. So, Candia, you're finished, and . . .'

'No arguments,' Llew heard her command as she steered John into the exodus for the buses. She was cradling his hand, the fingers of which were indeed swelling like a bunch of sausages. 'You're coming back to the hotel and I'm getting a doctor.'

'Bernard,' called John as they passed, 'tell Sarah I'm frightfully sorry, but I don't think–'

'What?' Bernard, who had been standing forlorn, cheated of his moment of glory on *Views North*, suddenly perceived the silver lining in this particular storm cloud. 'Forget the bloody bookcase,' he bellowed. 'You let her ladyship tuck you cosily up in –'

'A thunderstorm lashing the streets of Maltstone means the filming has ground to an unscheduled halt,' piped up the television reporter merrily. 'So I'm hoping this gives me a chance to seize a few words with the director, Mary Dance . . .'

His voice trickled to silence because she had turned to look at him. With just such a face, thought Llew with awe, might

Boadicea have transfixed an invading Roman. A couple of telly news boys were no match. 'God preserve me,' she could be heard to hiss as they slunk away, 'from stupid fucking journalists.'

Llew, turning up the collar of his jacket, decided on balance that fixing his feature could wait a couple of days.

Imagine a perfect English summer evening. Pigeons are croon-
ing in the tree-tops, the last of the lilac blossom is breathing
perfume into the breeze and a flagstoned terrace still glows
with the remembered warmth of the day. A couple – young,
handsome and, as any fool can see, very much in love – are
leaning across a lily pond. As a sinking sun shimmers across
the water, their profiles merge in a kiss.

Nauseating, muttered Llew. Although, in truth, he smiled
upon the lovers with a mellow and even proprietorial pride as
he strolled up the barbered lawn of the Maltstone Hall Hotel.
He was thinking that the scene reminded him of nothing so
much as the jacket of a (bestselling) novel penned by the likes
of Lavinia Stacey.

John heard the footsteps and rose, waving.

'No, please,' called Llew. 'I hate to gatecrash an idyll.'

'Piss off then,' retorted Candia and fished a bottle out of
the water. 'Glass of wine?'

'Make it a small one. I need my wits this evening. I just
called in to visit the invalid.'

This was not the whole truth. Llew was hoping he might,
as if by chance, bump into Mary Dance. It was now Thursday.
Since Sunday, when Candia had swept John out of the storm
and into residence at her hotel, Llew had telephoned there,
the London press office of Penhaligon Productions, and the
mobile phones of countless assistants to assistants, to be met
everywhere with the same polite stone wall. Just at present, it

seemed, Mary was working to an *awfully* tight schedule . . .

Since Llew, in the course, of the week, had himself become deeply enmeshed in a new and intriguing idea for a book, he had more or less decided to abandon the feature. Ironically enough, however, even as he did so, Phil Grimes warmed to the idea. Reared in the sturdy regional tradition which head-lines the battle of Alamein 'HUDDERSFIELD MAN LOST IN DESERT', Grimesy had got wind of a Yorkshire twig in the Dance woman's family tree.

'Make it a thousand words,' he'd said. 'Usual plus exes. I'll send a photographer.'

Llew knew better than to waste breath telling Phil King-of-the-Doorstep Grimes that the Dance woman didn't seem to want to be interviewed. Besides, he needed the money. But there was no sign of her here tonight, so he turned back to John. 'By the look of it, I needn't ask if you're recovered.'

John, who was indeed glowing with the rude health of a lifelong muesli eater, held up a bandaged hand. 'Skiving for Britain.'

'The doctor prescribed rest,' said Candia firmly. She handed Llew a glass of wine. 'Will you stay for dinner?'

'Thanks, but I can't. Anyway,' he said ruefully, 'much as I admire Charlie's genius, the prices in this place don't half take the edge off my appetite.'

'You're not joking,' grunted John. 'Home tomorrow or I'll be remortgaging the barn before –'

Candia had clamped a hand across his mouth. 'For the millionth time, this is on my bill.'

John detached her hand, kissing it. 'We'll argue later.'

'Tax deductible,' she said airily and turned to Llew. 'I've told this idiot if he wants to square up, he'll just have to drag me off to his cave in the hills. Baked beans over a camp fire will do, I'm easy to please.'

'Cassoulet simmered in the Aga?' suggested Llew and added some fatuous, flat-capped quip about fishing the coal out of the bath when he sensed John bristling. The joke might not have been funny but it was not, thought Llew, *that* unfunny.

'An *Aga*?' she carolled, her eyes widening. 'How very civilized. Has John been fibbing? Is he a good cook too?'

'Terrible. I, on the other hand –'

'Sure you won't stay to dinner?' interrupted John, rather rudely.

'Sorry.' Llew drained his glass. 'Going into town, aren't I? Far be it from me to flaunt my fame, but I'm starring this evening, live, on the Radio Dales arts programme.'

'Not you too?' exclaimed Candia. 'But so are Roddy and Mary. They left ten minutes ago. Oh Llew, for Christ's sake, don't tell her I was out here drinking. I only twisted her arm into standing in for me by swearing I was dying of a migraine.'

'You didn't,' said John, shocked.

'And she absolutely *hates* being interviewed,' gurgled Candia, blithely unaware of the would-be interviewer rising to his feet beside her. 'Still, Roddy can talk enough for three.'

So Llew was not surprised to find himself seated round a felt-covered table with Mary Dance and Roderick Chadderton. He was surprised though – and rather disappointed – to learn they were replacing his promised co-interviewee.

'Pre-recorded dear old Lavinia,' gabbled the presenter, shuffling her running order, lining up a disc, smiling dizzily at Roderick and disposing of a piece of chewing gum all, it seemed, in one movement. 'We can run that any time, but the filming's news. Adaptability's the name of the game in live radio.' She twitched back one of her earphones and blinked at Mary. 'You're not Candia Bingham, are you?'

Llew suppressed a laugh as Mary Dance agreed, tight-lipped, that she was not.

'Woman director? That's great. Brilliant. Nothing to get

nervous about, nothing heavy. Just a chat about what you've done, what you're up to here. Louie . . .'

'Llew.'

'Lou, a little bird tells me you live in the valley where it's all happening, right? So maybe I can ask you how it's affecting village life, that kind of thing. Feel free to chip in, we like to get a real round-table atmosphere rolling. We'll be talking about yourself, um, your . . .'

'Book?'

'. . . brilliant book, I mean, it looks terriff. Haven't managed to read it yet, you know how it is. Anyway, out of this disc then . . .' She put her finger to her lips, clamped the headphones back in place and her voice changed timbre with startling suddenness. 'Yes, it's nine o'clock here on Radio Dales, and a very good evening to you. I'm Gloria Black and this is *Artsround*. An action-packed programme tonight with . . .'

Llew had met Mary and Roderick amid the wilting rubber plants and grinning presenter mug-shots in the lobby. Mary Dance, he thought, looked as if she might even be pleased to see him. Or at least, not actively *dis*pleased, as she asked what brought him here.

'Oh, the usual.' He gave what he liked to think was the blasé shrug of a media-weary man of letters. 'Book out next week.'

'Really?' said Roderick, eyeing him as a farmer might inspect a potato weevil. 'Can't say I've run across your work.'

'Along with most of the British Reading Public,' said Llew cheerily, wondering what he could have done to offend this stuffed shirt.

'What is it you write exactly?'

'About a thousand words a day,' Llew retorted and, since Mary's face almost cracked into a smile, resolved that it was now or never. 'Actually, I also do a bit of freelance journalism . . .' Her smile had already glassed over but he ploughed on with the prepared spiel, finishing brightly: 'Just, you know, the local angle.'

'Was Jane Austen really a Yorkshire lass?' sneered Roderick.

'Ah, but wasn't your father, Mary?' said Llew, playing his trump card. 'Born up here, I mean? The Features Editor mentioned –'

'*What?*'

Llew nearly ducked for cover. Strewth, you'd think he'd asked if her Dad had run the local Gestapo.

'Just because my grandmother went into premature labour on a train,' she snarled. 'Far as I know or care, in sixty-nine years, he's never been back.'

'And who can blame him?' murmured Roddy happily, at which point they were ushered out of reception by – of all people – Christopher Nuttall. Who was also looking immensely pleased with himself.

'And I'll have you know I'm not just making the coffee,' he informed Llew, shepherding them along a luridly painted corridor whose carpet crackled with static. 'They've showed me how to cut tape, and Sasha – she's not local radio, she's *London*, telly too – anyhow, she's been giving me the real lowdown on breaking into network.'

'Oh yeah?' said Llew, dodging a fire-door as it swung back in his face. That's it, he was thinking. From now on, George does the schmoozing and Grimesy cobbles his own lousy copy. I'm calling a cease-fire on the charm offensive, here and now. And handing in my press card to boot. Stick to fiction. Your characters can't bite back . . .

'Stories with a youth angle,' Chris was saying. 'That's what I should be looking for if I want people to take notice. Through here. It was me set this piece up, you know.' He jerked his head proudly in the direction of Mary and Roddy.

'Give the boy a Pulitzer Prize,' muttered Llew.

'Sorry?' Waiting for them to catch up outside the studio

door, Chris leaned towards him and lowered his voice. 'Mind, I'm a bit gutted Candia Thingy pulled out.'

As the interview with Mary and Roderick proceeded, Llew decided, with a certain malicious enjoyment, that Gloria Black might be feeling pretty gutted too. Mary Dance was not a forthcoming interviewee. Her answers were economical, bordering on the monosyllabic, even before Gloria trilled she was sure Mary had a million hilarious stories about disasters on location. Roderick, however, was only too ready to raise the cultural tone of Radio Dales. At ear-numbing length. '. . . crucial axis of the plot is the verbal sparring between Darcy and Lizzy, rich as it is in sexual innuendo. In fact, one could argue that sex –'

'*Sex!*' cried Gloria, grabbing the word like a lifebelt. 'Would you call Jane Austen a sexy writer, Mary?'

Mary Dance shook her head. Great radio, thought Llew, feeling merrier by the minute. He glanced through to the cubicle where Chris was looking as woebegone as an animal trainer whose prize parrot's caught laryngitis. By nodding frantic encouragement, however, the presenter managed to extract from Mary an opinion that the book was about power. 'Power and money, anyway. Marriage was the only route open to a woman in eighteenth-century England to secure her future. It's a very cynical tale in that sense.' And this, apparently, was to be her last word.

Roderick was already leaning forward, mouth open, when devilry – or sympathy for the poor bloody presenter – inspired Llew to open his. 'Tosh,' he said. And there was a stunned silence. 'Well, honestly,' he continued. 'What is this, Jane Austen or an airport bonkbuster? Sex, power, money . . .'

'Local writer, um, Llewellyn Bevan,' chipped in Gloria.

'Call me a fuddy-duddy old romantic,' he said, beaming seraphically upon Mary Dance – if a man's going to burn his boats he may as well fire a few salvoes on the way down – 'but I've always read *Pride and Prejudice* as a comedy.'

Bang on target. 'I'm allergic to the word comedy,' Mary snorted. 'Play this story just for the glittering surface laughs and you risk obscuring the important themes of a great classic of English literature.'

'Surely there's not a theme in the universe,' countered Llew grandly, 'which isn't illuminated by a little wit?'

'Or trivialized?'

'Even Shakespeare had his fools and comedians.'

She stuck out her jaw. 'We're not all Shakespeare, buddy.'

'A lively debate here on Radio Dales,' intervened Gloria, glancing from Mary's scowl to Llew's impish grin with the air of a woman who prefers to buy her erudition at the glue counter. 'But, if I can just pick up what Roderick was saying, *sex*?'

Roddy smirked. 'The actual point I wanted to make is that Mr Darcy is surely the blueprint masculine sex symbol. The ultimate, once-and-for-all thinking girl's crumpet. Past, present and –'

'Hang on a minute, sunshine,' said Llew, enjoying himself, 'don't you think it's for women to pronounce on that? Mary? As a, if you'll forgive the phrase, *thinking girl*' – he rolled the offending words round his tongue with relish – 'would your, ah, crumpet have to be tall, dark and handsome?'

'Don't be ridiculous.'

Roderick's smile was irritatingly condescending. 'There's more to Darcy than looks.'

'Sure,' said Llew. 'He's arrogant, snobbish, self-opinionated –'

'Only because no one stands up to him, until Lizzy crosses his path. And why is she attracted to him? *Because*,' continued Roddy, steam-rollering over Llew's murmur that it might have something to do with the geezer being as rich as Croesus, 'he's cleverer than everyone round him and so is she. What could be more contemporary than that?' He turned to Mary. 'I mean, a man would have to be highly intelligent to attract a woman like you, wouldn't he? And as ambitious and success-ful as you are?'

Mary stiffened. 'I imagine no woman could love a man she didn't respect.'

A more perceptive man might have realized she didn't care for this personal tack, but Roderick was only just finding his rhetorical stride. 'Naturally, we're all ambitious in this busi-ness. Which, by the way, Gloria, I don't think it's stretching too much of a parallel to compare with the aristocracy of Jane Austen's day. National celebrities then were land-owners, peers and so forth. What are they today? Actors, media folk, the so-called tellystocracy.'

'Right,' said Gloria faintly.

Wrong, thought Llew gleefully, judging by Mary's flinty stare, but Roddy was unstoppable. 'As Mary said, the story's about power, and isn't power the ultimate aphrodisiac? Darcy was a rich, charismatic and immensely powerful man, and we can all imagine translating that allure into modern –'

'Garbage!' Mary snapped suddenly, with a force which must have rocked a few transmitters. 'This is the end of the twentieth century, dammit. No contemporary woman is looking for some God-like father figure, calling the shots and slapping down the million-dollar pay cheque every month. Is she?'

'No,' warbled Gloria, the contemporary woman at whom this question had been machine-gunned. 'I mean, well, mightn't she be?'

Mary's voice softened. 'Doesn't today's female want a man who can understand her?' The caring California-speak was belied by a distinctly ironic edge. 'Empathize with her? Be her best friend?'

'Well naturally,' began Roderick with the smug earnestness of a born-again New Man. 'And –'

'Blimey, is that all modern woman wants?' Llew interrupted rudely, grinning at Mary Dance. 'The physique of Superman, the brain of Einstein and the sensitivity of Jean-Paul Sartre?'

She returned his gaze limpidly. 'You're forgetting,' she drawled, 'the income of Jean Paul Getty. And anyone listening who fits the bill can put their name on a postcard and send it to me any old day.'

'Ho-ho, yes,' chortled Gloria gratefully, recognizing a good punch line when she heard one. 'Thank you, Mary Dance, Roderick Chadderton. We look forward very much to seeing *Pride and Prejudice* on our screens – some time next spring, did you say? More from Llew Bevan in a minute, but first some music from . . .'

'You bastard,' said Mary Dance amiably to Llew when the music had begun to ooze from the speaker. 'If you want to come down to the location to do your piece tomorrow, give Louisa Sharpe-Bresler a call. My PA. She'll fix anything you want.'

'What?' croaked Llew. 'I mean, um, thanks. Thanks very much.'

'But, love, you swore you weren't going to let another journalist near the place,' protested Roderick as the tall fair boy who, for some reason, looked familiar to Mary ushered them out of the studio.

'He's got more brain than most hacks,' she said. A speaker in the cubicle was relaying Llew's voice comparing the Welsh valley landscape of his childhood with the North Yorkshire Moors.

'Indeed to goodness,' mimicked Roderick. 'How green was my grammar school education, clever boyo that I am with my crow-black, sloe-black eyes, chipping the jetty treasure from the coal-face of the language and –'

'Yes,' said Mary.

Roderick abandoned the accent. 'Sorry, darling?'

'Remarkably clever eyes,' she said thoughtfully. 'Hasn't he?'

'I can't say I'd noticed.'

'No? I mean, I've never credited half the crap that's talked about eyes. What are they, after all, except globs of optical jelly? But his are quite something. They give you the feeling he's seeing everything and understanding twice as much again.'

'So do a spaniel's,' retorted Roderick, stalking ahead. As they quit the cubicle, Llew was talking about his devoted readership. All three of them. Mary, perhaps unwisely, laughed.

'Typical writer,' snapped Roddy. 'Peddling those tired old modest-little-me gags, when we know they've got egos the size of the Albert Hall.'

Mary smiled at him. 'We all have egos, baby,' she said. 'Maybe writers just have the wit to keep them better hidden.'

Oddly enough, Llew found himself contemplating his own ego the following afternoon. He was skulking on a bench behind a yew arbour at the time.

'Pride,' he said to himself. 'That's all you're suffering from, lovely boy: a nasty dent in the old vanity. Bevan, you're a plonker.'

As invited, he had telephoned Mary Dance's PA. Perversely, however, even as he agreed that three o'clock suited, he had found himself wishing it didn't. What was up with him? (Yes, he could find the vehicle entrance to Holly Lodge, yes, he looked forward to meeting her too . . .) As the clock was striking three, though, and he was gathering up tape-recorder and car keys, some impulse made him toss the keys back again. He would stroll down through the woods instead. This was not, he assured himself, a delaying tactic. Besides, who would care if he were a few minutes late? It just happened to be a particularly balmy afternoon . . .

He knew the rickety stile behind the church gave into the Lodge grounds. Unfortunately, he was less familiar with the maze of paths beyond and soon lost his bearings in an inky rhododendron jungle. He emerged unexpectedly into blinding sunshine to find a camera crane rearing above him like the head of a mechanical dinosaur. There was an equally startled cameraman aloft who requested Llew to remove his person from view. In less than civil terms.

And so Llew had dodged behind this yew arbour. The

twitter of human voices beyond the hedge hushed and only drowsy afternoon birdsong remained until someone far away said, 'Action'. Lying beside him on the bench was a thick, dog-eared script. Open, he read, at Episode I, Scene xi.

BINGLEY
My ideas flow so rapidly that I have not time to express them.

You and me both, Llew had thought, hearing the words filter across on the breeze as he read them. Except, having come up with a dumb idea like this feature, I've now got to express it in a thousand double-spaced words. By Monday.

LIZZY
Your humility, Mr Bingley, must disarm reproof.

I blame it all on George. I mean, was it ever exactly likely Mary Big Shot Dance would be so entranced by my interviewing technique she'd demand to see the books penned by a humble provincial journo?

DARCY
The appearance of humility may be deceitful. It is sometimes an indirect boast.

Spot on, Darcy, thought Llew. What stings is that, by setting up this piece, I've set myself up as some pig-price-reporting local hack, here to gawp at the glamorous invaders. Hell, if I'd stuck with the papers, I'd be in London now with my by-line plastered across a national. And there's boasting for you, Darcy old son. Instead, I'm stuck behind a hedge, eavesdropping on another world. And I am not talking about Jane Austen's England. No sir. God, there are times when I think I'm living in that now. I'm talking about *them*, the people, the buzz, the . . . Oh, the whole matey, multi-faceted, metropolitan, media merry-go-round. The world I quit.

... if, as you were mounting your horse, a friend
were to say: 'Bingley, you had better stay till next
week,' you would probably do it.

Llew sighed. Caro had told him to stay. Maybe she was
right. Maybe he really had been mad to chuck everything in
and come up here.

LIZZY

Surely, you prove only Mr Bingley's sweetness of
disposition in yielding to the persuasion of a friend.

'Cut,' snapped a voice he recognized as Mary Dance's, and
it jolted him out of his wallowings like a cold tap in a warm
bath. No sooner had he pronounced himself a plonker and
chucked aside the script wondering whether he now dared
venture from his hidey-hole, than a tall, Alice-banded young
woman rounded the hedge at a gallop.

'Llew Bevan? God, I'm most frightfully sorry.' She bore
down on him with a bulging file under one arm and a tea tray
balanced on the other. 'I'd no idea you were here. I'd been
patrolling the drive until someone said ... That *was* you
toddling in from the shrubbery?' She smiled toothily, dumped
the tray and shook his hand, all without pausing for breath.
'Anyway, hello, I'm Louisa Sharpe-Bresler, we spoke on the
telephone, terrifically nice to meet you, Llew, have you been
here ages? Honestly, if you'd only asked, we'd have sent a car
for you.' She had opened the file and was shuffling clipped
and labelled papers into his hands, swift as a conjurer dealing
cards. 'Now, these are all the press releases to date, just in
case you needed them, and I've run off biogs of the important
people, photocopies of recent cuttings and so forth. Got them
all? Lord, this is crazy, you can't see anything from here.' She
scooped up the tray again. 'Let's go round into the garden.
We're doing pretty well so far this afternoon, last two scenes

of the day. I've tea here, Earl Grey, or there's hot water and bags for a herby job if you prefer. Biscuit? *Gaspingly* warm weather, isn't it?'

Llew, juggling a polystyrene cup with a wonky lid, a lump of shortbread and a stack of photocopies, stumbled along the path in her wake. 'You really shouldn't have gone to so much trouble.'

'No trouble,' said Louisa gaily. 'Mary told me to lay on the works.'

She did?

'They'll be breaking for tea, once we've *finally* got this scene in the bag, so it'll be a good time for you to mingle and talk to anyone you want. Do you know Lady Willersley, owner of the house? Such a poppet, I told her you might like a word. I say,' continued Louisa, 'watch your step round this corner. Cables everywhere.'

But what Llew was seeing under his feet was not cables but a red carpet. Cars? Press-packs? Fancy teas? A minute ago he'd been lamenting his lowly status. Now he was frankly unnerved by the opposite. As he followed Louisa, he was combing his conscience. He'd made clear to Mary Dance this was a thousand words for the women's pull-out of the *North Yorkshire News*, hadn't he? Not a five-page splash in *The Sunday Times*. The *News* was a solidly worthy organ but . . .

'Hello, the one-rat pack's here,' called Candia as they rounded the hedge. Indistinctly, because a make-up girl was blotting her chin with a powder puff. Roderick was striking a Byronic pose against a tree and Patrick Mather, running a finger inside his starched white neckcloth, announced to no one in particular that he was sweating like a pig. Neither acknowledged Llew's arrival.

Mary Dance, however, amidst a thicket of frowning technicians, glanced round as Louisa ushered him to a canvas chair. 'Llew, hi. With you later.' She accompanied the greeting with a smile of very remarkable warmth.

And that was when Llew began to wonder . . .

'One more time. Are we rolling?' She was hopping backwards, as a youth darted out with a clapper board.

The visiting VIP treatment, that steamy smile . . . Could it possibly be that Mary Dance, not to put too fine a point on it, *fancied* him? This humble, clumsy, *halfway presentable* hack?

Her eyes were fixed on the cameraman. 'Thank you. Action.'

Patrick Mather, kiss curls a-quiver, neighed with laughter and again carolled: 'My ideas flow so rapidly that I have not time —'

The idea that Mary Dance would look twice at the likes of him flowed away faster than water down a plughole. Llew nearly ruined Roderick's lofty riposte by sniggering and buried his face in Louisa's sheaf of cuttings.

She was keen to supplement this compendium, between takes, with a whispered torrent of commentary: these scenes had to be shot mind-bogglingly out of plot order, what with the different locations and that filthy weather, 'But nothing could ever faze Mary, she has a memory like a computer . . .' Llew soon perceived Louisa was a fully paid-up member of the Mary Dance fan club. And said as much. *Oh absolutely*, hooted Louisa, but that was only because Mary was simply the best director she'd ever worked for, and she'd jolly well needed to be three times as good as any man. God, Llew simply wouldn't believe the macho games . . . Halfway through a libellously illustrative anecdote, Louisa seemed to recollect she was talking to a journalist and decided she was needed elsewhere.

'Don't worry,' murmured Llew to her departing figure. 'I'm hardly Nigel Dempster.' Too true, he thought, returning to the cuttings.

The journalists who had written about Mary Dance, however, were scarcely less adulatory. And as one mishap after another halted filming, and the scene was again repositioned and reshot, Llew could see why. Temperature and tempers simmered all round, but the woman stayed serene as a swan on a jacuzzi. She listened to suggestions, did not raise her voice, was smilingly polite – and, he thought, commanded events as intricately and absolutely as a grand-master behind a chess board.

'Talk about Captain fucking Bligh,' declared Candia, staggering over and draping herself across Louisa's empty chair when Mary finally pronounced herself satisfied and a tea break was called.

'Can I quote you?'

'Feel free.' She glanced beyond him and raised her voice. 'But you better add that I recognize Mary's a total genius, and none of it's her fault. Oh Mary, what about when that bird flew over and crapped on Darcy's shoulder . . .? I thought I'd *die* laughing.'

Mary Dance made a noise of disgust. 'Serve you right if you had. Roddy's coat wasn't in vision. The take would've been fine if you hadn't fouled up.'

'Fouled up,' wailed Candia. '*Fowled* . . .? Oh, never mind.' She mopped her eyes. 'Sorry. It's been a long day. For pity's sake don't quote me on anything. As Mary frequently points out, my mouth runs faster than my brain.'

'"My ideas flow so rapidly that I have not time to express them",' quoted Llew, with the ease of a man who had watched a scene played seven times in front of him.

'Smart arse,' said Candia. 'You know, I really hate writers. I'm always afraid anything I say may be taken down and used in episodes.' She chuckled, with disarming pleasure, at her own pun.

'Hoping it will, more like,' commented Mary.

'Piss off.' Candia turned to Llew. 'It's true what they say: this job's like war. Nine-tenths boredom, one-tenth terror and if you're still sane at the end, you need your head examining. And you *can* quote that.'

'Do you prefer the theatre then? To film or television?' Llew grimaced and produced his recorder. 'Sorry, I'm on business. I have to ask the stock questions.'

'And my stock answer is that I like best whatever I happen to be doing at the time.'

'Or whatever someone tells you you're best at,' chipped in Mary unexpectedly.

'So I'm persuadable. Anything wrong in that?'

'You know you're a good actor, Candia,' said Mary, with an audible edge of exasperation, waving the recorder away. 'Bloody good. But I warn you – because no one else will – you'll be hitting the sell-by date on a pretty face soon. It's a critical age for a woman. If you want people to treat you seriously, then damn well treat yourself seriously. Work at your career instead of bouncing from one job to another like a ball in a pinball machine. Some asshole says, "Why not try a musical, Candia?" Ping! Off you go.'

Llew had the mildly disorientating sense of having heard this dialogue before, too, if phrased rather more elegantly. 'Isn't that a tribute to her, um, sweet and yielding disposition?'

Absorbed in what was evidently a reprise of an old quarrel, Candia blinked for an instant before this prompted a reluctant laugh. 'Oh very clever. Hear that, Mary? Hoist on our own script.'

'If it weren't for me,' said Mary, unimpressed, 'Candia would be batting her eyelashes on a cruddy daytime West Coast soap at this minute. With a seven-year option on her contract.'

'Oodles of money and fabulous frocks . . .' But Candia caught the director's eye and shrugged. 'Thanks for saving me all the same. Trust Mary to know what's best for everyone. And me in particular. I'm going to get a tea. Anyone want one?'

'Reminds me of an old joke,' murmured Llew provocatively

as Candia, hitching her skirt round her knees, ran off across the grass. 'What's the difference between a director and God?'

'God doesn't think he's a director,' said Mary Dance, unmoved. 'Oh, is that for me?' Roderick had walked over holding out a phone. 'Hi . . . Yeah, Mary Dance speaking.' She moved a few paces away to the shade of a tree, clasping a hand over her free ear. 'Hal, thanks for returning my call.'

'Schwartz. As in Schwartz-Rota International,' whispered Roderick, and, evidently feeling Llew's face was registering insufficient awe, went on: 'She's trying to get the money together for a movie. Supposed to be a brilliant script: period piece, First World War. Candia's in, but they can't cast the rest until the deal's in place.' Roderick said this with the thoughtful air of a man who was seeing himself, noble and bloodied in khaki, even as he watched Mary mutter into the phone. 'You'd never guess she was playing poker with half a million dollars, would you?'

'Having read her CV,' said Llew with feeling, 'I could believe anything. Half a million, you say?'

Roderick saw the tiny tape-recorder and affected a wince. 'Strictly off the record. Mary's an intensely private person. She's only talked about this project to her closest friends.'

'Whose discretion,' retorted Llew, tiring of Roderick Chadderton, 'she can obviously trust absolutely.'

'I wouldn't mention it to her if I were you,' he snapped. 'She's famous for – as she would put it – chewing the balls off jumped-up two-bit hacks. I think that odd little man with a camera is calling to you.'

The *News* photographer. Llew, grinding his teeth, strode away to agree pictures. Correctly identifying as the owner of the house a stout figure in droopy cotton frock, muddy galoshes and battered trilby (unmistakably the gear of an English gentlewoman) who was standing in a tangle of terriers, surveying the havoc wrought in a herbaceous border, he began rethinking his feature along satisfyingly savage *would-you-hire-your-garden-to-this-gang-of-vandals?* lines.

Disappointingly, though, Lady Willersley was keen to assure him that the invasion had been the jolliest of larks. 'And, my dear, their catering facilities are miraculous. Toasted bacon sandwiches at all hours. Godfrey says he hasn't eaten so well in years.'

By the time Llew had had his ear bent by her, a gnarled old gardener and a small-part actress who, cooed the efficient Louisa, had actually been born in the village ('And that's what the local papers like, isn't it?'), he reckoned he'd more than a thousand words' worth of copy. In the meantime, the filming had ceased, cables were being wound up, Candia was chattering into the telephone and Roderick massaging the nape of Mary's neck with one long-fingered hand.

'. . . sick of the bunfight at the hotel,' Llew heard him say, in a whisper creamy as an ice-cream advert. 'If we could slip away for a quiet supper somewhere we could actually *talk* for once, then –' He broke off because he saw Llew.

'Don't let me interrupt,' said Llew hastily. 'I just wanted –'

'To grill me,' said Mary Dance, shrugging off Roderick's hand like an old scarf. 'Fine, I'm all yours, Llew Bevan.'

'Well actually . . .' Actually, since the woman clearly had matters a million times (and dollars) more pressing than the *North Yorkshire News* to engage her mega-watted brain, he had decided to cobble up her quotes from cuttings and memory and had intended only to say goodbye.

'Come back to the hotel for a beer,' she said. 'Do you want to run me up in your car?'

'Mary?' gasped Roderick. And his voice quivered with an outrage sweeter than music in the ears of a jumped-up two-bit hack – a hack who promptly decided old cuttings were no substitute for freshly garnered quotes.

Llew only wished he'd a cigarette drooping from the corner of his mouth, Humphrey Bogart-style. So he could have dropped it to the ground, mashed it under his heel and drawled: 'OK by me, shweetheart.'

As it was, he beamed upon Roddy, pocketed his tape-recorder with a flourish and purred: 'Walk this way. Whatever you like.'

12

'There's one tiny snag I've remembered,' said Llew as they walked together across the lawn.

Mary Dance, five foot ten inches of flawless, robotic efficiency, halted. 'Oh?'

Llew swallowed. 'I haven't actually got a car. With me, that is. I walked down here.'

'Terrific,' she said, striding on.

'Sorry, you must think me a complete idiot, I –'

'No, I meant it. I'd like to walk back to the hotel. Someone said there's a path by the stream. You know the way, don't you?'

'Sure,' said Llew. Path? *Stream?* Could she be referring to the noble River Malt? No doubt a mere brook to eyes which have feasted on the Mississippi, but big enough, he was sincerely trusting, to be unmissable if they headed south. 'This way, ma'am.' He led her down a weedy path and began, politely, to unhitch a gate. 'You know, I wouldn't have thought you were the country-walking type.'

She vaulted over the wall. 'That an interview question or just a personal observation?'

He felt obliged to refasten the gate and, clutching the bundle of photocopies, scrambled over the wall after her. His tape-recorder clunked out of his pocket and, as he dived to retrieve it, a bramble whipped round his arm, hooking talons into his flesh with malicious relish. She picked up the recorder and watched him untangle himself.

'You don't strike me as much of a country walker yourself.' She handed back the machine. 'Can you manage interviews on the hoof?'

'Standing on my head,' muttered Llew, eyeing the blood oozing through the sleeve of his (clean) shirt. 'But maybe I'll wait until we hit the riverbank.' She was already strolling away down the path. Heartless cow.

The path through the spinney was flanked with flowers; midges danced in shifting, green-filtered sunbeams and the trees echoed with birdsong – but neither of them remarked on the glories of nature. She seemed lost in thought. Llew, lost in a less metaphysical sphere, was squinting through the leaf canopy, trying to calculate the lie of the river from the position of the sun. Eventually he abandoned topography and studied her instead. She didn't notice that either.

His mother, he decided, would have tutted that the woman just didn't know how to make the best of herself. That hair, for example, glorious scads of the stuff, richly brown as a parlour piano, was yanked back in a loopy plait. Her only attempt at self-adornment, far as he could tell, was a phone number scribbled on the back of her hand. And yet, with a sweat-crumpled shirt reminiscent of cold porridge and boots you could mend the road in, she was striding along with the hip-swinging arrogance of any Dior-clad supermodel. There's class for you, Mam.

God knows how he could ever have imagined, even for a second, she'd look twice at him – or his books, come to that. He remembered Roddy's hapless struggle to define Mary's *beau idéal* and wanted to laugh. I'm not even taller than her, he thought, sneaking a sideways glance and straightening his spine, to no avail. Mind, she was an Amazon. One helluva handsome Amazon. Me, I'm *halfway presentable*, I'm also younger, poorer, red-brick to her Oxbridge and – in career terms – toddling up and down the village cricket pitch while she bestrides the International fucking Test Circuit. Collecting caps like other mortals collect stamps. Dammit, she even walks faster than me.

'That's pretty,' he heard her remark, a few paces ahead. She disappeared as the path twisted round a hawthorn thicket.

'Magic,' breathed Llew, when he caught up. This heartfelt response owed less to the view than to the fact that they had, actually, emerged on the riverbank. 'Left,' he pronounced, with new-found authority. 'OK to switch this on now?' He was holding out the recorder.

'Suit yourself.' She picked up a pebble and sent it scudding across the water. *Five* bounces. Never in his stone-skimming life had Llew managed more than four. He decided it would be quite easy to hate Mary Dance. She yawned. 'What do you want to know?'

Tell me, Ms Dance, has anyone ever tried to murder you?

No, no, better. Forgive me for mentioning this, but I notice your ears are quite large and I couldn't help wondering: are you actually human, or were you beamed down from some stony-faced galactic master race along with Mr Spock?

'So what made you choose to film in North Yorkshire?' Llew enquired politely.

But, as they strolled beside the river at (thank Heaven) a more leisurely pace, he barely listened to her answers. The recorder was mopping up platitudes about light, remoteness, some story of recceing a movie and God knows what else. Llew, however, had been struck by a charmingly offbeat intro for his feature: *Tall, dark and arrogantly handsome, not to mention distinguished, powerful and rolling in money. Mr Darcy? No, that's just the woman director of* Pride and Prejudice, *Mary . . .*

She had broken off in mid-sentence. 'What's so funny?'

'Sorry? Oh, um, nothing.'

'That machine is working, is it? The light keeps flicking.'

'Yes it is,' he retorted. 'It's voice-activated. So you were, um, attracted by the relative emptiness of this part of the world?'

'Aren't you? Isn't that why you came up here?'

'Yes,' said Llew, surprised. 'Yes, I guess so.'

She gazed at him measuringly. 'You really like it then?'

A breeze was teasing the trailing willow fronds; a fat duck led an arrow formation of self-important ducklings across the ripples. Llew gestured towards the scene as though this was answer enough. A wise hack, after all, doesn't fritter time and tape in personal chit-chat. But there was more to his silence than that. He'd done enough murky soul-stirring today. He loved this rural paradise, right? And if, stuck behind a yew hedge, he had for once found himself yearning for cities . . . No, not cities, just city people. What was it Roderick said? Like-minded souls? Kindred spirits? Dammit, he wasn't about to parrot anything that windbag preached.

'Well?' Mary Dance persisted.

Llew muttered something anodyne and, regardless of having collected already more material than he needed in a month of Sunday supplements, upped a few interviewing gears. 'What would you say are your strengths?'

A hardy old favourite, this question. Innocent, direct and guaranteed to floor nine out of ten unsuspecting interviewees.

'Conscientiousness,' said Mary Dance instantly. 'Determination. Energy.' She thought for a couple of seconds now. 'And probably bloody-mindedness.'

'Blimey,' said Llew. Most people, faced with this invitation, felt modestly obliged to flounder through the usual I'm-hardly-the-best-person-to-judge waffle before finally sinking their teeth into the full delicious catalogue. 'No one could accuse you of overselling yourself.'

She gave him the llama stare, blinking at him down her long nose. At these close quarters, he could see she even had the animal's sweepy eyelashes, lush as a pair of hairy caterpillars. 'What did you expect?'

'Vision? Imagination? Lord knows, startling originality? And that's straight from your press cuttings.'

'You can't have seen the ones saying I should stick to making toothpaste commercials. Besides, any jerk can have bright ideas. It's getting them realized separates the men from the boys.'

'So to speak.'

She flapped away a cloud of midges, although it might as well have been his fatuous comment. 'Do you really want to get into that sex-war crap? I'm a director. Male, female, who cares? You asked what I take a pride in, and I told you. I work my butt off getting every last detail the way I want it.'

'Genius being an infinite capacity for taking pains?'

'I didn't say that, either.'

They had reached the bridge. Llew was about to say they needed to cross the water here when she halted, deliberately barring his path. She leaned against the stone buttress. She was smiling oddly. Bloody unsettling it was, too. 'OK,' she said. 'I reckon you've had a fair innings. My turn to bowl. What are your strengths, Mr Llew Bevan?'

The look on his face nearly made her laugh aloud. The guy couldn't have been more startled if a duck had flapped up and bitten him.

'Sorry?'

'Typical,' she said. 'Journalists are just like doctors, scared stiff of taking their own medicine.'

'Hell.' He ran a hand through his hair which, God knows, looked wrecked enough already. What did he cut it with? Garden shears? 'You know, I'd just been thinking you were the first interviewee I'd ever met who wasn't silenced by that question,' he said. 'And here am I, struck dumb. Just like the rest.'

No he wasn't, thought Mary Dance. He wasn't at all like the rest. He didn't bore her, for a start, which was more than most people managed. And when he grinned, like he was doing now, she could even overlook the haircut. 'Think about it,' she said sweetly. 'I can wait.' They strolled across the bridge to the opposite bank.

'Humanity,' he said finally. 'I mean, I like people. And I'm eternally interested in what makes them tick. God, do I sound like a prick?'

'Why?'

'I've noticed that people who claim to be great listeners – fascinated by the human race – are always the gabbling bores who never shut up about themselves. And I hate talking about myself. Honest.'

'An acute observer of human nature,' she pronounced. And cute, she found herself thinking. And then winced at the word. *Cute?* Jesus -.

'Um, optimism,' he went on, his shoulders hunching higher with evident embarrassment. Like the wings of a well-ruffled little bird, she thought, amused. 'I'm a great one for the triumph of hope over experience. The original boy standing on the burning deck when anyone with a shred of sense has fled.'

'I thought that poem was supposed to illustrate mindless obedience, not to say stupidity. Never mind. Go on.'

He eyed her resentfully. 'Who's interviewing who round here?'

She resisted an impulse to pat his ruffled feathers. 'Don't try kidding me you need any more for the *North Yorkshire News.* Anyway, I can tell you're ducking the real answer. Come on. Numero Uno on your own little list. Give.'

All at once, he let out the most endearingly infectious chuckle. 'I'd say a sense of humour if I hadn't also noticed that people who pride themselves on a sense of humour are, without exception, the most po-faced, humourless wankers on God's earth. Let's say I have an enjoyment of the ridiculous.'

'You like laughing at people.'

'Starting with myself, I promise. If we climb this bank we should come out on the lane just beyond the Hall gates.'

She held out a hand both to steady herself and to haul him up the last few feet of the crumbling bank. His hand was warm, dry and felt good in hers. She released her grasp abruptly. 'Isn't that destructive?'

He shook his head. 'Strikes me as the only way to survive with sanity intact. And that's enough about me, so tell me –'

'No, let me guess what's coming.' Mary scrambled over a low stone wall into a tree-lined lane. 'You're going to give me another cutesy pat-a-cake smile and ask for my weaknesses. I've met your kind before. Well forget it, buster.'

'I wouldn't dare,' said Llew. And the smooth-tongued bastard was grinning at her. 'I'm sure you haven't got any.'

Mary grinned back. 'Ask Candia. She'll give you the full A to Z. At least, she's the only person who doesn't hesitate to tell me I'm being a pain in the arse.'

'And are you? A pain in the arse?'

She laughed. 'Shit yes. I guess so. When I have to be. It comes with the job. Do I frighten you?'

He was startled by the question, she could see that. She wouldn't have minded an instant denial, but he was actually thinking it over. 'No . . .'

'But?'

'I imagine you could be . . . unnerving. If you chose.'

Mary raised an eyebrow. 'Want to know what they call me in the unit? The Neutron Bomb. Destroys people but not buildings. Oh, thanks a bunch, brother. I'm glad you think it's funny.'

Maybe he wasn't wrong about his assets, though. That lopsided, crinkle-eyed laugh could melt hearts – well, the heart of any woman dumb enough not to vomit at the metaphor. They had arrived at the gates of the hotel and turned into the drive. Should she invite him to stop for dinner? 'I shouldn't worry,' he was saying cheerfully. (No way, she thought. Absolutely not.) 'The dangerous time is when they stop inventing names for you. That's when you've sunk beneath contempt.'

'I hope you're right,' she said, and found herself adding defensively: 'Anyway, I like to think I play fair. I try hard. Although I seem to recall Candia once saying she hoped she never really messed up on me because once someone was off my Christmas card list – I'm only quoting her, OK? This is definitely off the record – once someone had got on the wrong side of me, that was it. They were out for good. No second chances.'

He actually looked shocked. 'That's pretty damning. Is it true?'

What had inspired her to open this can of worms? 'How should I know?' she said, irritably. 'I've never bothered to think about it.' They were approaching the last curve of the drive. 'Self-analysis is as boring as watching your nail lacquer dry.' She saw him sneak a glance at her hands, and laughed. 'Correct. I don't go in for either. But if pushed, I'd sooner waste dollars on a manicurist than a shrink. And you can quote me. You're obviously good at your job, Llew Bevan. A dangerous operator with a tape-recorder.' The chimneys of the Hall were in view. Mary suddenly stopped and looked at him. So he halted too and stared right back.

'Something the matter?' he enquired.

'No – no, not at all . . .' I was just wondering, she thought, the words articulating perfectly clearly in her head, what else you might be good at. Specifically, what kind of an operator you'd be in bed . . . 'Actually, I was wondering –'

But at that instant, with a loud bip on its horn, a car rolled round the corner.

Llew recognized the car and waved. John drew up beside them and leaned out of the window. 'Amazing. When Candia told me you were walking back from Holly Lodge, I swore she was imagining things. D'you want a lift home, Llew? Or have you reformed your sedentary way of life?'

'Behold a knight in white Volvo come to your rescue,'

said Mary Dance, before he could get a word in. In a voice so changed from a moment ago it could have been a different woman. She seemed to be laughing at some private joke. 'Maybe we'll have that beer another time.' This, however, was offered with the polite social inflection which implies some time next century will do fine. 'You've everything you want for your piece, haven't you?'

'Well, yes . . .' said Llew.

'Then, if you'll forgive me, I'll go and collapse into my bath. Thanks for the walk.' And, with a brisk wave, she was off.

'Thank you and good night,' murmured Llew, snapping off his tape-recorder and walking round to the passenger door.

'Home for me tonight,' said John, leaning over and opening the door for him. 'I thought it was time I touched base.'

'Run out of clean socks?' Llew wasn't really listening. He was squirming round in his seat, watching Mary Dance vanish into the Hall.

'It's not just that. I've seen the doc this afternoon, and he's given me the all-clear to use my hand again. Well, God knows, there was little enough wrong in the first place.' John shoved the car into gear with a noticeably clumsy crunch, and pulled away. 'Convalescence over.'

'You know, I can't make that woman out,' said Llew. 'One minute she's –' He broke off, belatedly registering that John was sounding edgy. Not like himself. 'Sorry, what? You're not planning to start work this time of night are you?'

'Lord no.' John frowned into the rear-view mirror. 'Thing is, Llew, don't get me wrong. They're a great crowd back there, but they eat together every evening and split the bill – and you know the Hall. Costs an absolute fortune.'

So that was it. Nothing serious. 'Tricky,' agreed Llew, returning to wondering what Mary Dance had been about to say to him when John rolled up.

'And of course I won't allow Candia to sub me.'

'Why not? I could swallow a lot of scruples if Charlie was cooking them. Sorry, sorry.' John was not looking amused.

'It's not just money. I've explained to her I've got to water the plants, open a few windows, sort out the mail – I can't just desert the place.'

'Wheel the girl back to the homestead then. I'll don a white hat and chef for you, if you like.'

'Oh, I don't think so,' mumbled John. And rambled into some explanation about make-up calls at dawn which Llew barely heard. He was winding back his tape-recorder in search of the last few words he'd recorded.

'Something the matter?' he heard his own voice crackle. Sounding Welsher than his Dad. Was there some malign micro-chip in these gadgets designed to exaggerate accents?

'No – no, not at all,' drawled Mary Dance. He could hear the smile in her voice. 'Actually, I was wondering . . .'

She had been about to ask him to join her for dinner at the hotel. That was all. Big deal.

Except Mary Dance was honest enough to recognize that that was by no means all. It was not only dinner she'd had in mind. Just because he had pretty eyes and a sharp brain. She slammed the door of the hotel behind her. She must be going soft in the head. She hadn't the time or energy for a sex life in the middle of a shoot. Let alone with the likes of him. A nobody – worse, a joking yokel *content* to rot his life into the compost of this picturesque corner of nowheresville. John Hapgood had rolled along in the nick of time. He might or might not have saved Llew a walk. If he hadn't, then he'd saved her from some infinitely less advisable exercise.

Candia was sitting alone in the lobby with a large drink in front of her and an almost palpable cloud of gloom hanging over her. 'Enjoy your walk?'

'Yup. Something bugging you?'

'No.'

Candia couldn't lie, thought Mary, if her life depended on it. There was a bottle of wine in an ice bucket on a side table. She poured herself a glass.

Roddy strolled down the stairs. 'John about?'

'Gone home for the night,' said Candia flatly.

So that was it, thought Mary. Well, they'd been living in one another's pockets all week. All good things have to come to an interval. And if there was this level of misery over a night's separation, what would she be like when filming here ended? But then, to her amazement, she heard Candia petulantly asking Roddy if he was going to commission John to build the dresser in his kitchen or not.

'What's this?' said Mary sharply. 'Are you setting up as the guy's agent or something?'

'If John's coming to London,' said Candia, 'he might as well find some work.'

'You mean to *live?*' Mary was actually shocked. In her book, location flings came under the holiday-romance heading. And any fool knows the almond-eyed charmer on a moonlit beach is likely to look a damn sight less desirable on a rush-hour tube platform. Would John Hapgood transplant from the rolling hedgerows of North Yorkshire to a terracotta pot in Chelsea Reach? Frankly, she doubted it.

Roderick caught her eye and grimaced sympathetically. 'Now I insist,' he murmured to Candia, 'if there's to be a wedding, the delightful Bernard must preside as Master of Ceremonies. I'm sure his speech would be a riot.'

'Who's talking about weddings?' snapped Candia – to Mary's considerable relief. 'John's coming down for a few days once we're through in Derbyshire, course he is. And then, well, we'll just have to see what happens, won't we.'

Mary was prevented from offering some pointedly acid predictions by Roderick turning to her and asking where the dark-eyed silver-tongued newshound had got to.

'Llew hitched a ride home with John,' she said shortly.

Whereupon his smug smile annoyed her so much she found herself expressing a fervent hope Llew Bevan would be coming up to the hotel for dinner another day. Soon. And she realized she meant it. She perceived no contradiction between this and her disapproval of Candia's burgeoning romance. Mary was older, wiser, and knew how to organize a sex life.

'Don't leave us, darling,' protested Roddy as she picked up her glass and rose to her feet.

'I'm going to have a long bath, and to think about the letter scene tomorrow.'

Whereupon, as she climbed the stairs, Mary Dance reprogrammed her efficient brain to do exactly that.

13

It was a grey and soggy afternoon. Artie Shaw oozed moodily out of the hi-fi. Nicholas Llewellyn Bevan was hunched over his word-processor with a pencil chenched, cigar-style, between his teeth. He chewed it methodically. Here, unmistakably, was a writer in deep trouble.

He read through Chapter Twelve (umpteenth draft) again. And found himself smirking. A smirk which faded when he gathered up the printed-out spools of Chapter sodding Thirteen and began rereading that. Not that he was superstitious, but he was beginning to wonder whether he shouldn't have called it Twelve A. Oh, for a friendly terrorist to liven things up a bit. Personally, he'd always found Semtex more reliably explosive on the page than passion.

The letter scene. Did anyone actually write letters these days? Frankly, he doubted it. A fax then? But how many pubs could be expected to have fax machines? Hell, what about a plain old telephone call? Dimly, he registered the noise of a car revving round the bend at the foot of the hill. It gave him an idea.

'Time for a little variation on the theme,' he murmured, and began typing rapidly. 'Entering, unannounced, Stage Left . . .'

When Llew glanced up from his keyboard and saw the natty turquoise convertible parked at his gate he instantly, if irrationally, assumed such an exotic motor must belong to Mary

Dance. Although, as the doorbell trilled and he slithered down the rickety ladder to the landing – a quick if precipitous route to the front door – he found himself wondering if the flashy colour was quite her style.

Standing in his porch, however, was a woman he did not recognize. Middle-aged going on sixteen. Small and prominently brassièred, with white spike heels, streaky blonde hair and a streaky blonde Yorkshire terrier tucked under one bracelet-jingling arm. They both stared at him through their fringes.

'Hello,' said Llew. 'Can I help you?'

The pooch growled. She smiled coyly. 'Before you say another word: Aries?'

'Sorry?'

'I always like to guess. And you have that strong-minded but sensitive look.'

'Thanks,' said Llew. 'But I'm a Libran. I think.'

'Of course you are,' she declared. 'And you're racking your little brain, wondering who on earth this can be, popping up on your doorstep without so much as a by-your-leave. Well, I know we've never actually been introduced, Mr Hapgood, but –'

'Ah. No,' said Llew in some relief. 'Wrong house.'

The hand she was holding out dropped in a tinkle of gold. 'But they said at the pub . . . Cote Green Barn?'

'Farm. Actually, John used to live here. He moved across to the barn after . . .'

'His wife passed on?' She oozed compassion like jam out of a doughnut. 'I'd heard all about that, and believe me I feel for the poor lamb, having lost two husbands myself.'

How careless? 'How tragic.'

She leaned forward confidentially. 'How is he?'

Shagged? Gob-smacked, knock-kneed and starry-eyed? 'Well,' murmured Llew, reverent as an undertaker, 'it's nearly three years now.'

'As long as that? But he hasn't remarried, I gather.' Hello, hello . . . Was this a predatory gleam under the mascara? 'So that must be his barn.'

'It is,' he said, 'but I'm afraid you've missed him. Can I give him a message, um . . .?'

'Irene,' she said. 'Mrs Irene Cole.'

'Irene Cole?' echoed Llew, wondering why the name was familiar.

'Iren*ee*,' she corrected, stressing the third syllable. She fondled the dog. 'Your Uncle Kenny insists on the "e", doesn't he, Freddy? Do you know Sir Kenneth Burroughs at all?'

Llew blinked. 'The actor? Well, not personally, but . . .'

'My neighbour in the Cotswolds and a regular customer, in fact, more of a friend, I think he would allow me to say. I run a hotel, you know: small, but very select – just like me, Sir Kenneth jokes.'

'The Red Lion,' exclaimed Llew, placing the name at last. 'You own Bernie's pub, don't you?'

'I see our fame goes before us, Freddy.' Her smile was glossy and sharp-edged as a letter box. 'I inherited it from my late husband, bless his cottons. Doesn't Fate work in mysteri

The doorbell was ringing again. Really ringing this time. Nicholas Llewellyn Bevan cursed and cancelled the last few paragraphs. Crap: totally gratuitous introduction of Sir Kenneth whatever-his-name-was. He peered out of the window.

There actually was a car parked outside. A sports car, too. But it was red, snub-nosed, and instantly familiar. He slid down the ladder, cursed as a splinter snagged his finger and was sucking the injury as he flung open the front door. 'I might have known. Another plot's hitting the rocks and who should pop up, like the evil genie of the word-processor?'

As it chanced, this visitor was also female, diminutive and streaky blonde, but dogless, bangleless and would have blacked his eye if he described her as middle-aged. She was, as he well knew, thirty-eight. Thirty-nine next March. 'Thanks for the big welcome. You really know how to make an ex-wife feel wanted, Nick.'

'I wasn't expecting you.'

'That's no excuse.'

'It was the Reverend Collins who'd just washed up on my doorstep. So to speak. Mind, I'd been sneakily hoping it was Mary Dance. Conceited pig that I am.'

'I don't know what you're talking about.'

He sighed heavily and stepped back. 'That's the trouble. Neither do I. Well, come in then, since you're here.'

Caroline Bevan walked past him into the sitting room, sniffing the air. 'Back on the fags, are we?'

'It's all Christopher's fault. He left a packet when he was up here, half-term.'

'You've been letting him *smoke*? Honestly, Nick, I some-times wonder why I agreed to share custody.'

'If you've found any way of stopping a six-foot seventeen-year-old doing exactly what the fuck he likes, then kindly enlighten me.'

'Sure I have. I cut off the money supply..' Caroline caught the look in his face and bit her lip. 'Sorry – sorry. Below the belt. What're you writing, anyway?'

'A novel.'

'Why do I bother asking?'

'What you really mean is: why do I bother writing?'

'You said it, sweetheart. No, look, Nick, I haven't come to quarrel.'

'So why have you driven more than two hundred miles north of the last outpost of civilization as you now recognize it? By which I mean the M25.'

'It was the opening of Christopher's school play last night. I went to that.'

'That's only the first hundred-odd.'

'And I wanted to talk. To you.'

'OK, I'm listening.'

Caroline spun round to face him. 'No you're not. You're sniping. I mean talk. Seriously talk. Peace-offering: I've brought a couple of bottles of wine.'

He stared at her. 'Were you – are you – planning to stay here then?'

Caroline shrugged. 'You've got a spare room, haven't you? And I hope you've also got something to eat with the wine, because I'm famished. Except . . .' She caught herself up with a visible effort. 'Look, if you're really working, on a run with a book, I suppose I'd better not interrupt. I can always go round to John's.'

'I am writing as it happens but . . .' He stared at her, then up at the ceiling, as though he could see through to the sorry pile of manuscript strewn across the floor of his office. Finally he gave a weary shrug. 'You couldn't have come at a better time,' he said. 'I guess I was just about to jack the whole bloody story in anyway.'

Episode Two

From the *Sunday Chronicle*, Arts and Books Section, 26 June:

... nevertheless, it's hard to know how seriously to take Nick Llewellyn Bevan, whose latest spine-tingler *Snow Black* was published last week. He introduces his office (a charmingly converted hayloft with stunning views over the North Yorks Moors) as the Intensive Care Ward. This does not refer to the state of his liver, he hastens to add (emptying the bottle of wine between our glasses) but to the mounds of sickly manuscripts littering desk, floor and sofa. My glass is resting, he warns me, on a particularly tricky case.

'I've performed more heroic surgery there than Victor Frankenstein, but I'm afraid the poor bugger's failing fast.' He sighs. 'Any day now I'm going to have to declare brain death and pull out the word-processor plugs ...'

A tactful enquiry as to the nature of the, ah, ailment produces only a grin and an elliptical hint that writers should stick to their own patch of the literary pastures ...

14

'You're rewriting *Pride and Prejudice*,' Caroline exclaimed, walking into the kitchen with a handful of manuscript. 'In modern dress – and drag to boot.'

Nick Bevan spun round, outraged. 'Who said you could read that?'

'Don't bite my head off. I found it on the floor of your office. I've only skipped through.'

'I thought you'd gone up to have a bath.'

'I did – but you've known me long enough to realize I'm physically incapable of sitting in a bathtub or anywhere else for longer than two minutes without a supply of printed matter.'

'Could've read *War and Peace*, the time you've been up there.'

'Hell, I couldn't put it down, I was laughing so much.'

Nick looked hopeful. 'Thought it was funny, eh?'

'Hysterical. Such a *peculiar* sensation, finding one's ex-husband and brother striding across the pages of a novel. And as for the refs to yours truly –'

'I meant funny as in scintillatingly witty, not as in funny peculiar.'

Caroline took no notice. 'Downright creepy actually. Like reading schoolgirl fantasies. Or schoolboy in this case. Did you fancy her as you typed?'

'Who?'

'Ms Darcy. Sorry, *Dance*.'

'Neat that, don't you think?' said Nick. 'Mr Darcy – Mary Dance.'

'Oh very. And? Did you lust after your long-legged creation?'

'Actually she's called Hamilton.'

Caroline stared at him. 'Mary *Hamilton*? As in award-winning director of *Cambridge Nights, Hello Mr Good* –'

'Got it in one.' Nick tasted his sauce and frowned. 'She was filming round here a few weeks back. *Pride and Prejudice*, no less. And I did knock off a piece for the *Yorkshire Mail* – interviewed her, et cetera, et cetera.'

'As per page whatever?'

Nick sprinkled salt and stirred briskly. 'Word for bloody word. And scads more on the original tape, recycled into other scenes, naturally. Mind, I never used the tall-dark-and-have-some intro in real life. Too flip for the worthy *Yorkshire Mail*.'

'Just dashed off a novel instead? Casting yourself as blushing hero.'

Nick grinned. 'Naturally.'

'*Mister* Lizzy Bennet. Llew, indeed. No one's called you Llewellyn since your mother kicked the cauldron. What on earth gave you the idea?'

'I was christened Llew –'

'For the book, dimbo.'

He shrugged. 'You, actually.'

She gasped. 'I suggested you sit down and write a parody of –'

'Course not, but . . .' Nick put aside his spoon and leaned back against the sink. 'Look, don't get me wrong, Caro, but have you ever felt God was pointing you in a certain direction?'

'Now you're even talking like your Ma.'

'Fate then. What I'm saying is, few weeks back, when you phoned I really had hit rock bottom. Knee-deep in dead manuscripts. You were going on about the dosh romantic fiction pulls in, and, courtesy of BBC Radio Dales, I've got this DIY bodice-ripping manual by Lavinia what's-her-name.'

'Stacey. If this is going to be a long story I want a drink.'

Nick ignored her. 'That's what you should have taken up to your bath if you wanted a laugh. I tell you, she really got up my nose.'

'Her sales figures or her prose-style?'

'Both. Well, actually, as writing manuals go, it's not bad. And, I grant you, there's more to this romance business than meets the eye.'

'Steely, smouldering or . . . No, I remember: "blue as a postcard sea"? And as for the sun-gilded lovers smooching over the lily pond . . . Yuck-yuckety-yuck.'

'Piss off.'

She grinned. 'I never guessed that under such a ruggedly uncompromising exterior beat a heart of pure slush.'

'Oh come on, I was only playing by the rules – when in romance, do as the Lavinias do, and what have you. And she doesn't half lay down the law. Inscribed on tablets of bloody soap. Handsome, successful, older man meets . . .'

'Plucky, plain-Jane; she hates him for 249 pages, marries him page 250. I edit a woman's magazine and that scenario, let me tell you, is deader than Crimplene twinsets. Mills and Boon have them bonking by page ten these days. And with monotonous regularity thereafter.'

'Same formula,' said Nick, 'according to Lavinia. Quoting *Pride and Prejudice* throughout like the holy writ. Anyway, I'm pondering this – and if you'd seen the bills in my in-tray you'd know why – when this television crowd moves in, and what are they filming?'

'My tongue is hanging out.'

'I suddenly thought – blinding light – sod this for a lark, why not turn the classic formula upside down and inside out? Keep the plot, but reverse the sexes. Eat your heart out Jane Austen, this is your actual Twentieth-Century Equal

Opportunities romance: rich, rude and rakish women chasing shy, impoverished ... OK, OK, keep your hair on.' He rummaged in a cupboard and produced a bottle of Scotch and two glasses. 'But the amazing thing was, once I started writing, it was like letting off a fire-extinguisher. Honest, Caro, the words just gushed out, totally unstoppable. No wonder I hardly changed a name – there wasn't time. I was typing my fingers to the bone. Twelve chapters in, I was, and then ...'

'And then?'

Nick looked away. 'Oh, I dunno. Well, the new book came out for one thing and the publishers finally got their publicity act together so I was tied up with a load of interviews ... Want this neat?'

'I saw the piece in the *Chronicle* last Sunday. Quite entertaining. Ice and still water, please. And?'

'And I had to let it drop for a while. Then I felt I ought to go back to the beginning and tart up the story-so-far. Put more action in for a start. God knows, all they seem to do in the original is sit round yapping. But today, when I actually tried to move the story on ...' Nick swirled the whisky in his glass and swallowed a large mouthful. 'Well, it just seemed to have collapsed on me. Not funny any more. When you rolled up I was trying to write in old Charlie Meschia's appalling wife – you remember, Irene?'

'Sure but ... Good heavens, Charlie's not really moved up to Yorkshire, has he?'

'Course not. Haven't seen him in years. I just borrowed him to play Charlotte Lucas. Get it: Luciano – Lucas? Irene was to be the Reverend Collins, preaching astrology and ... Oh shit, never mind. Irene wasn't going to work, I could see that. None of it was. So joke over.'

'Well, well,' said Caroline. 'Fourteen years of marriage –'

'And three of non-marriage.'

'– and I'm discovering a whole new side to you.'

'Bollocks. It was an exercise, that's all. What's the novelty, anyway? Writers are supposed to mine their own lives for material. It's notoriously risky living with them. In case . . .' He chuckled. 'In case your words are taken down and used in episodes. I was pleased with that gag.'

'The old ones are always the best.' Caroline tore a corner off a French loaf and nibbled it, eyeing him satirically. 'You knocked a few years off your age, I notice.'

'So? I knocked some off Mary Hamilton's too. She's forty-two. Still four years older than me.'

'And *did* you fancy her? More to the point, am I to believe she was casting mean and hungry eyes at you?'

'You needn't sound quite so incredulous. She did actually invite me down to the location, red carpet treatment and all.' He looked a touch self-conscious. 'Although I can't answer for her privately lustful designs on my person.'

'Nor on your *œuvre*? Or are we breathlessly awaiting Nick Bevan, the movie?'

'Oh sure. Along with a cure for colds and the Second Coming. Only George could have been barmy enough to hope. And for your information, no, I bloody well didn't like her. *Don't* like her. In real life, she's a dangerous piece of work. Look, can we drop the subject now?'

Caroline ignored him. 'Some of it is quite funny actually. In a wacky sort of way. I mean, I can see it's an interesting experiment in sex-role reversal. By the way, is that loutish son of the pub supposed to be an accurate portrait of our own dear child?'

'I'd had a bellyful of Christopher when I started writing,' said Nick. 'He was a pain in the arse this half-term. So I gave him away. I reckoned he and Bernard Nugent deserved one another.'

'Bernard *Nugent*? There's even a Red Lion, too?'

'Black Lion. You must've driven past it on your way up. Known locally as the Fat Cat in honour of Bernard's beer belly. Mind, at a stroke, I'd deprived him and poor Sarah of their hard-earned freehold. Ah, the God-like power of the author. Come and sit down, love. The stew will cook by itself for a bit.'

She leaned over the pan, sniffing appreciatively. 'You know, I miss your cooking.'

'If nothing else. I've got the bottle, you bring the ice. Top-up?'

She followed him through to the sitting room. 'Bit weaker this time. And for your information, I don't earn fifty K. Or not yet, anyway. But as for writing poor John into your little fantasy . . .'

Nick stopped pouring and turned to stare at her. 'Shit, Caro, that's the *totally* true bit,' he said. He dropped some ice in the glass and handed it back to her. 'I thought you must have heard. Didn't your baby brother tell you he had a wing-ding affair with the lovely Candia Mayhew?'

'You're *joking*,' shrieked Caroline.

'I wish I were.' Nick settled himself into the armchair opposite her and held up his own glass, giving it a little shake. 'I tell you, he gave this stuff a bit of welly when they packed up their cameras and buggered off to locations new. Which of course they did.'

'For heaven's sake, Nick. You're telling me *Candia Mayhew* plucked my brother out of a crowded dance hall?'

'Amazing, eh? And none more gob-smacked than the boy scout himself. In fact, that was the real spark for me, come to think of it. Old John, standing in my kitchen, saying he felt like he'd been living in a novel ever since Candia –'

'I think,' interrupted Caroline forcefully, 'you'd better tell me exactly where fiction ends and fact starts.'

Nick waved an airy hand. 'I rearranged a few things. Details, that's all, to follow the shape of the original novel. You know, exercised a bit of artistic licence.'

'Like claiming you played jazz clarinet?'

He smirked. 'Ah, but if I'd ever learned, what a helluva performer I'd have been.'

'Not to mention cricket. Hitting sixes like – like Roy of the bloody Rovers. I don't believe you've wielded a cricket bat in your life.'

'So maybe I was only a spectator. Poetic truth – Bernie and his team are a metaphor for Mrs Bennet and her daughters, don't you see?'

'Sod poetic truth, I want the plain unvarnished.'

'The conversations are authentic,' protested Nick. 'The ones I'm in, anyhow. I just polished up the gags and spread 'em around a bit. Imported a few minor –'

'It's my little brother I want to know about,' cried Caroline, 'Candia Mayhew, of all people.' She shook her head wonderingly. 'I mean, don't get me wrong. Once he'd emerged from the shock after Sally died, John damn well needed a woman and I've been saying for ages –'

'No doubt to John himself. With the usual tact and discretion of a big sister.'

'I handle him with kid gloves.'

'I wish I could say the same about Candia Mayhew.'

'Is she a bitch? I once saw her at a party, actually. Some press launch. I can't claim we exchanged words, she was in a thicket of slavering reporters.'

'Not a bitch, no. Far from it. You can't help liking her. And John, well, he was besotted.'

'Oh God.'

'Like I said, he just couldn't believe her fancy had alighted on him. Walking round with an idiot grin and no idea what day it was.' Nick laughed. 'I remember Christopher asking quite seriously what Uncle John was taking. And I don't think he meant vitamin pills.'

'My son knew? Nick, when was all this?'

'I told you: three, four weeks ago. Started when Chris was up for half-term anyhow.'

'And I suppose it just slipped his mind to tell me his uncle was screwing Candia Mayhew?'

'I doubt if he realized.'

'He may be bone idle but he's not stupid.'

'At seventeen, if you remember back that far, it's flesh-creepingly impossible to believe your parents' generation could ever get up to anything sexual. I know I believed I had to be the product of immaculate conception.'

'And behaved like you could walk on water ever since.'

'I thought,' said Nick, 'we weren't fighting.'

'That was a joke.'

'Sorry.'

There was a silence.

'Christopher was hardly here actually,' said Nick in a neutrally informative tone which they both recognized as peace-making. 'Cadged a bed in town off Bernard's brother and spent most of the week hanging round the local radio station. Cheeky bugger.'

'Oh I'd already heard plenty about his glittering début on the wireless,' said Caro. 'Did you swing that?'

Nick shook his head. 'All his own work. I ask you, media studies.'

'That is what he wants to do, isn't it?'

'I'd rather he went to a decent university, wouldn't you?'

'Meaning?'

'Well, for heaven's sake, Oxford or Cambridge then. We pay enough for his bloody school – OK, sorry. You pay.'

'As a proportion of income, you contribute more than I do,' said his ex-wife generously. 'Anyway, Oxbridge isn't everything. If you didn't go there, it's easy to overrate the kudos. We enjoyed Manchester, didn't we?'

'The rate Christopher's going, he'll be lucky to get into the McDonald's Institute of Burger-Making.'

'And whose fault is that?'

Nick suddenly laughed. 'There are times when I feel bloody

sorry for the Mr Bennets of this world, with five kids. One's bad enough.' He rose, stretching. 'Spuds should be baked in about ten minutes. Another Scotch, or shall we move on to wine?'

'Glass of white for me. Got any crisps?' Caroline kicked off her shoes and curled her legs comfortably under her on the sofa. She waited until Nick returned with a bottle and glasses before asking: 'So who was the girl then?'

Nick suddenly looked wary. 'Girl?' He put the bottle on a sideboard and twisted a corkscrew into it.

'My son is still looking smug as a cat who's cornered the cream futures market. There was some female he'd met up here who was Big In Television, I forget the name, I'd swear it popped up in your manuscript somewhere . . .'

'Um, Sasha?'

'*Sasha*. One of your *Pride and Prejudice* crowd?'

The cork popped out. 'No,' said Nick forcefully. He poured out the wine and handed her a glass. 'No, nothing to do with them. At least, well, as it chanced, Sasha knew some of them. But that's neither here nor there. She just happened to be staying with an old friend at Radio Dales. Or so I gathered. Sasha Floyd, she's called. Quite attractive actually.'

'Oh ho. I recognize that tone of voice. Longing drips from every syllable.'

'Balls,' said Nick unconvincingly. 'I liked her, sure, but . . . Oh, it doesn't matter. She was far too old for Christopher, anyway.'

Caroline's eyes narrowed. 'But not for you? Don't tell me my little boy cut his father out? Oh, poor Nicky.'

'Nothing of the sort,' he said crossly. 'All she did for Chris was give him a bit of help, that's all. At Radio Dales. She'd worked in radio herself.'

'Where's she in the story?'

'She's not. Look, I've packed that thing in. Stupid bloody idea. Can we stop talking about it?'

'Most riveting tale you've ever written as far as I'm concerned,' said Caroline, grinning. She saw Nick's face and flung up a hand. 'OK, OK. Not another word.'

'You said you wanted to talk.'

Her grin froze. 'Oh – oh, yes. I suppose I did. Look, don't you want to eat first?'

'Up to you.'

'The thing is . . . Look, when I phoned the other week . . . Oh, Nick . . .'

Nick smiled sadly. 'Come on, love. Spit it out. Whatever it is.'

Caroline downed the contents of her glass defiantly. 'I want to be get married again. I mean – I *am* getting married again.'

Nick raised his glass. 'Congratulations.'

'Do you mean that?'

'No,' he said. 'But I'm prepared to work on it.'

15

Nick couldn't sleep. Too much to drink and too much to think about.

Not that he was particularly surprised by Caroline's announcement. What surprised him was how wickedly it hurt. They had been apart physically and legally for three whole years now. And severed emotionally – or so he'd thought – for much longer. Towards the end they had even given up fighting. The fights belonged in the early days when, fresh out of university, with jobs on the *Salford Advertiser* barely paying the rent on their slummy bedsit, they'd managed to conceive Christopher. Whereupon, in a flurry of infatuation, cheap fizz and downright pig-headedness – because everyone told them they were barmy – they had got married.

Shared passion for the child had outlived their passion for one another. The baby was now six feet tall and still growing. A clever, handsome, feckless cocktail of their genes. 'All the wrong ones,' Caro had once said. 'My ambition with your application.' Of course, as every accidental parent will always say, neither of them could regret Christopher's existence. And of course they didn't. Nick couldn't help feeling, though, that married life would have been easier, and maybe more enduring, if the same lovable bundle had rolled along ten years later. At the time when all their friends were settling down and sprouting families.

Caro, a mother at twenty-one, had found herself an object

of curiosity, if not actual pity, among her contemporaries. And she had furiously resented the obstacle to her career. Well, at least she'd made up for that now. The point at which her salary overtook Nick's had coincided almost exactly with the moment he decided to swap newspapers for novels. And nothing seemed to convince her that his defection wasn't inspired by macho jealousy. Within the year, she'd been offered the job in London and they'd parted. All of them. She moved south, Christopher had already started at boarding school and Nick came up here. Buying the farmhouse, ironically enough, from his wife's recently widowed brother.

Would anything have been different, Nick wondered now, if he'd made an instant success of the books? Four years since his riotous leaving party at the paper, and only three books published plus a motley heap of unfinished failures to show for it. This *Pride and Prejudice* spoof wouldn't be lonely in the rejects cupboard. But it was still early days – that's what George said. His agent was a great propper-up of bashed egos. Anyway, most writers have a tough time at the start. That was one thing he and Sasha Floyd had agreed about. One of the many things.

They had met, he and Sasha, at the Maltbury village fête, of all places. It was a Saturday afternoon, the very day after he had trotted along the riverbank with a tape-recorder and Mary Hamilton. He'd been intending to hammer the piece out that afternoon, but Christopher had demanded he come to the fête. Radio Dales had a bus parked in the corner of the green and Chris, inevitably, was on board with a stopwatch hung importantly round his neck and a clipboard in his hand.

'Still making the coffee?' Nick enquired. Which was a father's way of showing he was rather proud of his son's enterprise.

'Excuse me, squire,' retorted Christopher. 'You're talking to an Official Outside Broadcast Researcher here.'

This was to be his final voyage on the airwaves, however. Half-term was ending and his rucksack was also on board the bus. Having spent the week on a sofa in the pub belonging to Bernard's brother Ernie, he was, with extreme reluctance, returning to the farmhouse tonight so that Nick could deliver him back to school the following day. Nick had driven down this afternoon only (so he thought) to collect son and associated baggage. The stopwatch and clipboard suggested otherwise.

'I've a feature to write,' he complained, as Christopher confirmed his suspicions by saying he couldn't hang around talking to his parent when he had three hours' worth of interviews to line up.

'Haven't you knocked that off yet?' Chris said with the insouciance of a seasoned hack.

'I didn't pin Mary Hamilton down until yesterday afternoon.'

'Oh, *Mary Hamilton*,' said Chris grinning. 'And do you still think the sun shines out of her –'

'Chris!'

'Can't fool me. I clocked those goofy smiles across the studio table t'other night.'

Ahem, yes. Perhaps Nick had not been strictly truthful earlier this evening when he'd told Caroline he had not found Mary Hamilton attractive. Sure, he'd disliked the woman plenty at times, but mainly he'd liked her a lot. And there had been one moment – on that walk by the river as she turned on him laughing – when he'd suddenly found himself wanting her with the jelly-kneed urgency of a schoolboy. A fleeting aberration, that was all. The next afternoon, at the village fête, he'd seen sense again. With a vengeance.

And this had nothing to do with Chris confidentially informing him that the woman wasn't really such a big deal in the film world.

Nick raised an eyebrow. 'You reckon?'

'Everyone knows she's only got where she is because of family pull.'

'Thanks for keeping me in touch,' Nick said laconically, feeling older by the minute. 'Come and find me when you're through.'

So, expecting a wait of hours and idly watching fat gymkhana ponies being prodded and kicked over knee-high poles – and deciding Thelwell was less a cartoonist than a chronicler of social history – he'd been surprised to find Christopher at his elbow only minutes later urging him to come over and say hello to Sasha.

'Who?'

'I *told* you about her. When you came in for the arts prog. She's brilliant, Dad. Taught me loads.'

'More than your teachers ever have.'

Christopher snorted. 'She knows everything and everybody – and I mean *everybody* in the business. Including, you might be interested to hear, Mary megabucks Hamilton. She's even read your new book. Mind,' he added, as though this required excusing, 'she's a writer herself.'

She was a strange, leggy creature. At first glance, seeing her sprawled on the grass with a Coke can in her hand, Nick had thought she was barely older than his son, packaged as she was in the ubiquitous clinging black of youth. But her face, parchment pale under a scrambled nest of dark hair, was older – she was twenty-eight, he later learned – and she clambered to her feet as though she really did want to meet him. She also offered a few genuinely perceptive compliments (or so Nick flattered himself) on his not-quite published book. She told him, with disarming smugness, that she'd nicked the station's review copy and intended to keep it.

He smiled back. 'You're a writer too, I gather. Novels?'

'Television these days, actually. Mainly.'

'Ah,' said Nick. 'The big money.'

She pulled a face. 'When I can get the work. Look . . .' She leaned towards him confidentially, shaking the Coke can. 'If I have to swallow one more mouthful of this piss, I'm going to puke. Is there anywhere we can get a drink?'

'Bet your life,' said Nick, with enthusiasm.

Christopher looked from one to the other. 'Well,' he said, with a touch of uncertainty. 'Well, I'll leave you to it, then. See you later, Dad.'

Nick returned from the scrum in the beer tent with large and almost-chilled beakers of lager. Accepting one with a sigh of gratitude, Sasha produced a packet of cigarettes and thrust it towards him.

Nick grimaced. 'I've promised myself I won't smoke while Christopher's around. Setting a good example, you know.'

'Fuck that,' she retorted. 'Anyway, the kid smokes like a chimney.'

And so he accepted one fag – and Lord knows how many more. He'd even nipped across to the post office and bought another packet, as they wandered round the ground, chucking balls at skittles and darts at photographs of the Parish Council. He'd won her a bottle of fizzy wine, betting on ferrets, which she popped open when they finished the lager. She won a vast – and vastly ugly – teddy bear and insisted on presenting it to him. Even now it was lurking on top of his wardrobe. Lime green fur and purple paws. He was surprised the evil beast wasn't glowing in the dark.

As he lay in bed, he wondered what it was about her that was so seductive. Odd thing was – and he recalled thinking this even at the time – if you had to describe Sasha, feature for feature, she'd sound very like Mary Hamilton. Both were tall and thin with long dark hair and a sassy metropolitan buzz. And yet they could hardly have been less alike. Sasha was pretty, which was not an epithet you'd dream of applying to la Hamilton, and almost too thin. She had reminded him of a shivering whippet. Because, inside the spiky, wise-cracking shell, he glimpsed a rumpled, bruised vulnerability – and it had really got to him. Those big dark·eyes seemed to swim with a lifetime of tears. Even as she downed booze like a trooper and recounted stories about former colleagues in language that would have made a football hooligan blench, he found himself fighting an urge to wrap a protective arm round her bony shoulders.

Her English was immaculately unaccented although she was, he learned, half Persian. 'Persian' was her word, not Iranian. Her father had apparently been an engineering student in London, who had impregnated her mother and then (she said) fucked off back to his respectable Muslim wife and children in Tehran. Thus the semi-exotic Christian name, the ordinary surname and the entirely English upbringing.

'But I'm not English,' she said defiantly. 'And I'm not bloody well Persian. I'm lost in no-man's-land in between.'

She hadn't asked for sympathy, but Nick had read plenty of misery and confusion in that bald statement.

'I'm not English either,' he had said. 'But since I don't speak the language – well, apart from a bit of force-feeding at school – I'm not regarded as Welsh by certain of my compatriots.'

Christ, he thought now, twisting restlessly in his bed and watching the ceiling beams ooze in and out of focus in the moonlight, he must have been even drunker that afternoon than he was tonight if he'd got on to Wales and the Welsh.

Much of the conversation was lost for ever in a fug of alcohol, sun and smoke. When they'd tired of darts and skittles, they'd wandered away from the fête and found refuge – and large vodkas – in the garden of the Black Lion. Bernard had winked and raised an admiring thumb but had, thank God, been too busy serving other refugees from the festivities to join them. Nick remembered sitting side-by-side on the mossy grass under the apple tree, comparing life-stories. Like you always do in these situations. She'd read English at university, she said.

'So did I,' Nick declared. Pleased. Like you always are in these situations. 'Which university?'

Had she said Cambridge? He'd made the inevitable enquiries about a friend who might have been up at the same time but . . . Gone. He couldn't remember now. He thought she had started in radio, then moved to telly. Which she'd quit to help a group of friends set up an independent production company.

'I'm impressed,' said Nick.

'Shit, this was the time *everyone* was setting up as independents. The great eighties media euphemism. Nobody retired, nobody was sacked, they just turned indy. And look how many are left now. Nine out of ten sunk without trace.'

'Are you? I mean, how's your lot doing?'

'Fine,' she said, with a tiny acid smile. 'They're definitely among the floaters. But they had to jettison a bit of the excess cargo along the way. Like me.'

He had known – for no real reason he had *known*, from the moment she'd said the words 'independent company' – that it had to be the very company filming two miles down the valley. 'Pentagon?'

'How d'you guess?'

'Christopher said you were a friend of Mary Hamilton.'

He remembered now how he'd voiced the name rather self-consciously. Daft. He also remembered how Sasha's head had swivelled round, how her eyes had narrowed. 'You know Mary?'

'This time yesterday,' Nick had declared with alcohol-inflated grandeur, 'I was interviewing the woman.'

'Do you like her?'

Something in her tone of voice prompted caution. 'She's pretty damn impressive, wouldn't you say?'

'I certainly would,' agreed Sasha, blowing a long line of smoke.

'But you don't like her.'

'This is dumped cargo talking. And guess who did the dumping?' She grinned, not very convincingly. 'It's all right. I'm not bitter about it. I screwed up.'

'How?'

'A film about the Gulf War, sort of drama-doc. I mean, real-life background, but fiction. Well, it turned out it wasn't fictional enough. Like, there was a serious libel of at least two Very Important Pricks-in-uniform which the writer didn't get round to explaining. In fact, fed me a real pack of lies.' She shrugged. 'Don't bother racking your memory – it wasn't transmitted. Wasn't even filmed. The lawyers stepped in and we pulled out. But money was wasted. And guess whose head was on the chopping block?'

'I thought you were part of the company?'

'Yup. So did I. With a piece of the action. But contracts are full of small print. I mean, the others didn't blame it all on me. Andrew – you know Andrew too, one of the partners?'

Nick shook his head. 'Not personally, but –'

'Cool, but a real sweetheart underneath. Well, Andrew admitted the writer was a screwball. But Mary calls the shots and Mary said I wasn't to be trusted. No second chances in her book. Hey, is something the matter?'

He had flinched. What was it Candia said? One mistake and people were off Mary's Christmas-card list for good. Hell, it was Mary herself who had quoted it to him.

'I wouldn't mind so much,' said Sasha, drawing out another cigarette and leaning forward for him to light it, 'if she hadn't made it public round the industry that I'm a dangerous liability.'

'Has she?'

'I believe in speaking my goddamn mind,' drawled Sasha, in a sudden and uncanny impersonation of Mary's deep voice. 'If you can't be honest, then why bother to open your mouth?' She broke off and grinned. 'Do you want me to be a real bitch?'

'Shock me.'

'What made her really mad was that I'd walked off with her little friend.'

'Little friend?'

'Well, not so little, but *very* user-friendly. Assistant film editor, twenty-three, built like a Chippendale and – take it from me – hung like a prize ram. Don't get me wrong. I can see why she was pissed off. I'm sure she'd been having all kinds of fun and games on the cutting-room floor when she felt like it. Mary likes boys she can push around, you know.'

'Does she?' said Nick faintly. Then, with growing indignation as he remembered *exactly* the way she'd turned on him, laughing, on the riverbank, 'Does she indeed?'

And that was when Sasha had put her face close to his. So close he could taste the bitter tinge of tonic-water on her breath. 'But I don't,' she said. Her hand was on his thigh, dry and weightless as a leaf. 'Look ... Do you want to go somewhere else? A bit less public?'

You bet your life he did. He wanted nothing more in the world at that moment.

Even now, weeks later, he could see her sitting under that tree beside him, her T-shirt so flimsy he felt a nipple nudging his arm as she leaned towards him. He could still smell her perfume, feel the prickle of her hair on his cheek. The next minute, her mouth was open, her tongue flickering against his.

And he – prat – had pushed her away. Gently and, oh God, so very reluctantly. 'Christopher,' he'd croaked. 'My, um, my son.'

She had stared at him. 'I know he's your son. He introduced us remember? Nice kid.'

'He's coming home with me tonight.'

'He's a big boy, for Christ's sake. What does he think you do with your spare time, bake cakes?'

'Actually he's only seventeen. Just. I mean, well, I guess if

I had a long-term girlfriend it might be ... Oh blimey, you know what I'm talking about. He's probably searching round the fête for me even now. I couldn't roll home with a woman he's just introduced me to and ... I mean, could we?'

'You tell me,' she breathed.

But he hadn't. He'd just sat there, dumb as a sack of potatoes.

'Your loss, sweetheart,' she had said, gathering up her bag and brushing the grass off her leggings. 'Some other time, maybe?'

She had sounded more amused than annoyed.

Thinking about it now, he decided that was infinitely worse. And there had not, of course, been another time. With his son safely back at school and his heart thumping with excitement, Nick had rung Radio Dales first thing Monday morning. But Sasha Floyd had left for London.

He pulled the covers over his head and willed himself to sleep.

16

'Do you feel as bad as you look?' said Caroline when they met in the kitchen next morning. She had already boiled the kettle. 'Or as bad as I feel, come to that. Never – *ever* – let me get on to brandy again.'

'I'm unlikely to have the chance, am I?' said Nick hoarsely. 'Alka Seltzers in the cupboard on the right. Chuck me a couple, will you.'

'We're a bad influence on each other, Nicko. Always were.'

'If you say so.'

'Seconds out for round two?'

Nick shook his head – and winced. 'Sorry. It's me I'm pissed off with. Not you.'

'For that, I'll make you a bacon sandwich. Come on. Bit of food always makes you feel better.'

They drank and ate in what Nick thought was tolerably companionable silence.

'I'll have to walk across and see John,' she said. 'Should I mention anything? About Candia Mayhew, I mean.'

'If you do,' muttered Nick, 'you're a braver man than me, Gunga Din.'

'Thing is, it's pretty embarrassing knowing so much about it, from reading your manuscript. I feel like I've sneaked a look at his diary.'

'I didn't follow them into the bedroom,' he said virtuously.

'No,' she agreed. 'Shame really.'

'Caro!'

'Oh, not them,' she said impatiently. 'But I'd have given a lot to read about you bedding the awe-inspiring Mary Dance. Or vice versa.'

'And what makes you think we would have ended up in bed?'

'Oh come on. You always did like bossy women.'

'With yourself as the prime example?'

'Of course,' she said, not at all offended.

'Well you're wrong this time,' he said sharply. 'After that interview I only saw Mary Hamilton once. For precisely ten seconds. And if I never see her again, that's soon enough.'

The look on Caro's face showed she didn't believe him. Nick almost growled into his tea. 'Anyway,' she was saying, 'that's beside the point.'

'John?'

She buttered a piece of toast. 'I was glad you didn't mention the baby.'

'Baby? Oh, I see.' John's wife, when she cycled in front of the lorry, had been six months' pregnant with a long-awaited child. 'I'm not that much of a vulture,' he protested. 'Besides, I'd have changed all the names on a later draft. All the circumstances, everything. If I'd ever finished it.'

'So what actually went wrong in the end? Between Baby Bro and the divine Candia?'

Nick eyed his plate moodily. 'Life's not like fiction, is it? Tends to be a bit short on tidy endings. Let alone happy ones.'

'Too early in the morning for philosophy,' said Caroline. 'And I asked you a perfectly simple question.'

'Maybe, but there's no simple answer.' Nick pushed aside the plate. 'You tell me. Because I was there, and I haven't a fucking clue.'

It was quite by chance, but he had actually been present at John and Candia's final, brief meeting.

Far as Nick was concerned it was an unlucky chance because, after that memorable Saturday afternoon with Sasha, he'd spent the next week avoiding the visitors from Pentagon Television. This hadn't been hard. Tuesday saw the publication of *Snow Black* and, in the mysterious way these forces operate, there had been a surge – well, OK, a generous ripple – of media interest. Three more local radio interviews, several press pieces and even – oh, glory – one minute and thirty-two seconds (timed on the video clock) on regional television. The filming of which had occupied a whole afternoon. His accent sounded even worse on the box than on tape.

More than once, however, John had invited him to join Candia and her cronies. Drinks at the pub. A final meal (after the last day's shooting) in some Italian joint in York.

'Who with?'

'Oh, you know, Candia, Mary . . .'

Nick shook his head. 'Thanks, but no.'

John looked puzzled and even rather hurt. 'Something the matter, Nick?'

'Frankly, I'm a bit wary of Mary Hamilton. From what I hear, her managerial style makes Pol Pot sound like Mother Teresa.'

John laughed. 'Rubbish. I mean, I know Candia takes the piss, but that's all it is, joking. For goodness sake, I sometimes think she worships the ground Mary treads on. They all do.'

Exactly, thought Nick, feeling old and immensely wise. And we know how corrupting such power can be, don't we? But he hadn't the heart to throw this little spanner into John's affair which, far as he knew at the time, was ticking over nicely. So he'd kept *stumm* and given work as his excuse. To John – and to George who, on hearing that he was giving up on the Hamilton front, sighed with the stoicism of an agent inured to the pusillanimity of writers as a breed.

Nick had gone down to the pub, the morning after the planned farewell Italian meal, only to see if he could borrow

John's car. His own was going in for service. Service? Call it a fresh application of sticking plaster to a million rusting parts . . .

John was at the Black Lion because he was, finally, installing Sarah's precious bookcase in the sitting room. And standing there with him, to Nick's surprise, had been Candia Mayhew.

'We're packed up, checked out, and en route to Derbyshire for the Pemberley scenes even as I speak,' she explained. 'The crew left at dawn. I just called in to say a final goodbye. I haven't seen you for ages, Nick, what've you been up to?'

She was smiling at him, deliciously as ever, but Nick sensed trouble. Dammit, he'd known something was wrong the moment he'd opened the door. And John was burying his head in his toolbag . . . Before he could begin to guess what was going on, however, there was a clattering of feet in the corridor.

'They're down our end, in the sitting room,' he heard Bernard's voice call. 'Don't worry. I'll go and tear the lovebirds apart for you.' And he burst in. 'Oh, hello, Nick. Didn't expect to find you playing gooseberry.'

'Are they waiting for me?' said Candia.

They? thought Nick, with a start. He'd slipped into the pub through the kitchens. Was Mary Hamilton parked out front even now?

Bernard winked at the lovers. 'Take your time, I would.' He turned his back on them ostentatiously and addressed Nick. 'Saw you on the telly t'other night, sunshine. What's she really like, that Debby girl who interviewed you? You know, I fancy her something rotten . . .'

Bernard had plenty more to say on the subject. Nick was uneasily aware of John and Candia talking in low voices over by the bookcase. Was there something wrong? Oh God, thought Nick suddenly, surely she couldn't be ringing down the curtain on this little holiday romance? If so, he didn't want to be a witness.

'I guess I'd better be going,' he heard Candia say at length. Sounding miserable, yes, but was that from pain she was feeling or guilt at the pain she was inflicting?

'Not going for good though, are you?' said Bernard heartily. 'You'll be back, soon as you've finished your job.'

Candia smiled uncertainly. 'Well, I hope John might possibly come down to London when . . .'

Thank God, thought Nick.

'Bugger London,' roared Bernard. 'You like the fresh air up here, don't you, lass? And there can't be a grander little country pad in the North of England than John's barn. Our Sarah's told him, if ever he sells, she wants first refusal. For when we retire from this business, like. Mind, I'm hoping . . .' And Bernard chuntered on as ever.

Candia, Nick saw, was white as the bloody walls. Staring at John.

'Rubbish,' he was protesting distractedly, his gaze glued – wretchedly – on Candia. 'The barn's not finished, not really . . .'

'What d'you reckon to it then, Candia?' Bernard had enquired.

There were footsteps clipping impatiently down the corridor. Nick had even recognized the rhythm of the stride . . .

'Anyway,' he now said to Caroline, 'La Hamilton swept in and swept Candia out in ten seconds flat. Their car roared away into the sunset. Well, actually it was eleven o'clock in the morning but you get the picture. Fortnight ago yesterday.'

'And John never came to town?'

'Filming schedules changed or something. Or so he said.'

'And that was that?'

'Apparently. I mean, I didn't realize it then, exactly . . .'

Didn't think, more like. But John had just seemed to be rushing around, catching up on all the work he'd neglected while canoodling with Candia. He had even mentioned some commission in London for one of Candia's actor chums. So Nick, stupidly, had assumed things were all right. Let sleeping affairs lie and all that.

And then – ten days ago, was it? – he'd walked over to the barn and found John sprawled across his kitchen table with a three-quarters empty bottle of vodka beside him.

'John never drinks vodka,' protested Caroline.

'He had that night. Snoring like a bull elephant.'

'And?'

'And nothing. I mean, I put him to bed. Nothing else I could do. Next morning, by the time I woke up, he was out in the workshop. Looking like death, mark you, but chiselling away.'

'Surely you asked?'

'Course I bloody well asked. What do you think I am? But you know your brother. More protective cladding than an armadillo. Mind, he hadn't even realized it was me had packed him off to bed. Learning that mortified him to his respectable core. Even prompted him to admit – finally – he'd put a bit too much back because Candia had given him the big heave-ho. What you might call a Dear John telephone call. Shut up, Caro, of course I asked why. And he more or less said, well, these things happen. And I guess they do.'

Caroline's face twisted. 'My poor Johnny. But Nick, why do you think . . . ?'

He shrugged. 'I can only imagine it was, oh, you know, a fling for her. A lusty little diversion on location.'

'Fling? The way you wrote it up, it sounded like the love affair of the century. Rachmaninov was oozing off the page.'

'It looked that way. At the time. She seemed dotty as he did but . . . Shit, I've told you, I don't know the real ins and outs. How could I? John's made it daylight clear he doesn't want to talk about it. Upper lips don't come much stiffer.'

'Or hearts much softer,' said Caro quietly. She drained her

mug of tea. 'And he actually invited her up to the barn, did
he?' She shook her head wonderingly. 'My oh my. It must
have been serious.'

'Sorry? I'm not with you.'

'Taking her into the shrine to Sally?'

'Rubbish,' said Nick sharply. 'John doesn't even keep a
photo of Sally on view.'

Caroline gasped. 'How can men be so *blind*? Surely you
realize she created every pot in the place – every pot out in
that courtyard, too. Embroidered every damn cushion,
stitched every curtain, chose every picture. He moved out of
this house because he said he couldn't bear the memories,
then recreated it, piece by sodding piece.'

'Did he? I – I guess I'd never thought . . .' Nick thought
about it now. 'Actually, I don't know if Candia did come up
here. I mean, I never saw her, but she might've done. To be
honest, I was keeping out of their way. Not out of John and
Candia's way exactly . . .'

'But well away from Mary Hamilton,' said Caroline, with
disconcerting shrewdness. 'I wonder why?' But, to his relief,
this appeared to be a rhetorical question. She sighed. 'Another
man, do you suppose? A long-term boyfriend back home?'

'Candia? Well, it'd crossed my mind. While the cat's away
and all that. Anyway, no point in going on about it. The
thing's finished and that's that.'

'Poor boy.'

'He's thirty-four now,' said Nick. 'Old enough to take care
of himself. And – oh, you know – better to have loved and
lost and all that.'

'Is that your philosophy?'

Nick looked at her across the table. Undoubtedly it was the
brain-skewing effects of a hangover, but he felt as though he
was looking at her from a great distance. As though she was
behind glass. Remote, untouchable. She was still, he thought,
beautiful. In fact, more beautiful than when they'd first

married. She'd been pudgy and unformed then. Changing her hairstyle every two days. Wearing clothes as though she'd charged with outstretched arms through an Oxfam shop. She had gloss and polish now. And Christopher's cheekbones.

'Well?' she said.

'Yeah,' he answered at length. 'Better to have loved and lost than never to have loved at all.'

She leaned across and squeezed his hand. 'You always were a hopeless old romantic.'

She would drive back to London in the afternoon, she announced briskly as she washed up the breakfast pots. Once she could be sure her blood-alcohol count might be something closer to legality. In the meantime, she'd call in on Baby Bro and let Nick get back to his word-processor.

'Ha bloody ha,' he said. 'I know the annals of literature are full of alcoholic geniuses but I've never yet managed to write a coherent sentence with a hangover. I tell you, Caro, when I'm working full stretch I live like a sodding monk.'

'In all respects?'

'None of your business. Anyway, I'm fresh out of plots again. Let alone the one that'll rock the bestseller stalls.'

'I'm sure you will. Where does this go?'

'Cupboard under the sink. What, find a plot?'

'Rock the bestseller stalls. I think you were right to jack the newspapers in.'

Nick stared at her. 'You do?'

She nodded. 'The new book – the one that's just come out, the Welsh one, *Black Snow*?'

'*Snow Black*. You mean you've actually read it?'

'Seriously good. Best thing you've ever done.'

'Blimey.'

'And you look . . . really well. Oh I don't mean at this minute, with eyes like an albino rabbit and breath that would strip varnish. I mean since you came up here. Like – like a man who's found his vocation. I'm quite proud of you, actually. It can't have been easy.'

'Am I really hearing this?' Nick grinned. 'The softening effect of love, no doubt. What's he called again, remind me?'

'Daniel. As you well know.'

'Chris doesn't reckon much to him.'

'He's only saying that to keep you happy. Machiavellian little bastard. I promise you they get on a treat. Daniel's even proposing to invite him to fly out with us on our, er, honeymoon. What's so funny?'

'*Honeymoon?* Wasn't one enough for you?'

'Enough to put me off the idea for life, you mean? My God, four months pregnant and I let you drag me off to a leaky caravan in Snowdonia. In a blizzard . . .'

Nick sighed. 'Ah, Proust can keep his madeleines. It's the whiff of Camping Gaz stirs the cockles of my soul.'

'Well it doesn't stir mine,' she retorted firmly. 'So Daniel and I are going to the Caribbean. Cruising round the islands for three weeks in a personally chartered yacht. No butane, no chemical loos – and definitely no Welsh mountain sheep poking their noses in.'

'Very nice too. Actually, I'm returning to Welsh Mountain Sheep country myself soon,' said Nick, groping for a calendar. 'Crikey, very soon. Next week.'

'Not a nostalgia trip, I gather.'

'Llandudno in fact.'

Caroline frowned. 'Isn't that where Charlie Meschia lives these days?'

'As it happens – but this isn't a social jaunt. They've started a literary festival there, getting on the bandwagon. Smart way of filling hotels, I suppose.'

'And you're making a personal appearance? Well done.'

'Sharing a platform with two other thriller writers,' he said modestly. 'Rather, um, better-known writers. In a discussion on the art and craft of scaring people witless. I'm under no illusions. I'm only there because my middle name's Llewellyn and, when all's said and done, it's a Welsh festival. Still, as George says, it's free bed and booze, and all good publicity. And another excuse for not starting a new book until a week on Monday.'

'As if you needed one,' she said dryly. 'I'll see you later. I'm going over to John's.'

17

Postcard from Roderick Chad to John Hope-Simmonds:

Got your message on the answering machine — sorry for the time lag. The last days of the shoot were utterly ghastly. Still, P & P's finally all in the can now and we poor bloody actors can only cross our fingers and wait to see what emerges on screen. The dresser: actually, thanks for your drawings, but I think I'd better take a rain-check for the time being. There's so much going on, it could be Christmas before I'm back in the flat long enough to start thinking about home improvements. Although I lives in hopes, as they say. Anyway, I'm sure you're keeping busy. As ever, Roderick.

Letter from the Director, Llandudno Festival of Literature, to Nick Bevan:

Just to confirm that your hotel booking has been changed, as requested, to the Princess Royal Hotel on Marine Parade where a room with bath has been reserved for the nights of the 8th and 9th. We look forward to meeting you then. The secretary's office is just to the right of the main marquee and . . .

Letter from Christopher Bevan to Caro:

. . . although I think you're being pretty narrow-minded not let-ting me go away on my own this summer. I'm not a child, I'm seven-teen — and if even sixteen's legally old enough for lunatic activities like getting married . . . ??? Only joking, dearest mama.

Anyhow, you can tell Daniel it's really kind of him to invite me and all that, and offer to pay for the flights etc. etc., but I think you'd probably rather not have me under your espadrilles. It's your honeymoon, after all. AND I might be sea-sick. I was when you and Dad took me on that canal holiday (!!!) if you remember back that far, so I'll probably go up and do my dutiful son stint with him while you're away. Don't worry, I'll sort things out direct with Dad . . .

Letter from Nick Bevan to Christopher:

. . . entirely up to you, old son. Personally, for a free cruise round the Caribbean I wouldn't mind if I had to share the boat with Goebbels and Lucrezia Borgia. And if he's coughing up for the flights, you might consider just going out for a week or so. Anyway, plenty of time yet for you to make up your mind. Let me know. I dare say I'll be rotting away at the desk here all summer as usual – although all of a sudden there's talk from my agent of me going with him and Victoria to (wait for it) California for a few days. Via the Big Apple. No, seriously.

George says he has useful people he wants me to meet, but I'm not deceived. The invitation was issued the day after I told him about your mother's wedding plans. No doubt he thinks I might be slitting my wrists in a bath of warm gin up here while Caro's tying the knot in London, so he wants to keep an eye on his investment. Who am I to complain? Nothing confirmed yet and, in the meantime, I'm off to the Princess Royal Hotel, Llandudno. Yeah, I know, Llandudno sounds more my style than Los Angeles . . .

From the brochure of the Princess Royal Hotel, Marine Parade, Llandudno:

. . . a select establishment where panoramic views of the Irish Sea and the Welsh mountains combine with the sumptuous decor of an English country house. Fresh local produce is imaginatively

prepared by the Italian chef-proprietor, and the menus are complemented by fine wine from our cellars.

Some comments from our regular visitors:

'. . . magnificent food, superb wine, every attention to comfort; in short, a real home from home.' Sir Geraint Pryce-Evans, Chairman, Cambria Television.

Note scrawled on compliment slip accompanying brochure to Nick Bevan:

You jammy bugger. And since the festival of so-called literature (what are they inviting the likes of you for, then?) is footing the bill, I've put you in the Caernarfon Suite. Hot and cold running televisions, a phone in the bathroom, shag-piled jacuzzi, you name it, chum. And the Bollinger's on ice and on me — it's been too bloody long. See you Thursday. Charlie.

18

'Nick,' cried Charlie Meschia, throwing wide his arms in exactly the comic opera way his father used to. 'How long is it, then?'

'Feels like only yesterday,' said Nick with a faintly guilty grimace.

Which in truth it did, since for plot purposes he had recruited this drinking and jazz-clubbing mate of Manchester days on to the Maltbury cricket team, and invented and enjoyed several plausible conversations with him into the bargain. But the Charlie he remembered and had written about was younger. This Charlie was stouter and balder. In fact – Nick saw with a sudden stab of nostalgia – he looked just like his dad.

Charlie's father had owned a spaghetti joint down the road from Nick and Caroline's first flat. The Monte Bello was a popular establishment, not least because Meschia senior violently disapproved of the new-fangled ideas his son had acquired in catering college and their rows added regular spice and cabaret to the dinner menu. The golden days had ended, though, with Charlie's marriage; a late and (so the dejected diners muttered) more-prudent-than-romantic union with a widow who just happened to own a guest house in Colwyn Bay. This had enabled Charlie to set up in business for himself at last. The guest house had been traded for a small hotel and, subsequently, for the splendours of the Princess Royal.

'Hell, Charlie,' said Nick, waving a hand round an entrance hall chandeliered, swagged and Greek-columned like a film set, 'this is a bit of a step-up from the old Monte B., isn't it?'

'So are the mortgage repayments,' said Charlie, his face drooping into its usual basset hound lines. 'Ah well, never mind. Renee, *Renee*? Nick's here.'

Irene Meschia had not changed much. The blonde streaks had ripened into an improbable shade of auburn, but she still favoured towering stilettoes and tiny dogs. A pair of Yorkshire terriers snuffled in her wake like mobile doormats. 'Nicky, my favourite Libran,' she cooed, grazing his cheek with a razor-tipped earring as she pecked the air. 'And you're looking so *well* . . .'

Nick was not deceived. She was eyeing his jeans and holey-toed sneakers as though a slug was squirming across her crimson velour pile. Ever since Charlie's memorable stag night, Irene had had him marked down as a Dangerous Influence.

'Isn't he just?' agreed Charlie heartily. 'How's your sex-life then, mate?'

'I'm sorry there's nothing we can do about the suite, Nicky,' carolled Irene as though she hadn't heard. 'Has Charlie explained?'

Charlie's face fell. 'Oh aye, damn nuisance. But don't worry, chum, you'll be snug enough in Number –'

'The Pembroke,' corrected his wife with steely sweetness. 'Names are so much nicer than numbers, aren't they, Charlie?'

'Thing is, Nick, one of our regular old lags –'

'We are fortunate enough,' interrupted Irene again, laying a confiding hand on Nick's arm, 'to number among our most loyal customers Sir Geraint Pryce-Evans.'

The reverence with which this name was uttered evidently required some response. Nick, floundering, looked to Charlie.

'World famous in Aberystwyth,' he whispered. 'For his whisky consumption, if nothing else.'

Irene's laugh rattled colder than ice-cubes. 'Sir Geraint always stays with us, doesn't he, lovey? Whenever business or other interests bring him up here.'

Charlie winked. 'Like a new secretary. The old sod gets through more typists than the Alfred Marks Bureau.'

'And I'm afraid Sir Geraint,' concluded his wife, glowering at him, '*always* has the Caernarfon Suite.'

Sir Geraint Pryce-Evans was a short man. Short, stout and silver haired. In his voice resonated twenty generations of preachers. In his ripe strawberry of a nose shone a lifetime's defiance of their non-conformist strictures on alcohol.

'Nicholas Llewellyn Bevan,' he boomed when Irene, since Nick and he were the only customers in the bar, felt obliged to introduce them, a couple of hours later. '*Yodych chi yn siarad Cymraeg?*'

'Actually no,' said Nick. 'The bit of the language I learned at school, I've more or less forgotten. Sorry.'

'Shame on you. Bevan eh? Not related to the great —'

''Fraid not,' said Nick. 'Not to anyone great. I'm doomed to be the first celebrity of my line.'

'And you're speaking at our festival then? Splendid, splendid.'

'Sir Geraint,' trilled Irene, arranging whisky, olives and cocktail sticks on frilly mats at the great man's elbow, 'as well as being the Chairman of Cambria Television, is also Honorary President of the festival, aren't you, Sir Geraint?'

'For my sins,' he intoned.

'Generous of you to include us monoglot English speakers,' said Nick.

Sir Geraint's blue eyes bulged. 'This is a European festival, man. Not some tinpot eisteddfod. Damn, we have speakers from all over the world. Television coverage, press, radio . . .'

'In that case,' said Nick, 'it's generous of you to include the likes of me at all.'

Irene tittered flintily and said she was sure Nick's table was ready in the dining room.

'When are you speaking?' enquired Sir Geraint.

'Tomorrow. After lunch in, um, the main marquee.'

'I'll be there,' said Sir Geraint. It sounded more a threat than a promise.

Rather to Nick's surprise, Sir Geraint Pryce-Evans's silver mane was indeed to be seen amid the crowds clustered in the marquee entrance before the afternoon session. The tent was filling fast, but Nick did not flatter himself this was on his account. He was sharing the platform with a bearded face familiar from a thousand airport bookstands. The third panellist was also quite a celebrity, although more for a television talk show she used to present than for her dark and pacey novels.

Nick had met her at the buffet lunch beforehand. Built on unabashedly opulent lines and billowing acres of what looked like yellow silk pyjamas, the woman had a thicket of grey-black curls, a wide and merry mouth and eyes which twinkled like a well-sharpened carving knife.

Nick had felt he liked her even before they met because he'd always enjoyed her books so much. This warm predisposition was not at all diminished when she frankly confessed to having read none of his.

'But from a single glance at a dust-jacket, I can tell you that you're a damn sight better looking than your photograph. And probably, judging by the reviews of the new one pinned round the bookstall, a budding genius. How sickening. Hi, I'm Miriam Weissman.'

'I know that,' he said, putting down a sausage roll to shake hands. 'I'm a fan of yours.'

'I love you already. Have another glass of wine.'

She talked, ate and drank with a speed and gusto that left him reeling, and she listened with an alert intensity that charmed him utterly. Under her fast and frank interrogation, Nick found himself spilling out his entire literary career. Just as well the lunch was brief. Skewered on her intelligent sympathy and softened up by stories from her own riotous life (five delinquent kids, silver wedding in view, a mother-in-law from hell and three incontinent cats) he was being lured on to his own personal life.

'Such as it is. Or isn't.'

'Oh come on,' said Miriam, clucking maternally. 'A nice boy like you? I'm sure women come tumbling.'

'In droves,' said Nick, with a snort of laughter. 'All hoping for an introduction to my hunky brother-in-law.'

'I like you, Nick Bevan,' she declared, grinning. 'Strikes me you deserve a break. Come on, drink up. Our audience awaits.'

Nick drained his glass, even as she added a final top-up to her own. He glanced towards the door, 'Do you do a lot of these sort of events?' he asked, with more than a touch of nervousness.

'Depends. Don't worry. This lot are a load of pussy cats.' She shrugged. 'Anyway, once Big Bertha gets going . . .' she nodded in the direction of their fellow panellist, 'the likes of you and me can get the crossword out. Here's mud in your eye.'

Miriam Weissman was right, up to a point. The discussion meandered amiably round plot structures, characterization, planning.

'Novelists,' suggested the chairman, 'divide into two camps. Those who travel strictly according to their detailed road-map of a plan, and those who pack a metaphorical bag, as it were, with some interesting characters and plunge off into the unknown. I wonder how our panellists feel. Nick?'

'When I've found the right answer,' said Nick, caught off-guard, 'I'll let you know.'

At least it got a laugh. But it wasn't enough. Theory had never been his strong point. Where was Lavinia Stacey when he needed her? He cleared his throat. 'If I plan every step, the whole expedition's liable to die of boredom. When I don't . . .' He paused, remembering the recent jolly foray, thirty thousand words into the fictional forest, 'When I don't I just get hopelessly lost.'

More laughter. They thought he was joking.

Miriam swore by the plunge into the wilderness method, although she added that she needed a fix on her overall destination. The bearded bestseller, however, was a belt, compass and Ordnance Survey man. And held the floor for a long time on his meticulous card-index research methods. ('And why not?' whispered Miriam cheerfully, 'it's his robes they've come to touch.') He was, however, temporarily stumped by a question from the back row on whether the thriller was not quintessentially – in concept, content, and style – a masculine genre.

Even as the beard began to nod thoughtfully, Miriam stiffened like a terrier shown the rabbit. 'Bullshit,' she roared. And Nick choked back a laugh as grey heads in the front row, which had been drooping, jerked back to attention.

Miriam was firing the names of female thriller writers with the fluency of a Kalashnikov. Gathering momentum, she lobbed in psychological research which showed women's subtle brains were better suited than men's to work in the intelligence services, adding that girls were less squeamish than boys, being adapted by nature (as birth-givers) to dealing in life and death. Without drawing breath, she reminded would-be heroes that physical might gave no one any rights in an age of automatic weaponry, skidded through a potted guide to dangerous examples of the female of the species, ranging from a sixteenth-century pirate to the Baader–Meinhof gang, and concluded with the astonishing observation that the prime mover in Nick Bevan's latest novel was a women –

a Welsh housewife, if you please – and that it was one of the most gripping and genuinely thrilling stories she'd encountered in years.

'But you've never read any of my books,' said Nick later, under the cover of applause as they left the platform.

She guffawed. 'I didn't say "read" up there just now, did I? I said "encountered". So maybe I only encountered your feisty heroine on the dust-jacket blurb, but anything that rates as the most gripping yarn in ten years for a reviewer in the *TLS* is good enough for me. And for that gratuitous plug, sunshine, you owe me a large drink.'

But they were intercepted on their way to the bar by Sir Geraint who greeted Miriam as an old friend with a smacking kiss on each cheek.

'How are you, Geraint?' she said, untangling herself from his embrace. 'Have you met your compatriot here?'

'Yes, yes,' said Sir Geraint. 'Well done, boy. Good show. Ah, Miriam. What a performer. You should never have left us.'

'Why not? Even the BBC pays better than you do.'

'Is money everything?' asked Sir Geraint soulfully.

'You tell me,' said Miriam. 'You've had more experience of it.'

Sir Geraint turned to Nick. 'Such a ready wit. Worth her weight in gold on a live programme.'

Miriam snorted and glanced down. 'I should think I tip the scales at something approaching the National Debt. Anyway, the producers are starting to look younger than my kids and my morale can't take it. I'm concentrating on the writing these days. Screenplays even, would you believe.'

'Write them for us. We're always looking for original drama, aren't we?'

'You know, Geraint, call me an old cynic, but I never felt I quite fitted into the old boyo culture down here.'

'Miriam, Miriam, no one values the fairer sex more highly than I.'

She grinned. 'Quite. And I was going to add that Weissman isn't exactly a common name on the eisteddfod circuit, but far be it from me to make racist gags. However,' she said, unpeeling his hand which had found its way round her waist again, 'Bevan certainly is. I dare say your producers at Cambria are queueing up to grab the rights on his amazing new book, um . . .'

'*Snow Black*?' supplied Nick.

'. . . a brilliant study of the darker side of nationalism,' she quoted promptly. 'Fast, funny, *naturally* cinematic. Have I got that right, Nick? Ask him all about it, Geraint, but if you'll forgive me, I must dash.' She brushed past Nick whispering: 'My escape could be your lucky break. See you in the bar, baby.'

'Well, well,' said Sir Geraint. 'This sounds – ah – quite intriguing. Has there been any interest from television, I wonder?'

'You're joking,' said Nick before he'd had time to think of a smarter answer. 'At least . . .' He tried for an air of blasé indifference. 'Not that I know of, exactly. The book's only just published. So there's nothing – um – confirmed. As yet.' He wondered how he could imply that he was fighting off armies of avid producers. 'But my agent George Hillard seems to think –'

'Who? Who did you say?' Sir Geraint was already looking over his shoulder, waving to another acquaintance.

'Miller and Hillard?'

'Don't believe I know her, sorry. But I dare say here's someone who does. How are you, my lovely? More radiant than ever, I see.' He rolled the 'r' of radiant like a drainpipe gurgling whisky.

'*George* Hillard, actually . . .' Nick tried again, but his audience was lost. So he gave up and turned round.

And found himself nose to (long) nose with Mary Hamilton.

19

The amazing thing – the really amazing thing – was how pleased she looked to see him.

'Nick Bevan,' she exclaimed. 'What on earth are you doing here?' She leaned over and kissed him, and it *was* him she kissed, not politely adjacent airspace, but actually his cheek. Her mouth was dry. She smelled faintly of lemons. Or something equally sharp.

Nick swallowed. 'Not so much doing as just done. Actually. Thrillers, with, um, Miriam Weissman. Harold Crowe. It's in the programme. More to the point, what about you? I mean – you're not. In the programme. Are you?' He was incoherent as a bloody schoolboy.

'She's our salvation, isn't she?' said Sir Geraint. Embracing Mary was a problem because she towered comically tall over his stout little figure and made no effort to stoop. He fondled her hand proprietorially instead. 'She's debating the case for television and the book this evening. Translating the novel to other media. You mustn't miss it.'

'Oh I would if I were you,' said Mary cordially. 'Miss it, that is. I'm a lousy public speaker.'

'Nonsense,' blustered Sir Geraint.

'Whenever I let myself be talked into doing this kind of thing, I end up being blasted by a gale of Force Nine yawns. Someone once told me I'd a voice that makes a talking lift sound like Gielgud.' She shrugged. 'It was supposed to be Juliet Harman here tonight, but she had to drop out, and

Geraint rang and pulled the old pals act.'

'And why not indeed? I made this girl's career,' declared Sir Geraint. 'Damn, I've known Mary Hamilton since –'

'Don't say since I was knee-high to a grasshopper, because no one will believe you. I was taller than my teacher in First Grade.'

'Since my own far-off BBC days, when you came down to Cardiff on attachment. And what's more, Mary *bach*, I bet I can remember the very first programme you directed. Wasn't it . . .'

Mary pulled a face. And, as Sir Geraint reminisced, it struck Nick she was barely listening. Her eyes were continually straying back to meet his. Questioning? Amused? He couldn't guess. Frankly, it was unnerving.

He felt stunned enough, just meeting her. Shocked as any author must be to find himself swapping pleasantries with a character from his latest plot. It was as though he'd conjured up Mary's presence here. No, more than that, he half felt he'd *invented* the woman altogether. Oh sure, she had been real enough when she'd been working up in Maltbury. It was a flesh and blood creature who had argued across the studio table, prowled behind the cameras and skimmed stones on the river. In fact, had it not been for Sasha's revelations, he would have accepted John's invitations and seen a whole lot more of the real-life Mary Hamilton. As it was, after the fête, they'd only had the one briefest of brief encounters in Bernard's sitting room when she'd stalked in, stared at him . . . well, never mind that now.

The point was that, since then, the reality of a few hours here and there with Mary Hamilton had been overtaken by long days in the company of the fictional Mary Dance. Overtaken and swamped. He felt he only knew her now through his own word-processed pages. He'd merrily put words into her mouth, thoughts into her brain – and what thoughts. And he wished she'd stop eyeing him so peculiarly, as though she could read the lusty lines he'd written for her galloping across his forehead. He was glad he had sallow skin. If he were John, he'd be out-blushing the geranium tubs by now.

'I gave her a film to direct, didn't I, my lovely? And a roaring success it was too. Ah Mary, I only read about you in the newspapers these days. What is it you're doing now?'

'Four-part adaptation of *Pride and Prejudice*,' said Nick, who was (after all) quite in the habit of scripting answers for Mary Hamilton. He caught himself up guiltily. 'At least – sorry – you've probably finished that, haven't you?'

'The filming, sure,' said Mary. 'Post-production to come. Monday morning, I hit the Stygian blackness of an editing suite and won't see sunlight for heaven knows how long.' She smiled enigmatically. Straight at him.

And this was here and now, and she was definitely flesh and blood, and his own blood was pumping disconcertingly fast. Suddenly it was Sasha who was fading into the papery distance – poor, pale little ghost – as Mary declared: 'So I'm intending to enjoy these last few hours of freedom.'

'Starting with a drink now?' Nick found himself saying. 'If the bar's open.'

Wrong. Something had gone wrong. Mary Dance would have said 'terrific', and led the way. But this creature's smile switched off, sharp as a light. 'Thanks, but I've only just checked into my hotel. I want to find my cohorts in tonight's exercise in public humiliation and see what's in store. God, I hate these rituals. I just hope you're grateful, Geraint.' But, as she turned to go, she actually glanced back at Nick. If it were anyone else, he would have said she looked shy. Diffident at any rate. 'Will you will be around tonight, Nick?'

'Course he will,' boomed Sir Geraint.

'I don't know,' said Nick numbly. 'I mean, I guess ... Why not?' He felt like a rabbit who has strayed into the headlamps of a particularly powerful sports car and suspects whichever way he runs he might get splattered.

The neutron bomb, he remembered suddenly – and he hadn't invented that line, either, she'd said it herself – destroys people not buildings.

Actually Mary Hamilton was feeling neither shy nor diffident – just bloody irritated with herself. She had known perfectly well Nick Bevan was going to be here in Llandudno. She had seen his photograph and name in the programme Geraint Red-Starred to her office. And, while it would be an exaggeration to claim she had been persuaded to yield to the anguished plea in Geraint's accompanying letter by Nick's scowling portrait (who the hell shot *that?*), she was too honest to deny it might have tipped the balance.

Of course, the event also chanced to coincide with the one naked patch in her diary for months. A few days set aside at the insistence of her cautious (over-cautious) partner Andrew, in case of a shooting overrun. The shooting, she was gratified to have been able to inform Andrew, had not overrun. On the contrary, they had wrapped a full day ahead of schedule. So she had found herself with no real excuse for declining Geraint's invitation. The old stoat had certainly not made her career – nor her either, though he'd tried often enough – but he had given her an early break when plenty of others wouldn't, so she supposed she owed him a favour.

But if that explained why (against her better judgement) she had agreed to take part in this festival, it hardly justified turning up in the marquee at the conclusion of Nick Bevan's event. Let alone deliberately seeking him out. Which she had. She wasn't even sure what attracted her to him.

He was a nobody, right? A two-bit hack on a local paper. OK, a two-bit hack who apparently wrote novels as well. It had been a shock to find him staring out of Geraint's glossy programme. But so what? No one had heard of him. Well, Andrew hadn't. And Andrew devoured thrillers. When asked what he read at university, he was apt to answer John le

Carré. So she'd tried the name on him yesterday. Zilch reaction.

'Why do you ask?' he'd enquired, eyeing her with bright curiosity. 'Should Pentagon be interested in him?'

'No,' she'd snapped.

And, no, she shouldn't be interested in Nick Bevan either. He might be tolerably good-looking. Pretty, almost. Or he could be, if he stood up straight and dressed better. That tie he was wearing this afternoon for instance – terrible. And up home in Yorkshire, he'd given the impression of a man who didn't know what a tie was for. Slumming around in frayed shirts and droopy pullovers, looking for all the world like he'd rolled fresh out of a trashcan. But with a decent haircut? A well-cut suit?

Mary ruthlessly obliterated such fanciful visions. Besides – tramp, hack or nobody – it wasn't surprising she'd allowed herself to be amused by him on location. Briefly. While she was stranded up there, anyone who could string two intelligent words together and *wasn't* part of the unit, *wasn't* an actor needing tactful ego-bolstering, a crew member with a gremlin, an assistant mewing for a decision, Andrew at the end of the phone firing figures at her ... well, she'd have fallen on that creature, man or woman, like Stanley on Dr Livingstone. Any living, laughing soul who offered a few moments of distraction for her battered and overloaded brain. Under those circumstances, it was no wonder she had taken a shine to Nicholas Llewellyn Bevan.

But then, just when she was thinking there could be no real harm in having a little fun with the guy, he'd fucking well vanished, hadn't he? If the idea wasn't ridiculous, she'd have thought he was avoiding her. She knew Candia had issued invitations via John for Nick to join them. She knew because she had told Candia to. And did he ever show his face?

So, maybe he genuinely was working. Work, in Mary

Hamilton's book, was the single cast-iron excuse for anything. Work and maybe death. But it did not excuse – nothing could – that final morning, when they were leaving for Derbyshire. She'd walked into the sitting room of the pub and unexpectedly found him there with Candia and John bloody Hope-Simmonds. *Hopeless* Simmonds, more like.

Well, hello, stranger,' she'd said. (To Nick, of course.) 'How's the work going?'

And he'd snubbed her. No other way to describe it. He'd damn well turned his back on her and asked that foul-mouthed slob who ran the joint if it was too early for a drink. Was the bar open? Pretty much the same words as he'd used to her just now. And frankly, the memory still rankled. This time, she'd exited. That morning it was Nick who had stalked off, without another word. Now, preferring Bernard's company to hers was either a sure sign of a man not worth knowing – or a downright insult.

Since she couldn't imagine why the Nick Bevans of this world should deliberately want to insult her, she concluded his taste in people must be as appalling as his taste in clothes.

And that was why she was irritated with herself now.

20

The marquee during the afternoon session had exuded a homely, grassy air redolent of scout camps and flower shows. With nightfall, it took on a more glamorous guise. There were microphones dangling overhead. The stage had been banked with extra tubs of flowers. Corset-pink begonias and crimson geraniums flirted gaudily under a battalion of spotlights, and the front row was a-glitter with an armoury of mayoral chains.

Mary Dance – shit, thought Nick, Mary *Hamilton* – looked, well, splendid sitting up there under the lights. That was the very word which rose in his mind: splendid. Not simply beautiful, and nothing as milky-tame as pretty. God knows, even in Yorkshire, in her sweaty working gear, Nick had been aware the woman packed a magnetic charge that could halt a pacemaker. Sitting up there now, though, stiff-spined and proud-nosed in her plain black strip of a dress with yards of naked leg and even more yards of hair spilling down her back, she made him think of some warrior queen of pagan antiquity. Bloody magnificent.

Nevertheless, she was right: she was a lousy public speaker.

She was making more effort than she had on that memorable Radio Dales arts programme. What she had to say was interesting, intelligent and to the point – unlike the contributions of at least one of her colleagues on the platform who claimed every twist of the debate as a licence to exhume yet another anecdote from his long and gloriously funny career. Every one of which stories, admittedly, went down a treat with the audience. Mary's quieter and more abstract offerings, however, if not actually lulling them to sleep, noticeably failed to tickle the communal imagination. As she tackled the dilemma of translating into a dramatic medium a novelist's intentions – as opposed to the words actually printed on the page – Nick fancied a cartoonist would have sketched a giant question mark hovering over the body of the hall.

However, he was surprised, and also touched, when he found himself standing beside her in the crush round the stage at the end – nuts, he didn't *find* himself anywhere. He had elbowed a ruthless path through the crowds. Anyway there he was, next to this fierce empress of the media tribes, and he was touched to discover that she was actually trembling. Physically shaking.

'What do you expect?' she demanded. 'I told you. I hate these things.'

'You didn't *sound* nervous,' he protested. Which was true. She had sounded, if anything, faintly bored.

'I sounded arrogant,' she snapped. 'You needn't tell me, I already know. I always come across as some big-mouthed, big-headed, big-nosed American broad who can't be bothered to descend to the intellectual sub-life of the proletarian provinces.'

Since there was more than a little truth in this, Nick gulped, but recovered himself enough to say: 'I've always thought oratory's a con trick, a sign of a limited brain. If what you've got to say can be fitted into sock-'em-between-the-ears slogans, then it probably wasn't worth saying in the first place.'

She looked at him sideways. 'You've not got a bad way with words yourself.'

'It's how I earn my living, remember. Such as it is. I should think you need a drink.'

She shook her head. 'I need to get out of here. Fast.'

'I think Sir Geraint is trying –'

'Exactly,' she said. 'Are you coming?'

This end of the promenade was dark. A necklace of creamy lamps glittered round the still water of the bay. Behind them on the field, the marquee glowed fat and white like a descended spacecraft. There was a buzz of music rising from it. Bemused, Nick followed Mary Hamilton's leggy figure as she galloped across the empty road, over a stripe of grass and straight on to the beach.

'Ouch,' she shrieked. 'Man-eating pebbles.' But she kicked off her sandals nevertheless and, dangling them from one finger, picked a wobbling path down to the water's edge. 'Patch of sand down here,' she called. 'Christ, the sea's cold.'

And, as Nick watched in amazement, she tossed bag and sandals to the ground and waded out into the water until the waves were lapping round her knees, recklessly hiking an already short skirt higher up her thighs.

'What do you think you're doing, you idiot?' he yelled. 'This isn't California.'

'You're telling me. More like fucking Antarctica. Well, come on then. Aren't you going to paddle?'

'For Pete's sake, what do you expect me to do, roll my trousers up?'

'Take 'em off if you like. I won't faint.'

The moon was glinting across the glassy waters, Mary was gambolling in the waves like a demented mermaid and . . . I cannot, thought Nick, I simply cannot and will not figure as the juvenile romantic lead in this moonlit, sea-washed scenario with my trousers hitched up round my knees like Uncle Alun on a Bank Holiday at Barry Island. I have knobbly knees for a start.

'Coward,' she shouted.

'Bollocks,' he roared back, swaying like a drunken stork as

he removed one shoe and sock, then the other. And then, uneasily replanted on two pale and naked feet, he contemplated what to do next.

'After the first minute, you don't feel anything,' she sang, leaning down and swinging her hand across the surface of the sea like a propellor blade.

Nick, dropping his jacket on top of his shoes, was fully clad as he strode in after her. 'I hope you realize,' he said, gasping as the cold percolated up his legs, 'that I'm ruining my jeans.'

'Good. I hate them.'

'What d'you mean?'

'And that shirt is disgusting. You have the cruddiest taste in clothes I've ever seen.'

'You cow,' bellowed Nick, splashing her.

A mistake. His splash had been a gentlemanly affair, a mere playful spattering. Her retaliation was more in the nature of a tidal wave. Nick, drenched, seized her by the shoulders.

'He-man tactics?' she said, laughing. 'I warn you, buddy: I'm – no – pushover.'

She wasn't either. After a full minute's grim struggle, like two stags locked in combat, she sneakily managed to hook an ankle behind his calf and knock him off balance. But he was still clutching her shoulders so they toppled and capsized into the water together.

'Help,' gasped Nick, as he came up for air. 'I'm dying.'

'You can't drown in a foot of water,' she retorted, lying back and letting her hair float round her like black seaweed.

'Yes you bloody can. Anyway, it's not drowning I'm scared of. It's third-degree frostbite. Jeepers creepers. This is mad.'

'You asked for it,' she said, surfacing like a dark sea monster beside him, moonlight glinting on her teeth. She had too many teeth. Like all Americans. And, unlike his, they weren't clattering with cold.

'Well I'm asking now for b-brandy, blankets and immediate resuscitation.'

'Mouth-to-mouth?' she whispered. Against his mouth.

'Oh God, yes,' breathed Nick, shoving an arm round her. Her body was cold as a fish. 'Yes, I should bloody think so.'

'Shit,' she shrieked, slithering out of his grasp as an unexpected wave splintered over them. 'Any more of this and we'll both drown.'

'Come on,' said Nick, scrambling clumsily to his feet and seizing her arm.

Her fingers closed round his. 'My hotel's down the other end of the whatever you call it – esplanade.'

'Mine's closer. Hell, where are my shoes?'

He didn't bother putting them on. Carried them, swinging and banging from the laces as they leapt and shrieked over the pebbles, his jacket streaming from her shoulders. They startled a passing motorist into honking his horn as they raced across the road, yelping at sharp grit in the tarmac. Finally, breathless and shivering, they padded up to the entrance of the Princess Royal.

'So what now, Batman?' said Mary, dripping wet, grinning, her dress clinging like a shiny black skin to every angle of her body under his jacket. 'Nick? Oh for Christ's sake, wait until we get inside, can't you, not *here* . . . Nick!'

'I'm not raping you, you prat,' muttered Nick, silencing her with one hand over her mouth, as with the other he continued to grope in the pockets of his jacket. 'I'm trying to find my room key. There. Now, ready? Dignity is everything, got it?'

'Dignity.'

'You hold your head up high, walk past reception like nothing's happened, get to the stairs and then –'

'Run like hell?'

'Into the valley of death, rode the – Good evening, Irene,' Nick smiled radiantly. 'Sudden, um, rain shower. Forgive us. Must hurry upstairs and get out of these wet things.'

A minute later, Mary slammed the door labelled Pembroke behind them, coughing and weeping she was laughing so much. 'That woman's face . . . You were leaving goddamn puddles all the way across her floor. And you've got a huge glob of seaweed round your neck. Oh Nick. Oh . . . baby.'

'Must,' said Nick indistinctly, 'get out of these wet things.'

'Now – you *are* raping me.'

'Oh my God,' groaned Nick as, in a tangle of soggy clothing and clammy, grasping, hungry limbs they staggered towards the bed, 'I haven't – Mary, I haven't even got – a condom.'

Mary Hamilton grinned as she pulled off his tie. 'You must've been a lousy boy scout, honey,' she whispered. 'Lucky I came prepared.'

'You still taste of salt,' she murmured, licking his shoulder. 'Whenever I smell seaweed I shall think of you.'

'I'm underwhelmed.'

'I like the smell of seaweed.'

'I suppose I could acquire a taste for it,' said Nick, picking up a damp strand of her hair and sniffing it.

'That was good,' she said softly. 'You were good.'

'Bloody miraculous. After that immersion in ice, I thought my balls would never recover.'

'Must you laugh at everything?'

'Not at you,' he said suddenly. 'I'm not laughing at you. I've never felt less like . . . Mary? Hey, what are you doing? Oh God, you insatiable, ravening, she-wolf.'

She wanted to shut him up. The earnestness in his voice alarmed her. He'd been about to say something – she didn't know what, but *something*. Something that would spoil it all. Tonight was only going to happen once and she wanted pure, clean action – wham, bam and thanks-be-to-God for inventing sex – not stupid words they'd regret in the morning. No muddying of glorious sensation with cheap sentiment.

So she had clambered astride him, pinning him flat, smothering his words under kisses, biting the pale, salty flesh of his neck, breathing his hair. She clasped his hands over her breasts, felt his fingers close round her nipples and – with a shuddering whoop of triumph – impaled herself on him again.

'When all else fails,' murmured Nick, into her ear, 'I just like back and think of Wales. Oh Mary, *cariad* . . .'

'Carry-ad's Welsh, right?'

'Right. Love – darling – something like that. Ask Sir Geraint. He'd tell you.'

'Pompous little prick.'

'Are we speaking from first-hand experience here?'

Mary bit his earlobe so hard he yelped. 'You'd better believe I was talking metaphors.'

'Anyway,' he said, 'we men are always told it doesn't matter. Size.'

'You're fishing.'

'Who, me?'

'Of course it fucking matters. And your equipment, boy,' she drawled in the accents of the Deep South, 'is truly awesome. There, happy?'

But he had stopped grinning. In that instant he was remembering waif-faced Sasha and her description of the trainee film editor. *Hung like a prize ram. Mary likes boys she can push around.*

'Hey, I meant it,' she was protesting.

'Sorry. I mean, thanks. Actually . . . actually, I was thinking I could do with a fag. Would you mind?'

'Just as well I'm familiar with your cute English idioms,' she said. 'Although I didn't know you smoked.'

'I don't, often. But . . .' The twinge of unease had passed – no, not true, it hadn't simply passed. He was aware of stifling it, of deliberately shoving the image of Sasha beyond reach. Two sides to every story, right? And, for Christ's sake, this was no time for rattling closets in search of a skeleton. 'Tonight is by way of being a special occasion. Damn, I hope the box was in my jacket and not my jeans pocket.'

'Serve you right if it wasn't,' she said, uncoiling herself from the wrecked bed and prowling along the dressing table, poking open drawers. 'Is there a bar hidden here? Oh good. Champagne?'

'Why not?'

'And you can tell me how you survive, all alone in your little hut, in the wilderness, starved of people, culture, oh you know . . .'

'Sex?'

'*Sex?*'

'The sheep,' said Nick, 'are very friendly.'

'You must get lonely, though,' she insisted, as they sprawled on the bed, sipping champagne and trading lazy scraps of autobiography.

'Absolutely no,' said Nick. 'And at the same time, absolutely yes.'

That was typical of the guy, she thought. Incapable of giving a straight answer. What the hell had he meant a moment ago when he'd suddenly laughed and said something about being afraid he'd written all this? Afraid he'd wake up and find she was a sheaf of typescript. Joke, he'd said, kissing her (just to make sure she existed, he said), a stupid joke.

'I actually like being alone,' he was saying now. He was lying flat on his back, the wine glass balanced on his chest, a cigarette drooping from a hand flung (give the guy his due) as far away as he could manage. He had a really pleasing body, she thought, tracing the faint blue snake of a vein along his arm with one fingertip. Lean and tight-muscled as a boy's. Well, he wasn't a boy, but she had been amused – actually rather taken aback – to learn he was four years younger than she.

'In fact,' he went on, staring up at the ceiling, 'that's one of the reasons I quit the paper.'

'Were you any good?'

'Do you want the modest answer or the true one?'

She laughed. 'Then why not wave goodbye to the sheep

and hit Fleet Street?' She was thinking that, along with the suit and the haircut, a few by-lines in the national press could turn Nick Bevan into a respectable proposition. Well, almost.

'I told you. I like working alone. Work isn't stressful, it's people give you ulcers and cirrhosis. Now, it's just me and the keyboard and the keyboard can't answer back. Nor can –' He broke off with a choke of laughter.

'What's the big joke now?' enquired Mary, smiling but puzzled.

'I've always, um, argued that fictional characters can't object to what you write about 'em, unlike interviewees – but under the circumstances . . . Oh, never mind. Daft. Too daft to explain. Thing is,' he went on hastily, 'papers are like any other big organization: the only way is up. And then it's a different ballgame. At least a word-processor doesn't need staffing rotas, annual reports, sympathy for hangovers, pep-talks – and it doesn't have a wife, mortgage and three kids when some bugger in a grey suit tells you to sack it.'

'Same in any business,' she agreed absently, wondering what had amused him so much. Funny guy. 'Mine too, but it's worth it – shit, anything's got to be worth it, to make a movie. Even when I hate it most, I love it. When I'm putting a project together, I feel like, oh, like the Grand Old Duke of York, pulling and pushing, cherishing, bullying –'

'Bullying? *You?*'

'Is that sarcasm, Nick Bevan?'

'Don't hit me. I'm a devout coward. So, Madam B. de Mille, you march your ten thousand extras up to the top of the hill and –'

'Ah,' Mary found herself saying, 'but you never quite get there, do you?'

'Come again?'

She sighed. 'You make a film, you make a string of compromises. No other way. You have an idea and in your head it's magical, but actually realizing the thing . . . I mean, here's your frail, precious vision, but it's got to be transmitted through other people: their eyes behind the camera, their fingers on the script, their bodies on the screen. Like the movie I'm crazy to do next, I –' She broke off, irritated with herself. Much too heartfelt. This was a double bed, not an analyst's couch. Anyway, he couldn't begin to understand.

'The day any of us thinks we've finally got it right,' he offered flippantly, 'is the day we're washed up.'

'Which fortune cookie did that fall out of?'

'It's my consoling philosophy,' he retorted unabashed, 'every time I read through something I've written and decide it's crap.' He raised an eyebrow. 'What's this film then? First World War drama, didn't Roderick say?'

'What would Roddy know about it?' She fell back on the pillow, staring up at the ceiling which, like everything else in this gin palace, was gilded to kill. 'Well yes, I guess. Great War. Without a trench, a poppy, a single solitary tin helmet.'

'Tell me.'

Her voice was jeering. 'Yorkshire women running a sweet factory, that's the story. Sound as ludicrous to you as it apparently does to everyone else?'

'Yorkshire?' he said thoughtfully. 'So this was the idea brought you north in the first place. With your sceptical, sniffling partner.'

She glanced sideways. 'How d'you know that?'

'You shouldn't give interviews to strange pressmen. And?'

'And what?'

'What's the story?'

'The men volunteer, or get their papers,' she said reluctantly. 'The women have to take over the works. It's about them, their hearts and lives. Their sons, husbands, fiancés mainly don't come back. The girls just keep turning out Pontefract cakes.'

'Ah – *liquorice*,' said Nick with a faint smile.

She hoisted herself up on one elbow, glaring at him. 'Just

what, tell me, is so comic about liquorice, that everyone sniggers when I mention it? Is it the Brits' lavatorial obsession with laxatives or what?'

'You also mentioned the name, *The Liquorice Fields*,' he protested. 'I just didn't connect that with ... Besides, who's laughing? Liquorice is amazing stuff. Do you know they once made dresses out of it?'

'What?'

'Also an ingredient in fire extinguishers. And the finishing processes of steel. Introduced by Crusaders from the East. Miraculously cultivated by monks in the particular microclimate of South Yorkshire.'

She stared at him. 'How do you know all this bullshit?'

'Bullshit nothing. I did a feature on an exhibition last year. Anyway, your women are stuck on the homefront with the vast steaming vats of the stuff ...'

'It's not funny.'

'I told you, I'm not laughing. It was always a women's industry, far as I recall. Manned – womanned – by Amazons. Brewing, mixing ...'

'With flour and treacle and sugar.'

'Yuck.'

She settled her head against his shoulder. 'Thick and brown and viscous,' she said dreamily, 'just like the mud on the Somme. Churning and turning as the women learn week by week that another sweetheart, another son is dead, and what do they do? They weep but they just keep cutting and stamping the little cakes, a crest embossed by hand – *bang!* – on every one.' She was talking more to herself than him. 'The sweet boxes even had a picture of General Kitchener on them. And a royal crest. By appointment.'

'Just as they turned out sons?' Nick's voice was soft and sad in her ear. 'To be engulfed in the churning mud, to end up boxed, with a regimental crest on the lid. Maybe not even boxed. But by appointment to his august and imperial majesty nevertheless.'

'Yes,' said Mary, wonderingly. 'Yes, exactly.'

'Why are you sounding so surprised?'

'Am I? It's just . . .' She hadn't expected such ready understanding. It was as though he were seeing the pictures inside her head. 'Oh God, I suppose because all I've had from other people is whinges about parochialism, sneers about the littleness of the story, the Englishness. Worse, Northern bloody Englishness. Almost how *dare* someone like me suggest it.'

'Love and death. Nothing parochial about that. Has it been hard?' he asked unexpectedly. 'Your career as a whole, I'm talking about. Getting to be able to do what you want?'

'Is this an interview?' she said sharply. 'I thought we were fucking.'

He didn't flinch. His gaze met hers steadily across the pillow. 'I want to get inside your soul,' he said. 'As well.'

And for a wild fleeting instant, she wished he could. Those clever eyes, black as sodding liquorice, were fixed on her, silently urging her to spill the very essence of her being. She almost blurted out her perpetual terror that she would never, ultimately, be good enough. Fail her own standards – Dad's standards. She was even tempted to confess just how bloody some of the last twenty years had been. This country with its obscure rituals and schoolboy clubbery. The fights, the failures, the downright futility of so many jobs taken just to keep working. To keep working, more to the point, this side of the Atlantic. And now, at last, doing what she passionately wanted, she could tell him about the nights she was so weary – aching in bone and soul – she could hardly drag herself up from car park to flat. Her echoing, empty flat.

Sanity snapped back just in time. She *liked* her flat being empty. She *hated* the ever more rare nights when some man's clothes were littering her floor, when there was a mess of shaving stuff on her shelf, someone else's tidemark round her bath, foreign hair in the plughole. She'd decided long ago sex was only to be played as an away game.

And *game* was the right word. Not that she had anything against long-term relationships. Nor marriage even. In principle. On the contrary, she sometimes fancied she was reserving marriage – along with gardening, cathedrals and portrait-painting – as a pleasure for her declining years. Nice to have something to look forward to.

She reached across him, took Nick's cigarette and inhaled deeply. She did not cough.

'Do you smoke?' he asked curiously.

'Not for years,' she said, 'but if I'm going to choke from passive inhalation tonight, I may as well get a kick out of it along the way.'

They hardly slept. They played and argued and laughed and fucked – and smoked and drank – and fucked some more. Under the shower, on the floor, sprawled over the armchair. Nick was to look back on that wild night with awe. They'd behaved like delinquent children let loose in a fairground. And, as a young sun peered gold between the curtains, they were lying entwined, gorged and exhausted, amid the wreckage.

Mary was still asleep. Her face, in repose, was smooth, almost childlike. A sad child? Nick traced the angle of her jaw with one finger and gently, without waking her, slid from under her arm and walked across to the window.

A seagull shrieked, startlingly close. The cry evoked childhood holidays with sudden, piercing nostalgia.

I'm happy, he thought. The actual words formed in his brain with a banality that made him smile out into the sun. Purely, simply, uncomplicatedly happy like I've hardly been since I was a kid.

'Nick?' She was stirring, blinking. 'Is it morning?'

'Been morning for hours,' he said and padded round the room, lifting bits of clothing, patting pockets, knocking over an empty glass, until he found his watch. 'Half past seven.'

'Help.'

'Help?' he said, returning to the bed and cradling her face in one hand. 'What kind of help?'

'I'm stranded, here, you idiot. I haven't got anything, not even a toothbrush.'

He laughed. 'Use mine. Anything you can catch off a toothbrush, you've got already.'

'With one sodden little dress.' She stretched out an arm, plucking a limp black rag from the carpet. 'Now totally ruined. Know how much that cost?'

'As a proportion of my annual earnings? Better not tell me. I might feel obliged to string your gorgeous capitalist corpse up the nearest lamppost.'

She fell back on the bed. 'Are you expecting me to walk out of this hotel and across Lan – clan – how the fuck do you pronounce it anyhow?'

'Llandudno.'

'Wearing that?'

'Sweetheart,' said Nick, smiling tenderly, 'tell me your hotel name and your room number, and I will put on my, um, cruddy jeans . . .'

'Well, they are cruddy.'

'Also now salt-stained and stinking. And I'll walk to wherever your hotel is and bring back whatever you require to make yourself respectable enough to face the world.'

'Know what, Nick *Thcloo-ellen* Bevan? You're my knight in shining armour. Come here.'

'Shouldn't the reward wait until I, um, gallop back from the quest to rescue your dignity?'

Mary's mouth curved wickedly. 'Just call me Lady Bountiful, baby.'

22

Mary felt as though a steam-roller had run over her. Every limb ached, she suspected she might not be able to sit down again for a week, her throat was raw from cigarette smoke and there were, she noticed, examining her body with detached interest, some pinkish bruises in the most embarrassing places.

She was lying in the bath.

The guy was amazing. Simply amazing. She hadn't had sex like that for . . . for ever. Even as she found herself framing those words, another part of her brain whispered cynically that good sex always felt unique. It induced an amnesia of all the other good times. Nevertheless . . .

She unwrapped the tiny free tablet of Rose-yucky-Geranium and began, lazily, to soap her shoulders. But as she did so, she was feeling Nick Bevan's hands again. Wow, this was like the aftershocks of an earthquake. She hoped he wouldn't take long collecting her gear. It wasn't the clothes or her damn toothbrush she wanted back here urgently now, it was him. She couldn't do without him for ten minutes.

The idea startled her so much she dropped the soap.

But however much she told herself she was going crazy, that she was contemplating her biggest mistake in years – decades; that she would regret it, that it would all end in tears; *however* fiercely she argued with herself, there was no escaping it. She knew, the minute Nick Bevan walked back into the room, she was going to invite him down to London. To move in with her.

Only for a while, of course. A weekend? A month? A *night* . . .
See how it went. He'd probably hate her friends. What – oh
no – what would they make of him? Andrew? The others?
Her *father*? Well, he just wouldn't have to meet them. Course
he would have to meet them. Not her father (definitely not
Pa, no way), but the guys she worked with – hell, she spent
nine-tenths of her waking life with them. They might even
like him. They might not. The point was, they'd know,
recognize at a glance, Nick Bevan wasn't her type. Absolutely
not. Too young, too shabby, too . . . well, just too unlike any
previous man in her life. They'd think she'd run mad. In fact,
the whole idea was mad. Stark, staring, barking, raving
crackers.

But she was already deciding that he could have the spare
bedroom for his study. There was a desk in there for his
word-processor and bookshelves a-plenty.

She was smiling as she bit the corner off the free sachet of
shampoo. By the time she began lathering her hair, she was
laughing aloud.

'Room, um, twenty-three,' said Nick. 'Miss Hamilton asked
me to call in and, well, collect one or two things for her.'

The receptionist gaped at him.

For the first time it occured to Nick he must look pretty
disreputable. No such potential embarrassment had crossed
his mind as he skipped along the sunny promenade, kicking
stray pebbles back towards the sea, beaming at innocent
early-morning dog-walkers and envying the seagulls their
free-wheeling dives across the sky. He rather fancied, if he
really tried, he could leap free of the paving stones and join
them up there in the blue eternities, weightlessly dodging the
shreds of cloud.

Now he realized he was crumpled, unshaven, lacking any
means of identification – his own or Mary's – and was
demanding access to someone else's hotel room.

'She's – ah – a friend of mine,' he began. 'Maybe . . . Look, ring the Princess Royal Hotel, if you like. Ask for Nick Bevan's room.'

'Nick Bevan?' she echoed, glancing over her shoulder as though hoping her manager might materialize to rescue her. 'Who exactly is Nick Bevan?'

'Me, of course.'

'I can vouch for that,' said a wryly amused voice at his shoulder. He spun round to find Miriam Weissman, startlingly clad in pink shorts and jungle-print shirt, standing behind him.

'And you want to get into Mary's room?' she said, the eyes more alarmingly sharp than ever. 'Well, well, well . . . Look,' she said, turning to the receptionist, 'they're both friends of mine. You can give me the key. I take total responsibility.' And she tucked her arm into Nick's. 'I'll show you up, doll.'

'Are you?' whispered Nick. 'A friend of Mary's, I mean?'

'Sure. Known her for ever. Don't look so stunned. Television's just a very small and very incestuous global village, remember. Besides, Mary and I have been working together recently. Matter of fact, it was me suggested to Geraint he rope her in on this jamboree. More to the point . . .' She paused and pressed a button to open the lift doors, 'I didn't know *you* were a friend of the mighty Snow Queen. And, far as I can gather, a pretty *close* friend. I should tell you I'd asked Mary to meet me for a drink after the debate yesterday evening. Not just girlie gossip either: serious business. And I rang her room for the last time at – oh – something like midnight. Mary Hamilton, let me tell you, has never been known to forget a meeting in her entire turbo-charged life.'

Nick grinned.

'Ugh, don't,' she said, screwing up her face in horror. 'Young love makes me want to throw up. Stand clear of the doors, please. Second floor, ladies' lingerie.'

'Dead right,' said Nick, with a laugh. 'Lingerie, soapbag, hairdryer, the works. I've been despatched to retrieve them.'

'Well I guessed that,' she said, bustling along the corridor ahead of him. 'But what you haven't told me is how *you* come to know Mary in the first place. Unless you just coincided yesterday evening and *kapow*, lightning struck?'

'Felt like it,' murmured Nick.

'No gory details please. I've just breakfasted.'

'No, actually, we met up in Yorkshire. She was filming in our village.'

'Aha,' exclaimed Miriam. 'Now I understand all. Here we are.' She unlocked the door and ushered him in. 'I feel I'm responsible for your good conduct and checking that you don't steal the television,' she murmured. 'My goodness, the Yorkshire connection, eh? That explains a lot. I'd heard there'd been no end of stormy passions unleashed on the Heathcliffe-blasted moors.'

'Oh, that was nothing to do with me,' said Nick jovially. 'Do you know Candia Mayhew too?'

'Not well. But I gather that little fiasco fizzled out harmlessly enough in the end, didn't it?' she said. 'Thank the Lord. I think I might just as well stick everything back in the suitcase, and you can take it round to Madam lock, stockings and barrel. OK?'

'What? Oh, sure.' Nick brushed these irrelevancies aside. 'Miriam, what exactly did you mean? About Candia. A fiasco?'

Miriam spun round, her eyes shiny with mischief. 'Whoops, have I plunged my size seven in, as per usual? Anyway, it's water under the bridge now. Candia's such a flighty piece, it's a hundred-to-one she wasn't pregnant anyway.'

'*Pregnant?*'

'Well, *quite*,' Miriam shrieked back, misunderstanding his shock. 'I promise poor Mary nearly had a heart attack, because she's sold *Liquorice Fields* almost entirely on the strength of Candia's name. That's a movie we've been moving heaven and earth for, as she must have told you. No one wanted to touch it and –'

'I know all about it,' he said impatiently. 'But she didn't mention Candia.'

'Oh Lord, I just assumed . . . Well, never mind. I declare an interest in this affair, by the way. You're talking to the poor bloody writer. I'm into draft 503, Mary's had her partners' arms twisted twice round their backs for months, finance is finally in prospect, and there was La Mayhew calmly announcing she fancied settling into a cottage for a few years and rearing crèchefuls of babies. The complete roses-round-the-door routine.'

'Sorry? Look, let me get this straight . . .' Nick had grasped the back of a chair. Stupid, but the floor felt shifty as a mattress. Hell, if it was John hearing this, the guy would have passed out cold. 'You're telling me Candia's – having a baby?'

'Course she isn't,' declared Miriam exasperatedly, returning to her packing. 'That's the whole point. And Mary reckoned she never was. You know actresses. They can think themselves into hysteria, illness, religious mania, you name it. A two-day phantom pregnancy should be a walk-over. But it did create one Godalmighty row, with Mary telling her – well . . .'

'To have an abortion?' gasped Nick.

'Oh come on,' said Miriam, glancing over her shoulder at him. 'Not a Catholic, are you?'

Nick shook his head.

'I mean, no woman could ever say outright to another . . . Anyway, whatever, the next morning Candia was bleeding. Two-day wonder, the whole thing, like I said. She hadn't even had time to do a test.'

'I see,' said Nick. No, he was thinking, I don't see at all. Could Candia really, seriously, have been talking about settling down with John, and then . . . ?

'Course, I didn't know a thing about it until afterwards,' Miriam observed from the depths of the wardrobe. 'But I could see Mary was terribly shaken up.'

'With her precious film at risk?' Nick muttered before he could stop himself. Don't be an idiot, he told himself. He couldn't – wouldn't – believe the woman waiting in his bed would care more about a bloody film than . . .

'Not just that,' protested Miriam. 'She's very attached to Candia, and she hates rows. Still, all's well that ends well and what have you.'

Nick stiffened. 'Ends well for who exactly?' He was seeing John sprawled, dead drunk, across a kitchen table. John, haggard and red-eyed the next morning, saying nothing and radiating an agony that would melt stones.

'Everyone concerned, by all accounts.' Fortunately Miriam was bending over the case and couldn't see Nick's face. 'Sure, Candia didn't think so at the time, by all accounts, but Mary gave her a zonking great gin and the courage to offload this no-hoper.'

No-hoper, thought Nick wrathfully. Who the fuck had dared to call John a *no-hoper*? Who . . . ?

'No, I can't bear it: look at the size of these knickers,' Miriam was continuing merrily. 'Wouldn't fit round my ankle. And, my dear, the brand-names . . . Well, they always say you can tell a woman's income by her underwear.'

She chattered on, but Nick didn't hear. He was recalling conversations in Maltbury. Dialogue chronicled, word for telltale word, by him. Sell-by dates on pretty faces . . . Crucial age for an actress . . . Candia ought to work at her goddamn career . . . And Candia – he could see her now – grinning and parroting that Mary always knew what was best for everyone, and her in particular. *So I'm persuadable*, she'd said. And she really had said that. No embroidery by the author. *Anything wrong in that?*

'Anyhow, the film's scheduled to shoot next spring, please

God, touch wood, chuck salt, et cetera. And Candia's safely out of mischief for a bit.'

'What?'

Miriam slammed shut the lid of the case and snapped the lock. 'Only joking. But Mary found her a dolly little job in New York for a few weeks. To cheer her up, you know.'

To *cheer her up*? Like a sweetie for a grazed knee? A ticket to New York for a broken heart? The snarling, spitting surge of his own anger shocked Nick as much as what he was hearing. 'I suppose she just waved a magic bloody wand?'

'Telephoned Poppa,' said Miriam absently, tugging a strap closed on the case. 'Which amounts to the same thing, natch.'

'Does it?'

Miriam turned to look at him. 'Didn't you know? About Mary's father?'

Nick didn't and he didn't care either. Dumb with outrage, he managed a shrug.

'Only one of the biggest bugs in the whole East Coast media ant-heap.' Miriam fastened the other strap and hoisted the bag on to the floor. 'Known to his friends as God. Hell, if you don't know about Mary's papa, you don't know *nothing*, sunshine. You should ask her.'

'I don't think so,' he hissed.

Miriam's smile suddenly vanished. 'Nick? Something the matter?'

'What? Oh ...' He mustn't lose his grip. His quarrel wasn't with Miriam. In fact, there was going to be no quarrel. Two sides to every story. And he was going to ask Mary Hamilton – sweetly, quietly and perfectly reasonably – for side two, wasn't he? And then ... Big breath now. Compose face into a smile. 'No, of course not. Is that all packed? Great. I'll – I'll take it back to the Princess Royal then.' Walking towards the door, a thought halted him and he turned. 'Miriam,' he said slowly. He didn't want to ask. He desperately didn't want to ask. But he could no more

have shut up now than willed his heart to stop beating. 'I
don't suppose, by any chance, you ever knew a girl who used
to work with Mary at Pentagon, um, Sasha Floyd?'

Miriam frowned.

'Thin,' pursued Nick, hating himself, hoping wildly Miriam
would say no. 'Black hair. Bit exotic-looking.'

'Oh *her*,' said Miriam, and all at once her expression was
wary. 'No, I didn't. Not personally. And I think Mary – all of
them – are doing their best to forget her. At least . . . I mean,
one can't exactly say it turned out all right in the end but, one
has to thank God, because it could have been so much worse.
You mustn't hold it against her,' she added earnestly. 'I know
they've tried to hush it up, but by all accounts Sasha behaved
truly wickedly. Mary was genuinely fond of the boy. She was
heartbroken.'

'Was she indeed?' hissed Nick, and was unable to prevent
himself adding: 'And what about Sasha?'

Miriam's plump face was troubled. 'Well – I guess she has
her problems, poor stupid kid, but . . . Nick? Hey, there *is*
something wrong. What've I said?'

'Nothing,' he snapped. 'At least – oh Christ, it's nothing to
do with you, Miriam. I'll get a move on. Thanks, thanks a
lot.'

For ruining my life, he thought. And this melodramatic
declaration didn't strike him as remotely comic. It sounded
about right under the circumstances.

23

'Baby,' exclaimed Mary, beaming up at him, 'you've been gone *hours.*'

He had been gone a little more than one hour in fact. After leaving Miriam, he had pelted down to the beach and capsized, winded, on the pebbles, with Mary's bloody suitcase beside him. He'd watched the waves smashing at his feet and hated them for reminding him of last night. When they'd frolicked in the sea like a couple of randy seals. He had felt physically sick.

He was seeing Mary as he'd left her, sprawled across the bed, flushed and fluffy as a kitten. A six-foot, man-eating fucking tiger kitten. And he'd known it. Thanks to Sasha Floyd, he'd known the nature of the beast all along, but preferred to kid himself he'd got through to some soft, sensitive and even rather sad inner creature. Sentimental claptrap. Anger with himself made him even angrier on behalf of John.

One thing he was sure of: John couldn't have known about the pregnancy scare. God, if the poor fool had even suspected, nothing on earth would have stopped him racing to the woman. And never mind whether it was imaginary or not, the point was Candia had actually wanted to give the relationship a go. Settle down with him. And they could have. Oh, maybe not in Yorkshire: forget the roses round the cottage door. But John would have upped chisels and followed the woman to Scunthorpe, Siberia or the other side of the sun. If he'd only been given the chance. And why shouldn't he have had that chance? He'd lost a wife and unborn child already. He and Candia were created for one another. Any idiot could see that.

Nick had seen it. Written about it with, according to Caro, string orchestras sighing off the page. But he'd been forced to conclude he'd got it wrong. And what's more, been cynically ready to agree with Caro that there must be a man waiting for Candia back in town, a shadowy third party in the wings, blighting the affair.

He was sourly ashamed of that cynicism now, because there damn well *had* been a third party to the affair. Not in the least shadowy, and not a lover. Feeding Candia gin and the courage to give this *no-hoper* the push. Field Marshal bloody Hamilton, driving her army onwards and upwards, taking no prisoners, brooking no deserters – and dumping inconvenient little embryos along the way. The woman was a she-devil.

But then memories of last night flooded back, agonizing in their sweetness, and he'd caught himself up, telling himself there must be some excuse, some other explanation. He'd grabbed the case, started walking up the beach, gathering pace, running by the time he reached the promenade. She wouldn't sacrifice John – the pair of them – on the great celluloid altar. Just because he might get in the way of Candia's career, of her own precious film. (*Anything's got to be worth it, to make a movie* . . .) No, there was another side to this story. Had to be. He would ask her. Calmly. Reasonably.

And what about poor Sasha? Sasha and her film editor chum. *Mary likes boys she can push around.* He was spitting curses as he raced across the road, reckless of traffic, dodging pedestrians.

Here was one *boy* she was not going to push around. He blundered into a litter bin, grazing his elbow and stopped. He was not going to lose his temper. We're two adults, right?

We can deal with this in an adult way, right? Be calm. Be reasonable. He was muttering this like a mantra as he strode up to the door of the hotel. Oh shit . . . 'Sorry, sorry, didn't see you.'

He'd collided with Sir Geraint on the step. The old fool was bumbling on about something, grabbing his arm. Nick managed to shake him off and barged through the doors into the lobby, up the stairs three at a time – and ran smash into Charlie at the top.

'Who is she, then?' demanded Charlie. 'The six-foot Venus who dripped sand and sea water all over Irene's carpet last night?'

'Not now,' Nick had gasped, pushing past him and pausing for a minute, to order his thoughts, catch his breath before he opened the door to the room.

And now here she was, sitting at the dressing table, swathed in one huge towel, with another turbanning her head. Smiling at him like – just like a bloody tiger, waiting for the next feeding time.

'So where've you been?' she repeated.

Calm. Calm and reasonable. 'I went for – a walk.'

She raised her eyebrows: 'A *walk*? Haven't you had enough exercise for one night?'

'Yes,' gasped Nick. He could hear the blood pounding inside his ears. 'Yes, I have as a matter of fact. More than enough.' Stay calm. For pity's sake . . .

'You look like a tramp,' she sighed, grinning. 'Know what the first thing I'm going to do is? Take you to a hairdresser's and then buy you some halfway respectable jeans and . . . Nick? Nick, what's the matter?'

Suddenly he couldn't speak at all. Rage and bitter bewilderment were choking him.

'Anyway, I'm jumping the gun,' she said with a little laugh. 'Thing is, ah, I've got a proposition to put to you. Don't faint. I just wondered . . . Well, I mean, a writer can live anywhere, can't they? You only need somewhere to park your typewriter and a bit of peace and quiet – and I can promise plenty of that. I'm hardly ever there when I'm busy, which is always, well, except at night, and I usually –'

'What? What are you saying?'

She shrugged, smiled. 'I'm suggesting you might like to move in with me, dimbo. Only for a while, if you –'

He was still in control. Well, so help him, he wasn't actually shouting. 'Until you get bored with me? Or I get in the way of more important things in life?'

'Sorry?'

'But I suppose I strike you as easy to push around too, do I? Good-tempered, house-trained. You could keep me in the flat like – like one of Irene's bloody Yorkshire terriers. Something to amuse you, warm your bed and – and fetch your slippers when you deign to return after a hard day in the cutting room? I'm a good cook, too, matter of fact, although you probably didn't even know that.'

'I don't know what you're talking about at all. Look, if you're offended just because I mentioned giving you a pair of pants – hell, it was me wrecked them, I just wanted –'

The blood was pounding louder. 'Pygmalion, is it?'

'Oh, for Christ's sake.'

'Given a bit of polish, I might not be a complete – what is it – no-hoper?'

Her gaze dropped. And the woman was actually *blushing*. Looking guilty as all hell. 'Look, Nick, you mustn't be offended just because I might have had a few qualms, dammit, some perfectly sensible reservations, about –'

And the cork finally blew. 'Only a few?' he snarled. 'Well, frankly, I'm amazed. After all, if John was going to be such an impediment to Candia's glittering career, then I'd have thought the likes of me would be a fucking death knell to yours.'

She stood up. 'John?' she echoed blankly. 'Oh, you mean John . . . Lord, what's his other name?'

'Jesus wept,' roared Nick. 'You can't even remember the poor bastard's name!'

'Simmonds,' she snapped exasperatedly. 'John Hope-Simmonds.'

'He was crazy about Candia, did you know that? His wife – and his child – were mashed to pulp under a lorry three years ago, and when he met Candia that's the first time – *the first time* – he's ever looked halfway like a member of the human race again.'

She stared at him. 'Wife? I didn't know that. Candia never mentioned . . .' She sounded shocked, but Nick was beyond caring.

'You don't think John talks about it, do you? He was as likely to tell Candia about that as tell her he'd got AIDS. There isn't even a photograph of Sally in his house. He can't bear to be reminded. But what's mere life and death compared to your filming schedules? Apparently John was just an obstacle that might have got in the way, not to mention the baby, so –'

'Oh, for God's sake.' Her voice was rising now. 'They're two adults, they had a good time for a while. These things happen on location.'

'Or at literary festivals?'

'What the hell's it got to do with me – us?'

'Us!' He spat the word at her. 'It's you I'm talking about. You mean you didn't do your very efficient best to smash them apart?'

She was flushed. 'I told Candia she was mad if she dropped everything for a family at this particular moment, sure. And why not? She's just about to make it big. Seriously big. She could screw everything. Strange as it might seem to you, I'm very fond of Candia.'

'Yeah, it does seem pretty strange. So fond you don't hesitate to tell her to have an abortion.'

'You bastard.' The towel, which had been uncoiling from

her head, flopped to the carpet. 'I did·nothing of the sort. What kind of a monster do you think I am?'

'You tell me. And what about Sasha Floyd? You saw her off pretty smartly too, didn't you? Sasha and her pretty film editor chum.'

'What?' Now she was screaming like a banshee. 'What the *fuck* are you talking about?'

'Hung like a prize ram? Did you have as much fun with him as you did with me?'

'Get out,' she shrieked. 'Get out of here or, so help me, I'll kill you.'

'Don't worry, I'm going.'

Something actually thumped against the door as he slammed it behind him.

He slumped against the wall, eyes closed, gasping for breath. Only a rattle of crockery against metal roused him.

'Romantic breakfast for two in bed?' Charlie, in full spanking-white chef's regalia, was wheeling a trolley along the corridor towards him. The trolley was loaded with a champagne bucket, a single red rose, an ice-tinkling pitcher of orange juice, a mountain range of silver salvers . . . 'Bacon, eggs, mushrooms,' Charlie was listing with relish, 'black pudding, tomato . . .'

'No,' groaned Nick, unhearing. 'No, no, no . . .'

'Blimey, what did you expect? Fried bloody flamingo?' Charlie stared at him. 'Hey, are you all right, chum?'

'What does it look like?'

'Ah,' said Charlie. And sighed. 'Do I gather my champagne breakfast for two is, ahem, not required?'

'You could say that,' hissed Nick, and collected himself enough to attempt a smile. 'But the thought was – very kind.' He hoisted himself away from the wall, and cleared his throat. 'My, um, companion should be gone soon. That is . . .' He glared at the door. 'She'll probably fly out of the window on her fucking broomstick. In the meantime, I'm going out.' He winced. 'And I may – as they say in all the best movies – be some time.'

Episode Three

From the *Cocktail Menu*, Princess Royal Hotel:

Y **HEARTBREAK HOTEL:** *equal measures white rum and fresh mango juice shaken in crushed ice, topped with a bitter twist of lemon and a sweet dash of* Parfait Amour.

May not mend a broken heart but, taken in quantity, guarantees temporary anaesthesia.

24

'Well hello there,' said John, strolling into the kitchen. 'The wanderer returns.'

'Just,' said Nick. 'I only walked in five minutes ago. I, um, I decided to stay on a couple of days longer with Charlie. You remember old Charlie Meschia?'

He had, in fact, got himself so rip-roaringly, dangerously, *manically* drunk after Mary had left the hotel that Charlie (who generously kept pace with him at least halfway to oblivion) had refused to let him attempt the journey home until a full thirty-six hours later. Irene was frozen in silent outrage throughout.

'Sure I remember Charlie,' said John. 'How is he? How was Llandudno?'

'Oh, you know. OK.' Nick tried to order his still-reeling brain. He wondered how many grey cells he'd managed to pickle in the course of the last couple of days. 'I ran into, um, Mary Hamilton over there. Would you believe.'

It hurt enough just to pronounce her name, let alone with such magnificent indifference. But the spasm of anguish which twisted John's face told him he should have kept his mouth shut. At least until he'd had a chance to prepare the script.

'Small world,' John was saying now, with an indifference almost as impressive as his own. 'Talk to her at all?'

Oh blimey. Get out of this one, Bevan. 'Yeah, yeah, I did. Matter of fact we had . . .' The night of a lifetime? Ten hours of wild, unbridled, mind-wrecking, soul-ripping lust? '. . . a few drinks.'

'I don't suppose' – John was staring out of the window – 'she mentioned Candia at all?'

'Not really. Only in passing.' That at least was the simple truth.

'Yes, sure, why should she? Well, I'm glad to see you back.'

Having got this far, however, Nick couldn't just quit. Not after John himself had raised the woman's name. 'Actually, John, look, mate, I don't want to pry, but . . .'

'But what?' John turned back to look at him and his face was wary.

'I've been wondering . . .' (Wondering how I tackle this hornets' nest?) 'When Candia finished it, when she phoned you . . .' (Full of gin? With Mary Hamilton standing over her?) 'Thing is, what exactly did she have to say for herself?'

John flinched as though Nick had struck him. 'If you don't mind, I'd rather not. Talk about it, I mean. I was sorry you had to find me afterwards in such a filthy state but –'

'As if I'd care, you chump. I'm just asking why she suddenly gave you the boot?'

'It wasn't as simple as that,' said John sharply. 'I dare say it was my own fault.'

'I can't believe that.'

John ignored him. 'We were supposed to be getting to-gether for the weekend. I thought – I thought I was going down to town to join her. After Derbyshire, they had a few final days' shooting near London. But the schedules changed and she . . .' He was gripping the back of a chair, white-knuckled. 'Anyway, she phoned and we agreed – well, it was perfectly obvious – there was no point. Trying to fix anything else. That's all there is to say. Clear as daylight there was no future in it. Silly to expect anything different. With someone like her.'

Easy, lovely boy, easy now. 'What do you mean?'

'Don't pretend to be stupid,' hissed John. 'Who she is. *What* she is. Sure, we seemed to get on ...' His mouth tightened. He could hardly get the words out. 'We got on pretty well for a − a fortnight up here. But I should have guessed the end was inevitable, once she left.'

'Have you rung her?' demanded Nick. 'Tried again? After she gave you the heave-ho?'

'God, no.'

'Why not?'

'You don't understand. When she rang, it was like talking to a complete stranger. Anyway − anyway I hate the telephone.'

'Oh come on,' cried Nick before he could stop himself, 'write her a bloody letter then.' Wrong. This was like performing open-heart surgery with garden tools.

'I don't want to bug her like some demented fan. If a thing's over, it's over. And so is this conversation, OK?'

And John was looking not simply upset but ... angry? It occurred to some distant corner of Nick's soggy brain that he had never actually seen John angry. Never. Not in the near twenty years he'd known him. 'No, listen a minute, please.' This needed delicate phrasing. Oh Lord, where had his wits gone? 'You don't think someone might have, um, persuaded her to drop you?'

'*What?*'

'It's just that I happened to hear Mary Hamilton's flogging a film on the strength of her name.'

'So? What the hell's that to do with me?'

'So,' said Nick eagerly, 'the whole project's riding on Candia being free and available. I mean, just suppose she settled down with you −'

'Can't you get it into your thick skull? She doesn't' − John's face contorted − 'doesn't bloody want to settle down with me. Doesn't want me at all.'

'She's a very persuadable girl. She –'

'I've never heard such unutterable balls,' roared John. 'You can't talk people out of love.'

'Well maybe, but –'

'Or into it. And frankly, I'm finding this whole conversation pretty fucking excruciating, so can we please drop it?' If those eyes were the blue of a postcard sea, then there was a typhoon brewing. A prudent man would stop right here.

'I'm only suggesting –' And then, Nick broke off. It was not prudence silenced him, however, but sudden doubt. He blinked stupidly. Was there, could there possibly be, some sneaking logic in what John said? After all, Candia was a grown woman. Persuadable she might be over refusing parts in soap operas, but over a lover? If she had cared at all for John, would she really have dumped him just because Mary Hamilton gave the imperial thumbs-down? His brain felt like suet pudding. Nothing – quite – made sense. And John was looking like the last of the crusaders, ready to die in the cause. A prudent man would stop right here . . .

'I'm only suggesting you should try again.'

The manly jaw was jutting out in a most uncharacteristically pugnacious fashion. 'Nick, I really, seriously, do not want to discuss this.'

'You can't just give up. I mean –'

'I'm warning you, Nick . . .' His fists were actually bunching. But John would never hit him. Never. Nick dodged behind the kitchen table.

'Look, you're in London yourself soon, aren't you? For Caro's wedding?'

'So?' The guy was actually growling.

Gordon Bennett, thought Nick, I've had enough rows this week to last a lifetime. How did I get myself into this one? 'So – go and see her?'

'For Christ's sake,' roared John. 'The girl's pissed off to New York, hasn't she?' And wham, the fist was out. Except it was the door he punched. The door to the hall. And his hand sledgehammered clean through.

There was a moment of stunned silence.

'Ouch,' said John faintly. In as slow a double-take as any cartoon character ever managed.

Nick was staring at the dresser where the plates were still quivering. A framed photograph of Christopher gently, almost balletically, keeled over and flopped face-downwards on the floor. 'Bloody Nora.' He glanced at his own hand and winced in sympathy. 'Are you OK, chum?'

John was retrieving his arm from the splintering hole, looking dazed and disbelieving as a sleepwalker who's surfaced in the middle of Piccadilly Circus. 'What? Um . . . fine. I think. Sorry. About the door. Don't worry. I'll fix it for you.'

Nick managed a wavering grin. 'Think nothing of it. You always said it was a cheap door.'

'Even so . . .'

'I'm just grateful it wasn't me on the receiving end.'

John grimaced. 'Don't be daft. I just – oh, I suppose I needed to let off steam.' He shook his hand pensively. 'Bloody silly thing to do.'

'Was it . . .' Nick cleared his throat. 'Is it the same hand?' He was thinking – and he dared say John was too – of the last time he'd injured a hand. Only then there was Candia fussing over him like a mother hen. Such a loving little hen. Who had now flitted off to the far side of the Atlantic. Nick should have remembered that, at least. *Safely out of mischief*, as Miriam had so merrily put it. The memory still smarted.

'What? Oh no, no. Left hand, that was. Look, I really am ashamed of myself, Nick. I don't know what came over me.'

Oh I do, thought Nick cordially. Forty-eight hours ago, I could have punched a few doors myself. Except, with my puny paws, I'd have smashed bones instead of pine panels. 'Entirely my fault,' he said swiftly. 'I lumbered straight in

195

where angels fear and what have you.' But at least he'd had sufficient wit to stop short of the phantom pregnancy. He'd have to think very carefully about opening that can of snakes. Anyway, his own certainties were crumbling. How could a woman be talking crèches and roses one day and cheerfully setting off for New York the next? Could anyone be that fickle?

'I'd better go and find some Dettol,' John was saying, turning towards the door.

'I'm –' Nick wanted to apologize for his tactlessness. John interrupted.

'Please. There's nothing more to say.'

'Look, do you want a drink?'

John actually managed a smile. 'At this hour of the afternoon?'

Nick recognized that smile. Warm and welcoming as steel shutters. Frankly, he preferred the clenched fists. At least they were honest. 'Medicinal?'

'Later, maybe. I've got, um, things to do.'

'Like what?'

But John only shook his head and vanished.

Nick, already opening the drinks cupboard, halted. Then he sighed resignedly and reached for the tea bags instead. After all, if there were answers lurking in bottles, he would surely have found them by now.

25

Did he ever get lonely?

She had asked him that. Lying there, smiling at him over the rim of her champagne glass.

No, he'd said at the time.

Yes, he said now. Four days and forty gallons of sodding tea later.

You bet your life he did. Bitterly, miserably, self-loathingly, furniture-kickingly lonely. The blackness might have been more bearable if he could have talked to someone about it.

But John had sorrows enough of his own, well stirred and bitterly seasoned by Nick's bludgeoning attempt to help. Not that Nick was giving up on the Candia front. Yes, her behaviour left a few questions unanswered (a few?) but he was still prepared to give the woman a chance. Once she returned to this country, he reckoned he would find a plausible pretext for contacting her. (Such as?) He would also dream up some subtle and oblique way (ho ho) of sussing out her feelings. While he was about it, he might slip in a discreet inquiry about Mary Ham— Oh no he would not. No way.

Nor, naturally, would he mention these plots to John. Not that he was likely to be given an opportunity. In fact he was beginning to wonder if John and he would ever settle back into their cosy old ways. Take the morning after Nick's return home. In an attempt to re-establish normal relations – and, OK, to cadge some milk – he had strolled across the courtyard and was astonished to find John knee deep in packing cases.

'Shit, you're not moving out, are you?'

John had actually laughed. Sounding as mirthful as a machine-gun. 'Don't be an idiot. Just sorting myself out. Bit of spring-cleaning.'

In July? 'Need a hand?'

'I'm fine, thanks,' John had said. 'Just rather busy.' Pressing the milk into his hand. Standing by the door. Waiting, oh-so-politely, for him to piss off.

An Englishman's castle, thought Nick, is his good manners. Impregnable as stone, and more daunting than the most towering rage. He considered ringing Caro for a few tips on tactics. He realized that, in the week before her wedding, she might not exactly welcome a heart-to-heart with her ex-husband, but that did not of itself deter him. More to the point was the inescapable necessity of sourcing his information. Which would entail naming Mary Hamilton. Caroline could infallibly be depended on to put two and two together and make *soixante-neuf*.

So he tried softening John up with alcohol instead. Managed to cart him down to the Black Lion a couple of times. Where he sipped orange juice and sat in the corner like – muttered Bernard – the corpse at a bloody wake.

'It's hit him very hard,' Nick explained to Sarah one lunchtime when, the bar being empty, he had sought company and consolation in her kitchen. 'You know; the Candia Mayhew business.'

'As if I hadn't guessed.' Sarah, rolling a slab of yellow pastry, paused. 'And if you ask me, it's done him a power of good.'

Nick's jaw clunked open. 'You're joking, of course.'

'I am not. It's like stubbing your toe when you've got a thumping migraine. Distracts you from the real pain, doesn't it? This has finally got him over Sally, mark my words.'

'And broken his poor old heart again?'

'Hearts aren't eggs. More like rubber balls. The harder you chuck 'em the higher they bounce back.'

'Says who?'

'You.'

'I never.'

'In your last book. Someone said it, I forget who.'

'Wasn't the author,' muttered Nick. 'Besides –'

'Anyway,' Sarah was continuing with a wry glance towards the doorway where Bernard could be seen polishing glasses in the bar, 'it's a sight better to grieve for what you've not got, than weep for what you have.'

'Sorry?'

'And better yet to do neither,' she concluded serenely. 'Like you and me, love.'

'What? Well, it's not quite –'

She was attacking the pastry again. 'Not that I'm saying anything against the woman. I liked her well enough. But these things happen, don't they?' She glanced sideways at him. 'John tells me he's going down to London this weekend.'

'Nothing to do with Candia,' retorted Nick. 'She's not there.'

'No, he told me it was because your . . . his sister, I should say, is, well, getting herself married again.'

'Oh, *that*,' said Nick dismissively.

Sarah smiled. 'That's the spirit, lovey. I mean, once John mentioned it, I realized like a shot why you've been looking wet as a Bank Holiday Monday. Poor old sausage.'

'No, no, you don't understand at all.' Nick heaved a sigh. A great cathartic wave of confession was surging inexorably upwards: 'Sure, I'm miserable as hell, but the truth of it is, Sarah –' But she was rolling vigorously and didn't hear.

'I just thank the Lord you've more sense than your brother-in-law. At least you don't wear your heart on your sleeve. I couldn't be doing with two of you through there weeping into your orange juice.'

'I sure as hell don't weep into orange juice,' muttered Nick, gazing down at the beer mug in his hand.

'Exactly,' agreed Sarah, in blithe misunderstanding. 'You've got a brain on you. You wouldn't go howling after what you can't have like a dog after the moon.'

'No,' said Nick forlornly. 'At least . . . *no.*' On second thoughts, he wasn't going to weep on Sarah's shoulder either. He drained his glass and stood up. 'I think I'd better get back to the word-processor.'

Sarah smiled. 'Don't work too hard, love.'

Chance would be a fine thing. John seemed to be finding consolation in sweated labour. Nick's door had been replaced within two days and when he wasn't tapping and whirring away in his workshop, the guy could be seen trotting around behind the newly curtainless windows of the barn with dusters and papers and boxes, and then paint-brushes and ladders. Mole to the life, thought Nick. Only he wasn't looking for a Ratty to wheel out the picnics and hang the spring-cleaning. John's brow was heavy with purpose.

Nick wished his was. God knows he should be writing. But what? He tinkered with old plot ideas. Dead as last week's newspapers. It was as though every word had drained out of holes in his skull like water from a colander. He abandoned the blank, winking, *waiting* screen of the word-processor and tried writing with his old Parker, which took more effort and was equally fruitless. When the pen ran out of ink and he found the remains in the bottle had dried up, it seemed poetically apposite.

He felt *used.* However he rationalized events, telling himself irritably that he'd had the fuck of a lifetime and he should be *grateful,* he could neither forget it and get on with life, nor remember it without flinching. He had embarked on that night knowing enough about Mary Hamilton to have known better. Or at least to have thought twice before plunging into the briny after her, like a randy sailor-boy after a mermaid. Mermaid? More of a great white she-shark. Even in bed with her, he had remembered Sasha and her disquieting tales, but he'd chosen to ignore them. So whatever happened had served him right. Mary Hamilton had got her good time out of him – hell, she had even wanted more. Snapping her fingers and expecting him to toddle down to her flat. Would she have tied a bow round his neck? Round his prick, more like.

For the first time in his life, Nick Bevan began to comprehend the attractions of becoming a monk. And said as much when his agent telephoned.

'Careful, my boy,' boomed George's fruity voice down the line. 'You're beginning to sound dangerously embittered. Anyway, I ring with glad tidings.'

And immediately Nick thought of Mary Hamilton. And just as immediately cursed himself. Nothing about that woman could be good news except possibly an obituary notice. Anyway, George was talking about the new novel and . . . Geraint Pryce-Evans?

'Yeah, that's right,' Nick confirmed. 'I did run into the man when I was in Llandudno.' Literally, he recalled. Now it seemed that what the old codger had been trying to say when Nick had so rudely smashed past him on the hotel doorstep was that Cambria Television might possibly be interested in taking up an option on *Snow Black*. Three-part serialization, subject to suitable co-producers, et cetera et cetera.

'Great,' said Nick listlessly, hardly hearing as George reeled off Sir Geraint's ideas for adaptors, actors, directors – no, Mary Hamilton's name was not mentioned. Some Welsh geezer he'd never heard of.

Mind, it was all pie in the sky yet, George warned. An option meant nothing really. But an encouraging development nevertheless, was it not?

'Very,' said Nick.

'Cheer up, old fellow,' said George breezily. 'Only a couple more days and you'll be flying off into the sunshine with Victoria and me, remember? The golden beaches and equally golden, ah, broads of California will soon put the heart back into you.'

California, thought Nick, where everyone fools around in the sea at ten o'clock at night. With no pebbles and less risk of frostbite. 'Sorry?'

George was rattling on about internal flights, meetings, schedules, Victoria's friends, Very Important Parties . . .

'Look,' said Nick, when George eventually paused for breath. 'Just tell me where to turn up and when. I'm in your hands.'

'That's the spirit. Heathrow, British Airways Terminal 4, not a minute after one-fifteen. I'll be wearing a white carnation.'

'Very funny.'

'Look, Nick,' said George in a less boisterous tone of voice, 'I know you must be feeling pretty down in the mouth.'

'Understatement of the year.'

'Sorry? Oh I see, yes, probably more than down in the mouth. But you mustn't let this business defeat you. We've all been through it – or at least I have.'

'What?'

'And you'll feel a hundred times better once you're safely on the other side of the Pond. Change and distance are nature's anaesthetics. Along with a few stiff cocktails. And you'll have them all by Friday – that's what matters, isn't it? Toodle-pip.'

By Friday? It said everything for Nick's state of mind that it was a full five minutes before he realized George had been talking about Caro's wedding. Which was also scheduled for Friday. George was as daft as Sarah. So, Caroline was getting married. So what.

He wondered gloomily what time she would be checking in at the Registrar's desk and went to find his passport.

26

'You're flying to the States this afternoon, right?'

Why did Christopher sound so full of the joys of spring? This was eight o'clock in the morning. The boy didn't usually start functioning until noon. He had been staying with a schoolfriend in Hampstead for the first week of his summer holiday, having found the atmosphere at home with Caroline (so he'd disgustedly said to Nick in a previous phone call) just too hearts-and-flowersy to stomach. With the wedding imminent and all. Anyone would think Ma and Daniel had not been bonking each other silly for the past year.

'I'm amazed you're accompanying them on honeymoon then,' Nick had observed at the time.

'Only for a week or so,' Chris had responded airily. 'Besides, you said it yourself. A man can suffer a lot for ten days in the Caribbean.'

'I'm actually leaving for Heathrow in twenty minutes,' Nick said now. 'Which is why I'm ringing. And at this ungodly hour too, since you've signally failed to let me know when I'm to expect the pleasure of your company up here with me, and you have been – according to your friend Rupert's amazingly tolerant mother – out on the razzle at every other hour of the day and night I've telephoned. Which I have, let me tell you, about twenty times.'

'On the razzle?' echoed Christopher indignantly. 'Excuse me, squire, I've been working.'

'You amaze me. Not actually earning money?'

'Experience in the right field is more valuable than a pay packet.'

'Not earning money. And not swotting for your A-levels, I suppose?'

'You are joking.'

'I was joking.'

'Pretty amazing project actually.'

'Amaze me.'

'I will, Dad, I will. Just you wait. And in the meantime I'm getting all my expenses paid.'

'What sort of expenses? Bar bills? Oh, hang on a minute, Christopher – thanks, Pete.' This was a shouted aside to the postman who stuck his head round the door and waved as he dropped the mail on to the draining board. Nick, clenching the phone between jaw and shoulder, reached across and plucked up the bundle. Bills, more unrepeatable opportunities to win a fortune, an envelope postmarked London, addressed by hand in a writing he . . . didn't recognize. 'What? Sorry, Christopher. Look, I didn't actually call to offer the regular vacation lecture on working for your exams.'

'I should hope not.'

Bold black handwriting, italicized, slight forward slant.

'I just wanted to know when you're coming up here. I won't be back from the States until a week on Monday.'

'OK by me,' said Christopher cheerily. 'I won't be back until after that either.'

Very fat envelope. Firmly glued down. Thick ribbed paper. Nick groped for a knife. '*When?* I want to know when to expect you. Flight times . . .'

'I've got them.'

'Fire away.'

'But not just here at this moment.'

Nick, engaged in slitting open the envelope, dropped the receiver. Propping it on his shoulder again he snapped: 'Look, do you want me to ring your mother?'

'Oh come on, no need for that,' said Christopher. 'On her wedding morning? She's running round in circles as it is. Anyway – anyway, she's probably down the beauty parlour by now, having the Polyfilla trowelled on. Look, just leave it to me, will you, Dad?'

'I'm quitting this place in twenty minutes exactly.'

'What a pain. Is there anywhere I can get in touch with you next week?'

'No,' said Nick, uncompromisingly. 'I want to know now. Dates, times, the lot, and . . .' He was ripping the letter out of the envelope – *Dear Nick* . . . – riffling through three . . . four . . . *five* closely typed pages to the end. *Yours, Mary.* Mary? Holy shit. 'What? Oh, for God's sake, I suppose you can get in touch with me via George's office, if needs be, they'll always know where to find him . . . You're *sure* you've got the number? That's the one, yes . . . What?'

'I said, do you want me to give any message to the happy couple? It is this lunchtime, you know.'

'Give – give Caro my love,' said Nick distractedly. 'Or, well, maybe not. Just – wish her better luck this time than last. If that doesn't sound too embittered.'

'Hey, are you all right, Dad?'

'Fine. Yes, I'm fine.'

'You sound peculiar.'

'It's my age.'

Christopher's voice softened unexpectedly. All at once he sounded much younger. 'Look, just don't worry, OK? I'll keep in touch.'

'What?'

'See you in a bit. Have fun in the States. Cheers.'

Nick let the phone drop and walked across to the kitchen table where, very slowly, he sat down in a chair.

It was several minutes before he could bring himself to spread the letter out in front of him.

27

Dear Nick . . .

Mary had written those words several times in the course of the past week. And each time, after a few more stilted sentences, she had flung down the pen in a fresh outburst of quivering fury with him – or exasperation with herself.

The bin in her flat was clogged with crumpled pages. With every abandoned attempt she had sworn that this time she was giving up for good and all. Let the screwed-up, foul-minded bastard rot. What did it matter what he thought about her? If he was prepared to believe *that* then he wasn't worth wasting a second over, let alone the sweat and, goddammit, the humiliation of writing him a letter.

But the business was driving her nuts. She couldn't even function in work. She knew she was rattling them in the cutting room. She knew because her partner Andrew had told her. In the friendliest possible way. As though he were afraid she'd bite his head off. Which she had.

'Bullshit,' she'd screamed.

He had shrugged. Nothing ruffled Andrew's suited cool. He was a walking, talking calculator. Creative genius, he had once observed thoughtfully, was rather like potted plants in Reception. Pleasant and classy, but not strictly essential and short on reliable shelf-life. *Ergo*, an expensive luxury for a small outfit. No one was sure whether he'd been joking. 'You know what the editing costs are. We're ticking over within budget but . . .'

'But what?'

He smiled enigmatically. He didn't have to explain. He meant they couldn't afford risks on projects like (say) *The Liquorice Fields*. Which (as Mary knew) he'd said from the start was a dodgy notion, unlikely to sell in the States, blah blah blah. And definitely not to be contemplated without a fat profit in the kitty from *Pride and Prejudice*. Blah blah fucking blah.

'Don't you read anything but balance sheets?' she snarled.

'Sure. Nick thingummy Bevan over the weekend,' he said calmly, and it felled her in mid-tirade like a mallet between the eyes. '*Snow Black*. Terrific. Thanks for recommending it.'

'I recommended *nothing*,' she hissed. 'I wouldn't touch a word that bastard had written if — if it was a cheque for a million dollars made out to cash.'

Andrew's eyebrows raised a millimetre. Which, for him, signified profound perturbation. 'Mary ... Look, do you think you should take a couple of days off?'

'Is this some kind of a joke?'

'I happened to be talking to your father ...'

'Pa?' She heard her voice rising to hysteria pitch. 'You were talking to my bloody *father*? About me?'

'He rang here, trying to get hold of you. Said you'd been sounding odd on the telephone since you got back from Wales and I just promised him —'

'I'm not listening to another word.' She was shrieking her head off. Any more of this and Andrew would be summoning stretchers and strait-jackets. She swallowed hard. 'I am walking out of this office,' she concluded tightly. 'And I am returning to my editing. OK?'

But she was appalled, when she arrived back in the cutting room, to realize she was being handled with care. The real kid-glove treatment. People were talking quietly around her, obviously convinced she was going to snap. *She*, who was always so meticulously controlled, a byword for reasoned politeness in an environment where screaming obscenities were common currency. She'd nearly thrown a clipboard at Louisa yesterday. Poor girl. She looked like a dog that had been kicked.

No, she had to get the whole messy affair out of her system. That was what she concluded on returning to her flat in the evening. Exorcize it once and for all. And if it meant swallowing her pride and writing to Nick Bevan, well then, so be it. It wasn't as though she was apologizing, she damn well was not. She was just putting him in possession of a few pertinent facts, that was all.

She poured herself a large vodka. Barely waved a vermouth bottle over it. And switched on her word-processor.

Dear Nick . . .

There were pages and pages of it, thought Nick, groping for a cigarette and cursing as he remembered he hadn't got any. Had forbidden himself nicotine ever since the night in Llandudno.

Dear Nick, I realize your first instinct might be to chuck this letter in the trash . . .

Too true, muttered Nick aloud. Although it wasn't, of course. He could no more have thrown this letter out unread than chopped off the hand which held it. His curiosity, though, was laced with apprehension. She might be about to resume the screamed insults at the point she'd left off. He began skimming down the page. For goodness' sake, he only had time to skim. He needed to get on the road within minutes and his case wasn't shut, the plants weren't watered, the alarm needed setting . . .

But no sooner had his eye reached the bottom of the first page than he found himself returning to the opening of the letter, and he began again, studying every word this time with glaring intensity.

. . . I realize your first instinct might be to chuck this letter in the trash. I understand that, I guess. But hear me out. All I want to do is set the record straight because — although I may have got one or two things wrong — I think there are even more things you don't understand. In fact, I know there are.

Sasha Floyd. From the way you said 'poor little Sasha' I imagine you've met her. I'd heard she was up in Yorkshire. It's amazing how often she does just happen to be hanging around wherever we're working. Still, it may be coincidence. Let's stick to fact.

I don't know what she told you about her background. I've heard several versions. Whatever, it will probably surprise you to learn that she's the daughter of Tom and Lucinda Scarrington — Lord Scarrington, former Chairman of North-East Television, Lucinda Harris, gardening writer. Not, in other words, the orphaned child of a South African mixed marriage, or the abandoned bastard of an Afghan mining engineer, or whatever. She has two parents still living, and several brothers and sisters, all considerably older than her. I think Floyd's a middle name. I remember admiring her for not trying to cash in on the family name. Or so I thought.

I know the whole family because Tom Scarrington has been a friend of my own father for just about ever. Since they were at college together. You may know my father is in television too, back in the States. Anyway, Tom was kind to me when I first came over to this country although, to be honest, I tried to steer clear of him once I left Oxford and started work. Which may sound perverse, but I didn't want to get any favours round the industry because of who my father is. Still, this letter isn't about me and my hang-ups.

Sasha. I'd always vaguely gathered from Lucinda she was the mixed-up kid of the family. She was expelled from a couple of schools, flunked her place at university, that kind of thing. But she's years younger than me, and I doubt if I'd have recognized her when Tom took me out to lunch and asked if I'd consider *giving her a job. Must be about six years ago. Pentagon was up and running anyhow. She was bright, he said. She'd done some research for religious affairs at the BBC, a stint in independent local radio, the usual kind of short-contract stuff. I think he possibly mentioned she'd had one or two problems, but that was all.*

I guess I can't blame him. She's his daughter. He was just doing his best for her, and it gave me such a kick to be able to dish out a favour to one of Pa's friends – after years of refusing to accept any – that I agreed. Sasha came to work for us, as a sort of general assistant/researcher. Tom actually offered to put some money into Pentagon, but at least I had the sense to turn that down. No, let's be honest, good sense had nothing to do with it. It was sheer pig-headed obstinacy about not taking favours, and my partners were ready to kill me at the time. It was only afterwards they were glad.

And Sasha seemed like good news round the place. She's bright enough, and funny. We all liked her. But she was unreliable. And that's the unforgivable sin. One day you'd ask her to set something up and she'd do it brilliantly. The next time, she'd tell you it was all set up, but nothing would materialize. And then she'd vanish. Without a word for days on end.

We put up with a lot. This business isn't staffed by routine-bashers and people do disappear occasionally. After a crucifying stretch of work you might need to crash out for a few days. But, by and large, most people don't leave their colleagues in the shit quite as often as Sasha did. There was one mess-up over a script which she was supposed to have put through the lawyers. It cost us a packet and nearly cost Sasha her job. But Tom got on the phone and, driven more by a heady sense of my own almighty power than any compassion, I promised him we'd give her another chance.

Sure, I've wished often, and bitterly, I'd dealt with Sasha the way I would with any other employee. But she was the daughter of Dad's old buddy, so I didn't. And however often I tell myself the same thing might have happened even if she hadn't come back to work for us, I still feel guilty as hell.

What I hadn't realized, and didn't realize until it was much too late, was that Sasha is a junkie.

And I don't mean she snorts the odd line of coke. She did that, for sure. But then so do a lot of other stupid bastards who aren't junkies. I mean heroin. Needles, tourniquets, busted veins, the works. Tom knew all right. He and Lucinda had been nearly out of their minds. When Sasha came to us, she was fresh from two months in a classy rehabilitation joint in the country at his expense. She told someone it was like an upmarket health farm only with better food.

But I – we – didn't know about that then. And I realize I was incredibly naïve. Junkies, in my book, were shot-up, emaciated, gibbering wrecks. Sasha was just a bit skinny and prone to mood swings. Aren't we all? Seems she had a good regular supplier and was careful about her needles. One thing I have learned is that Sasha Floyd has a strong sense of self-preservation.

There was a young film editor working for us, though not part of our company. We use outside facilities; this guy was at Worldtime, and they do a lot for us so we all knew him well. David Tattenshall. Tad, we called him. He and I sweated long hours on a serial together. He was sharp-eyed and sunny-tempered and I was very fond of him. I'm not even going to bother telling you our relationship never went beyond a work basis. I hope, in the light of the rest of this letter, you'll take that as read.

Anyway, Sasha and he knocked around together and she invited him on holiday. Thailand. Coming home – I have to rely on Tad's account – there was some cock-up over the tickets. Sasha had booked it all, and apparently told him not to worry. He would just have to catch the flight after hers. He did. And, being the honest boy he is, stopped to tell Customs in London about the camcorder he'd bought en route *in Hong Kong.*

Which was when, quite by chance, they found the three kilos of heroin in his suitcase. No coup of investigative policing was required, I have to tell you. The package toppled to the floor when he opened his case and split right across. If you'd ever met Tad you'd understand it. He was that kind of guy. Someone once said if you put Tad and a single banana skin in Wembley Stadium he'd manage to fall on it.

They let him off lightly, considering. Everyone from his Sunday-school teacher onwards swore he'd never touched drugs and never would. But it goes without saying that anyone found with a whacking brick of raw heroin in their luggage is going to claim they've no idea how it found its way there. He got three years. Out in eighteen months. By which time he looked ten years older, poor bastard.

Sasha, who was supposed to be waiting for him at the airport, melted into thin air. Her parents were nearly demented with worry. That's when we found out about her habit and put two and two together. Even Tad hadn't realized what she was up to. He'd believed her when she'd told him she was diabetic. He was young and, as you might have gathered, not the smartest thinker.

The point is, as I'm sure you're working out for yourself already, Tad got picked up at Heathrow. But just suppose it had been Bangkok airport? Even now I can't bear to think about it. Every time I read a case in the papers about drug-smugglers out there, on death row, or rotting from disease in some lousy prison, I could weep. Even Tad said it made him almost glad to be in Wormwood Scrubs — and if you've ever been inside that shit hole, then you'd realize how much it meant. Anyway, they moved him to an open place down in Sussex as soon as he was sentenced, thank God.

But we hadn't seen the last of Sasha. She swanned back to the office one day, with some story of a nervous breakdown, actually expecting to pick up her job where she'd left off. But of course, by then, I'd spoken to Tom. We nearly took her apart. At first she denied the whole thing. Then admitted, OK, she was a user. Finally she got as far as saying it was possible some of the people she'd met in Thailand might have slipped the stuff into Tad's bag. How was she to know? She didn't ask too many questions. You just didn't, she said. One thing was clear, she was scared witless. Presumably of the dealer, or whoever it was behind her. Someone was pulling her strings, but there was no way she was telling.

Andrew (my partner) still says we should have turned her over to the police. Told them everything we'd guessed. But, as I said at the time, what could we prove? Far as they were concerned, they'd got their mule behind bars and they'd as good as said they recognized Tad was no more than a dupe: his sentence was rock-bottom minimum. Nothing we could have done would get him out earlier, short of a full and frank confession from Sasha, and there wasn't a hope in hell.

But I suppose, if I'm honest, I held out against going to the police because I couldn't bring myself to do it to Tom and Lucinda. And even Andrew had to admit Pentagon could do without being embroiled in a narcotics scandal. So I read the riot act to Sasha. Let her know it was only thanks to me she wasn't being visited by the Boys in Blue, that she must get help to kick the habit, et cetera, et cetera. Obviously I should have saved my breath. From what I hear, she seems to have decided in some mysterious way that this makes me personally responsible for all her troubles. What the hell. She's off my hands. It's her parents I pity, and I do pity them, from the bottom of my heart.

So that's Sasha. Perhaps, now, you can understand why I was so bloody angry.

With regard to your friend — sorry, brother-in-law — John: look, if I read this wrong, I apologize. That's all I can say. Candia had a long heart-to-heart with me when we left York-shire. She really liked the guy, but she didn't know how she stood with him. Honestly. She said she felt he just kept shutting off from her. Those were her words. Whenever she felt she was *getting close to him, a sort of barrier would come down — bang — and she was left on the outside.*

I even felt a certain sympathy for him when we were in Maltbury. Candia has no half-measures. She demands a hundred and ten per cent and, far as I could see, was creating dust-ups whenever he tried to get on with his own life. I could see he was embarrassed about money, too. Candia earns plenty and spends even more. But that was before the crunch came, over his house.

You know she was always pestering him about going there? Or maybe you didn't know. You weren't at the hotel with us. The point is, John gave us the impression he was living in a hovel, which he was converting to be fit for human habitation, so he couldn't expect Candia to slum it, and so forth. Even though (typical Candia) she swore a shack with hens was fine by her. Then, the day we left, that guy who runs the pub (Bernard?) blew the story sky-high. Raving about John's fantastic pad. Just at the moment Candia had been saying there was a slim chance she could get back for the weekend and John had been trotting out the old excuses.

Maybe, given what you say about his wife — presumably it was her house? — it's understandable. Up to a point. But Candia didn't know that, and neither did I. What I did know about and, yes, what I told Candia in no uncertain terms, is exactly what it means when a man (or a woman) only plays away from home. It means they're playing games. They are definitely not serious.

So when Candia decided she might be pregnant, and announced, in a mad panic, that she would ring John and that would surely bring him racing down to join her, I freely admit I told her she was off her head. If there's one sure-fire guaranteed way not to glue up a rocky relationship, then it's got to be a baby on the way. And, yes, I also said she'd be crazy to opt out on her career at this moment. Particularly since, as I saw it, chances were she'd end up a single mother. The fact that she'd agreed to do a movie for me was only a tiny part of my reasons for saying all this. I hope you believe that, because it's true.

But she was a wreck. Candia lives on her nerves, on her emotions. There's no logic. She was appalled to think she was pregnant, and devastated that she wasn't. Schedules changed. I changed them, in fact, to give her a few days off between Derbyshire and London. So she rang John and said she was coming up to Yorkshire. And he said maybe that wasn't such a good idea . . . Which was when she concluded he was just stringing her along and told him he could rot in his bloody barn. By this time, she was hysterical. I practically had to carry her through the last days of the filming. At the end, I genuinely thought it would do her good to get away, see some new faces. I accept I may have fouled up badly. Trust me when I say I'll do what I can to put things right there at least. If it's not too late.

And that's about it. It was stupid of me to ask you down to London. Stupid, and arrogant, because I assumed you'd jump at it. All I can say is that, at the time, I believed I genuinely did want you to come. In other words, I wasn't playing games.

Sorry about the length of this letter. Don't trouble to reply. I don't think there's anything more to be said. We've probably both said more than enough already — some pretty harsh things too. Now, perhaps, we can draw a civilized line under it all.

With best wishes for your future career,
Yours, Mary

28

. . . Yours, Mary.

Nick's first thought – no, his *second* thought – was that he must get hold of John. Stiff-lipped, thick-headed, self-deprecating, self-destructive clot that he was.

'Spring-cleaning, my arse,' roared Nick, slamming down the pages. 'Deconsecrating the shrine, more like. Why couldn't you have done it before, you great idiot? Talk about shutting the stable door. Or opening it – but too late either way. Well, sunshine, it's time you got off your high horse and on your bike.'

He was halfway out of the kitchen before he remembered John had left for London the previous afternoon. To attend his sister's wedding. Frustration made Nick thump the door frame. Had John left a telephone number? Had he hell. And he was planning to stay down there for several days, too. Nick strained to recall the names of the friends he'd said he was staying with. Not friends, cousins. Cousin Henry, that was it. Henry and Alice . . . Thompson. Oh terrific. A Mr H. Thompson, somewhere – anywhere – in Greater London.

And Nick should, in fact *must*, be on the road south himself in . . . blimey, in no time at all. He should be leaving now. This instant. He rampaged round the house plants like a two-legged monsoon, slammed shut his case, threw it into the car and had the burglar alarm set and un-set twice within five minutes as vital omissions from his packing occurred to him. Lord knows what else he'd managed to forget. At least he had the sense to check he was in possession of his passport. Passport and fountain pen.

'Poor darling,' said Victoria Hillard compassionately, settling into the seat beside him on the plane and taking out a small embroidery frame. 'You do look an absolute wreck. Was the traffic so terrible?'

Traffic? Nick had barely noticed the traffic. It was a miracle he had arrived at Heathrow at all. He'd driven five hours down juggernaut-infested motorways in his rattling heap of motorized rust on some kind of automatic pilot, conscious of little beyond the letter rustling in his breast pocket, struggling to remember the exact words, hungry to read it again. In the terminal building Victoria, with the unflappable competence of a nanny, had taken charge of both him and her husband George (who suffered from a phobia about flying) and gently steered Nick towards the desk for the New York flight murmuring: 'No, darling, over here. George told you the plan, surely, New York until Monday, then . . . Nick? Good heavens.'

Nick was embracing her. New York, he told her ecstatically, was exactly the place in the whole wide world he most wanted to visit at this moment. 'New York, New York!' He hadn't actually broken into a song and tap-dance routine, but almost.

Victoria, keeping a restraining hand on Nick, mouthed very visibly at her husband: '*Woman?*'

And George, pale and clammy of face, mimed ignorance.

'No,' Nick had said, answering for him. 'At least – a woman, yes. But nothing to do with me. It's . . . Oh, never mind.'

Between him and Mary, he felt, there was a skull-and-crossboned minefield which was going to require the most delicate of negotiation. Bashing John and Candia's silly heads together, on the other hand, struck him as an easy and immediate outlet for his frustration in the meantime. The task of locating one actress in New York City – and at a weekend to boot – daunted him not at all. He was a journalist, wasn't he? Piece of cake. He'd, um, he'd ring Pentagon Productions back in London . . . Damn, he'd had the number when he was fixing the feature for the *Mail*. And chucked it. Might as well look it up now, then, before they left. Even as he instinctively veered away in search of a phone box with directories, Victoria grabbed him and hustled him back towards the check-in desk. Anyway, he rationalized, Pentagon was no problem. He could track them down from New York as easily as from here. They'd give him Candia's whereabouts in New York – he would *make* them – and he would go and tell her everything. And John, at least, could be happy.

'You're talking to yourself,' Victoria observed, handing him luggage labels and a pen and instructing him to use block capitals as though he were a particularly dim-witted child. 'It doesn't worry me in the least, but poor dear George is in a pathetic enough state as it is without attracting general suspicion that we're the travelling guardians of a lunatic.'

'Shop,' said Nick suddenly, handing back the biro. 'Just give me a minute. I need somewhere selling ink.'

That telephoning Pentagon might mean talking to Mary – hell, he *wanted* to talk to Mary. That had been his first impulse at home, even before he got to the end of the letter. To ring her at once. Beg, grovel, for forgiveness. And then what? Well, they would fall weeping and laughing into one another's arms . . . OK, *arrange* to fall weeping and laughing into one another's arms when he got back from the States. (Did he have to go? Yes, dammit but . . .) Fix a date then, to fall, etc., etc? When he returned? If she wasn't too busy? When she could find a space in the diary?

Reality, seeping damply through the cracks in this romantically impetuous scenario, swiftly engulfed it. Would Mary *want* to see him? Speak to him even, let alone fall into his arms. *Don't trouble to reply* . . . Maybe she'd seen sense. Was even now marvelling — as, frankly, he was — that someone like her could ever have wasted a second of her high-octane time on a nobody like . . . *I don't think there's anything more to be said. We've probably both said more than enough already* . . . Hell, she would write that, wouldn't she? *Wouldn't* she? After all, she'd made the first move. It was up to him to follow through. And he intended to. Nothing on earth was going to stop him. Standing in the kitchen, he'd had the telephone in his hand before he began to wonder whether it was practical, or even remotely possible, to convey everything that needed conveying in the few minutes left to him at home.

That was when he'd first had the vision of the skull-and-crossbone warnings strung round this particular emotional minefield. Finding a safe path across was not to be accomplished in a hurried phone chat. And he bloody well had to get to Heathrow. George and Victoria would be waiting for him. Heavens, they'd more or less set up the whole jaunt for his benefit.

So he would write to Mary. That was it. Soon as he got on to the plane. He must take paper and pen with him instead of a novel. Whereupon he had hastily un-set the burglar alarm for the second time and raced up to his desk. And remembered there was no damn ink in his Parker. It was unthinkable he should compose such a crucial document in plebeian biro. Only the hope that there must, somewhere in the whole vast complex of Heathrow Airport, be a shop selling ink, had persuaded him to punch the code back into the alarm and scramble into the car.

It was the sight of Victoria's biro at the check-in desk which, fortunately, had reminded him of this most pressing requirement.

'I say,' said George faintly, as with seat-belts fastened, hand luggage secured and no cigarettes to extinguish, he glanced across his wife and saw Nick calmly produce a brand-new bottle of permanent black from his pocket. 'Don't fountain pens explode at a certain altitude?'

Victoria patted her husband's hand as it kneaded the arm rest. 'Aircraft are pressurized these days, darling. I even believe,' she added with a malicious smile, 'they've dispensed with the rubber bands to turn the propellors.'

'It's not funny,' said George darkly. 'Just remember this next time you want a spider removing from your bath.'

'That's it,' said Nick, with satisfaction, mopping the pen tip on a tissue silently handed to him by a fascinated Victoria.

'I don't suppose,' said George, hope kindling momentarily in his woebegone face, 'you're drafting the new novel?'

'Nope,' said Nick.

'Didn't think so.'

'Just the next chapter of my life.'

'Ah,' said George, leaning back and closing his eyes. 'But will it sell?'

29

That weekend, Nick was later to swear, was the most soul-sappingly, mind-numbingly, head-bangingly maddening of his whole life. Leaving Heathrow after lunch, they had limped into their hotel eight and a half hours later, disorientatingly in time for afternoon tea. Served (this was an establishment which prided itself on old-world connections) with silver-handled cake forks and lace-edged napkins. Victoria and George were pale and yawning. All Nick wanted was to get his hands on a telephone.

He was going to ring her. Stuff this letter-writing lark.

'Forgive me, dear boy,' George had remarked, four or so hours into the flight, 'but the next chapter of your life doesn't appear to be very *long*.'

A writer – calling himself a writer anyway – and all Nick had managed was:

Thanks for your letter. I really appreciate it. Can we meet? There's a lot I want to say, and even more I need to apologize for. I'm in the States for ten days but I'll be in touch as soon as I get back, if I may. In the meantime, with luck, I'll have got hold of Candia over the weekend.

And that little masterpiece had taken upwards of half-a-dozen drafts and as many gins.

'Alcohol is terribly dehydrating on long flights,' Victoria had murmured.

'Ah,' said George with an air of enlightenment, 'so that's

why I'm so thirsty.' And ordered himself and Nick a refill.

Only when he'd finished and reluctantly sealed the miserable scrap of a letter did Nick, boggling at his own stupidity, realize he had nothing beyond a name to inscribe on the envelope. Mary's letter began *Dear Nick*; not so much as a date, let alone an address. (She didn't want him to answer, did she? Course she did – why write in the first place?) That was when he decided a phone call had to be preferable after all.

So, while George and Victoria bathed and unpacked and patiently consumed cocktails in the lobby bar, Nick began to run up a phone bill the settlement of which, by the end of the weekend, seemed likely to require immediate delivery of a new novel. Obtaining the telephone number of Pentagon Productions was straightforward. British Directory Enquiries even, kindly, allowed him to inveigle an address out of them as well. Also a fax number. Nick considered walking down to Reception and asking them to fax his letter. Then quailed at the prospect of his pathetic little note passing under public scrutiny in a production office, and boldly punched in the boggling string of digits for Pentagon.

Even though he'd calculated it was getting on for midnight in London, he managed to feel aggrieved that a machine answered. Wasn't Mary forever boasting about the outrageous hours she and her colleagues worked? He slammed down the receiver, and, after rummaging through his wallet until, in triumph, he extracted a very old dinner bill with, yes, the phone number top right, he proceeded to root Dorothy Judson out of bed at the Maltbury Hall Hotel.

No, she snapped, with possibly forgivable exasperation, none of the television people would have given home telephone numbers, all rooms had been booked in the name of the company.

'Addresses then?' pleaded Nick. 'Surely they might have signed the register with home addresses?'

'Maybe they did at that,' said Dorothy. And Nick's still-elastic spirits bounced back. 'But the register's locked away in t'office downstairs, and if you think I'm traipsing down there this time of night looking for it, you've got another think coming, young man. Ring back at a decent hour, if you must.'

'I will,' Nick promised.

Time was short. It wasn't simply a matter of wanting to talk to Mary. In fact, he was ricocheting crazily between a longing to speak to her and fear that the handicaps of a three-thousand-mile telephone line might scupper his hopes for good. But there was the more immediate problem of Candia. Her whereabouts. He was only in New York for two days. So he steeled himself and rang Pentagon again. And of course, the same mechanical voice answered. He felt irritably convinced there was intelligent life somewhere in those offices still. They were just ignoring the phone. He managed to compose a semi-coherent message asking someone – anyone – to ring Nick Bevan at this hotel. Any time.

Then, reluctantly, he retrieved his letter from the bin. Scrawled Pentagon's address on it. Added PERSONAL, AIRMAIL, and URGENT in capitals. Childishly huge capitals. Dammit, the thing looked like any schoolboy love-letter. He might as well have printed SWALK over the seal and have done with it. He galloped downstairs to reception to buy a stamp and post it before his nerve faltered.

No sooner had he watched it slip, irrevocably, into the shiny brass mouth of the hotel's post box than Victoria captured him and bore him off to dinner.

'Dear boy,' George hissed on Sunday evening, 'you know, this is not entirely a *pleasure* jaunt.'

'You're telling me,' muttered Nick.

They were at a party. Yet another sodding party. Standing under a palm tree on the umpteen-hundredth floor of some glassy apartment block, with the city lights glittering without and the city literati glittering within.

'Totally devoted as I am to your interests' – George was hissing the words out of the corner of his mouth because his finest social smile was pinned in place – 'I just thought I'd mention . . . Harvey, my dear chap. What a delightful surprise. How are you? I wonder, have you met Nick Bevan?'

Nick bared his teeth dutifully and pretended to be studying the twilit panorama outside. The most famous skyline in the world and all he was thinking was that somewhere in that vast, angular jungle, one of those million tiny lights was twinkling over the head of Candia Mayhew. Somewhere. And to think he used to call himself a journalist. How had he managed to fall down on the job so completely and totally and utterly for forty-eight hours?

Nobody at Pentagon had returned his call. No one *anywhere* was answering his pleas. No, that wasn't quite true. Dorothy Judson had grudgingly supplied an address for Mary Hamilton. A flat in East London. Mega-bucks Docklands? He wouldn't be at all surprised. Nor was he surprised to find, referring to Enquiries, that her telephone number was ex-directory. But he ploughed on doggedly and said he wanted a Llandudno number instead then, please. The hotel where she had *not* stayed was even less helpful and directed him to the Literary Festival office. Which was shut. It was the weekend. Everyone in the whole wide world was away for the weekend.

Still, ever more urgently, as Saturday lurched into Sunday, via restaurants, art galleries, inky-drinkies with George's publishing chums, and a musical of Wagnerian tedium, he had kept right on trying – and failing – to locate a single person who might know where Candia Mayhew was hiding. He couldn't even trace John, and the silly clot wasn't due home until the middle of next week. If he heard another answering machine – by now he could recite Pentagon Productions' glib message from memory – he might just smash the telephone.

'. . . very charming people.' George had waved away his acquaintance and was now hissing plantively at Nick again. 'Some of whom, though far be it from me to sound reproachful, *some* of whom might just be useful for you to know.'

'Sure,' said Nick. 'Sorry. Look, I don't want to screw things up for you. Great weekend. Great party.'

He had already combed the crowded, furiously chattering room with some barmy hope that, in all the parties in all the giant metropolis, Candia Mayhew might just be nibbling a canapé at this one. Fat chance.

'Well, I'm enjoying myself hugely,' observed Victoria, drifting across to join them with a frosty drink and a sunny smile. 'I think the line of Nick's I most relished was when I pointed out that the cab was taking us past Times Square, and he muttered: "Yeah, looks better in the movies." And promptly returned to chewing his fingernails.'

'Just now, I introduced him to Harvey Topolski,' sighed George, 'and did he so much as open his mouth? My witty, clever, budding writer of international bestsellers here. Do you know who Harvey Topolski is?'

'A publisher, didn't you say?'

'He's a television executive,' wailed George. 'A very *important* television producer, as it happens. Call me a cock-eyed optimist, but I just thought –'

'George, hush!' said his wife with a spurt of laughter. 'I think darling Nick may possibly be having a heart attack.'

Actually, Nick felt as though a fire alarm had exploded in his head. Television . . . Mary's father conjuring up the job . . . For Heaven's sake, he was the key to the whole bloody maze. He'd know where to find Candia. Would have a home number for Mary too, come to that . . .

'Do you know someone in television called Hamilton?' he demanded.

'Someone in television called Hamilton,' echoed George without interest. 'Haven't we had this conversation already?'

'Not Mary,' said Nick impatiently.

'No, I thought that would be too much to hope for. Victoria darling, who's the siren in the lurex *décolletage* pressing her, er, considerable charms on our host?'

'George, this is serious. Man called Hamilton. English, but works over here. Big in the industry. Or so I gather.'

'No,' said George. 'Well, I'm sorry, Nick, but I don't know *everyone*. Not in television. Publishing, maybe . . .'

'Your friend Topolski?'

And so, protesting, George allowed himself to be hauled across the room in search of Harvey Topolski. Whom they found, moodily eyeing a plate of what looked like raw fish. He swallowed a couple of slivers as Nick explained his mission. And then pretended to choke.

'Hamilton?' he said. He was a small man with huge spectacles and a tie of eye-watering vividness. 'You're kidding, right?'

'He's serious,' said George resignedly. 'Believe me, Harvey, he's serious.'

'*Max* Hamilton?'

'Max Hamilton,' echoed Nick eagerly. 'Is he in television?'

Harvey's smile was pitying. 'Is the Pope in the Vatican?'

Whereupon George twitched as though his batteries had been switched back on.

'You wouldn't, I suppose,' said Nick, 'have a phone number for him, would you?'

Harvey shrugged. 'Not on me. But there's plenty here who will. George, you know Rosie Martinez, don't you?'

'Through three husbands, twenty years and uncountable bottles.' George tweaked his bow tie and beamed at Nick. 'Leave this to your Uncle George, my boy.'

Twenty minutes later, he returned to Nick and Victoria with a piece of paper rolled between his fingers.

'Mr Max Hamilton,' he said slowly, savouring the syllables

with the air of a man sampling vintage port. 'Father of the blessed Mary and a *very* big cheese, it seems.'

'The biggest bug,' said Nick, remembering Miriam Weissman, 'in the whole damn ant hill.'

'Quite. And, just for you, I have the numbers of his palatial offices, his even more palatial home, and his Connecticut holiday pad (no details available) where, according to my informant, Mr Max Hamilton is likely to be found this evening.' He handed over the piece of paper and tucked his arm into Nick's. 'We have been invited to use the telephone out here. Ah, thank you.' This was addressed to a white-jacketed waiter who ushered them through a doorway into the hush of a lamp-lit anteroom.

All at once, Nick's mouth was as dry as sacking. Along the trail, he'd just followed his hunting instincts. Only now did it occur to him that he was proposing to telephone, out of the blue, Mary's father. What would she think if she found out? Without even noticing, he'd advanced fifty paces into the minefield.

'Go on then,' said George. 'I'm not being put to all this trouble for nothing.'

Nick picked up the receiver. Dialled. For the first time in a weekend of abortive telephone calls, he hoped this one wouldn't be answered. Or that it would be a machine. But a woman's voice said, yes, sure he could speak to Mr Hamilton and who was calling?

'Nick Bevan,' he muttered. 'He doesn't know me. I'm – um – a friend of his daughter's.' As soon as the words were out, he cursed himself. Why couldn't he have said a friend of Candia's? Already there was a man's voice on the line.

'Hello?'

Nick, glowering at George who had leaned closer to the receiver with the alertness of a terrier attuned to his master's voice, began to explain that he was anxious to track down Candia Mayhew who was, he understood . . .

'Hey, you're Welsh, right?'

'Yes. Yes, um, why?'

'Oh, good to hear the accent, that's all. Brings back happy days at the Arms Park. And you say you're a friend of Mary's?'

Nick shut his eyes. No going back. Just hold your breath and tread as lightly as possible. 'We met when she was filming in Yorkshire.' Worse and worse. Having claimed to be a friend, he could hardly demand her home number. George was watching the contortions of his face with every appearance of malicious pleasure.

'You're in this business?'

Nick gulped. 'No. No, as a matter of fact I'm a writer.'

'That's my boy,' whispered George.

'Shut up,' hissed Nick. 'Sorry. Interference on the line. Thing is, I'm very anxious to get in touch with Candia Mayhew. I gather she's in New York.'

'Sure she is. I forget where she's staying. They'll know in the office but I won't be back there myself until . . .' He broke off. 'Well, matter of fact, she'll be coming out here tomorrow.'

'She will?'

'I'm having a small lunch party. God knows why. Birthdays shouldn't be celebrated when you reach my age. Look, why don't you drive out and join us?'

'Oh I couldn't do that,' said Nick hastily, ignoring George's glare.

'Why not? Any friend of Mary's – or Candia come to that. Besides, I think little Candia's lonely. She'll be glad to see a friendly face from home.'

His accent was an easy mix of East Coast American and English, his warmth all American.

'I'm travelling with friends,' protested Nick. 'My agent and his wife.'

'Great. Bring them along.'

Nick cringed. 'But we're flying to LA tomorrow morning . . .'

'We'll get a later flight,' said George loudly.

'Terrific,' said an amused voice in Nick's ear. 'Look . . .'

And he proceeded to give directions for reaching his home. Mary's home. Hour and a half's drive. Say two. That was all. All?

'How very kind of Mr Hamilton,' purred George after Nick, pale and clammy-fisted, had replaced the receiver. 'Now, a man who can hold a birthday party on a Monday lunchtime two hours outside New York is a man worth meeting. Vicky, my angel, you know all about car-hire firms, don't you?' He turned back to Nick and sighed contentedly. 'For this, dear boy, I am prepared to forgive you a very great deal.'

30

Mary was standing alone on a lawn as smooth and emerald bright as a billiard table. The pillared mansion behind her had been filched off the lot of *Gone with the Wind*. She was wearing the skinny black dress again and her hair was whipping out on the breeze. She stretched long yearning arms towards him and began to gallop across the grass . . .

'Shame Mary isn't over here,' said Max Hamilton, shaking hands.

Well, that was real life for you. Nick had twisted and sweated in his hotel room all night, irrationally convinced that Mary, somehow, would be there. That her father, somehow, had forgotten to mention her impending arrival.

'And Candia's delayed, but don't worry, Nick, she's on her way, I promise. George, is it? And Victoria, good to meet you. Come in, all of you. Let me fix you some drinks.'

No lawns either. The house – more weather-boarded bungalow than mansion – sprawled amid almost-convincing wilderness with the Atlantic growling stage right.

Mary's father was . . . unmistakably Mary's father. Which only increased Nick's discomfiture at having hustled his way in here. Of much the same height as his daughter, if considerably broader, he had her long limbs, her Roman nose and looked, in spite of a glossily bald head, absurdly young to be celebrating the seventieth birthday he assured them this was. He even talked like Mary, if an octave lower, and threw back his head in uncannily the same way when he laughed. There were more subtle differences, though. Like her, this guy radiated his own energy field, but whereas the tension hummed and resonated from her thin frame like the harmonics from an overtuned violin, Dad was more laid back than a jazz bass. He eyed Nick with lazy but undisguised curiosity.

'Seen my girl recently?'

Nick swallowed nervously. 'A week – well, maybe ten days ago.'

'That so?' His eyes were the exact grey of Mary's. And at this moment they were trained on Nick like the twin steel muzzles of a shotgun. 'Ten days, you say?'

'Something like that,' he stammered, flunking the mental arithmetic. 'In – in North Wales.'

'*Wales*, eh?' drawled Max, and he invested the word with a downright sinister significance.

'We both, um, happened to be involved in a literary festival.'

'Did you now? The week before last . . .' Max smiled. The transition back from inquisitor to genial host was so abrupt Nick blinked. 'And here you are now on my doorstep. Well, isn't that great? Matter of fact, we've had another of Mary's friends roll up today to see Candia. Through here.' He ushered them into a comfortable, sun-flooded, white-plastered room with sliding glass doors open to a Sahara-sized beach. The ornaments might be driftwood logs, and the wall-hangings rugs that could have been woven by drunken, not to say myopic, sheep-farmers on a rainy night, but the place *reeked* money. Money and power.

Nick no longer wondered at an out-of-town birthday party on a Monday lunchtime. Any fool could see that if this guy felt like celebrating, a snap of his fingers would conjure up a crowd in an Arctic dawn in Alaska. Help. But he could practically hear George purring as he adjusted the old bow tie and upped gears into full-throttle social drive. Clusters of under-dressed men and under-nourished women turned as they approached, with shiny smiles on tight-jawed faces. Nick got the impression people always smiled wherever Max walked. He followed numbly, aware that every step was leading him further out of his depth, as Max glided between his guests with a touch on the shoulder here, a kiss there, halting only when he reached a particularly elegantly posed figure. Handsome as a shop-window dummy. Tall, dark and – God – horribly familiar. Not in the least disguised by (pretentious) black sunglasses which he shoved on top of his head as Max approached. 'Now then, Roddy. You and Nick acquainted?'

Roderick Chad gaped at him.

And in that instant, even as Nick was praying that this might turn out to be just one more in a long night of bad dreams, something inside him seemed to snap. Most probably his hold on common sense. Because a strange and dangerous recklessness began to bubble in his veins. After all, he was here now. There was no retreating. Word would undoubtedly get back to Mary. He'd just have to tell her (if ever he got the chance) it was all for Candia's sake. So, instead of bolting, he found himself beaming as toothily as a crocodile. 'Roddy! What a delightful surprise.' Max was nodding avuncular approval, so he continued sunnily: 'And what brings you over to this side of the Atlantic? Visiting Candia, I gather?'

'Old friends, I see,' murmured Max with the oddest little chuckle. 'And both old friends of my little Mary, too. Now isn't that a coincidence?'

'Isn't it just?' agreed Nick promptly. In for a penny, in for a mortgage.

'Nothing of the sort,' snapped Roddy.

Max raised his eyebrows. 'Oh, hang on a minute, fellah,' he drawled, with a folksy naïvety as convincing as an antique Shaker video cabinet. 'You kidding a wise old owl like me you've not been a-pining after my li'l gal for years?'

'Sorry?' squawked Roderick, caught unawares. 'No, that is, well . . .' Give the guy his due, he recovered fast. Too fast. 'I meant Nick wouldn't claim to be an old friend.' And he turned, smiling faint and damning incredulity. 'Surely you hardly know Mary?'

'That right?' said Max composedly, before Nick could frame any sort of riposte. 'You do surprise me. Excuse me, you guys, I must circulate.' And he turned to shepherd George and Victoria into a group of crumpled linen shirts by the window.

'Shit,' breathed Nick, wondering how he'd escaped un-scathed, 'I wouldn't like to play poker with that one.' He was speaking to himself, but Roderick heard.

'Max? Oh, he's a terrific chap. Once you get to know him.' The smugness with which he said this would have kindled an itch in the fists of an angel. 'I must say you're the last person I'd have expected to run into here.'

'Oh yeah?' said Nick, rising to the fly like a piranha. And he nodded in George's direction. 'Actually I'm en route to LA with my agent . . .' George, he noted without surprise, was already engaged in beaming, arm-waggling discourse with Max Hamilton and the crumpled linens. 'But you know old Max, he absolutely *insisted* we drop in here for his party on the way.' His sense of do-or-die devilry was gathering perilous momentum. 'And, of course, Mary, when we were in Llandudno together recently, said that –'

'*Llandudno?*'

'It's in North Wales,' explained Nick helpfully, savouring the chagrin in Roderick's ridiculously clean-chiselled features. 'Charming resort. Perfect for a quiet weekend *a deux*. Anyway,' he finished hurriedly, feeling this might be pushing his luck, 'she suggested I look Candia up when I was over here.'

'Well now's your chance,' hissed Roddy, dodging aside and, with outstretched arms, reassembled his glowering features into saccharine-kiss mode. 'Here she is at last. Hello, my old darling.'

And indeed, here she was. At last. Candia: sun-tanned and maybe a touch thinner. But she was giving Nick the famous, snub-nosed grin; in fact she was flinging her arms round his neck like he was her long-lost brother.

'Nick Bevan!' she shrieked. 'How completely and utterly amazing. How are you? How's John?'

In that instant, in the very way she said 'John', everything began to seem worthwhile. The wasted, frustrated weekend, the risk of infuriating Mary, the whole shooting match. Nick wrapped an arm round Candia's shoulders, neatly excluding Roderick from the conversation.

'To be perfectly honest,' he said, 'John is awful. In fact, John is miserable as all hell.'

Candia's eyes were fixed on him. 'M-miserable?'

'Sui-bloody-cidal.'

'Not – not . . .'

'Compared with my poor brother-in-law in recent weeks,' said Nick, 'Romeo's a stand-up comic.'

She laughed uncertainly. 'Are you saying . . . John's missed me? A bit?'

Nick turned and gripped both her shoulders. 'Just tell me one thing, Candia: have you missed him? Because frankly I don't think John can take –'

'Missed him?' She snorted. 'Oh for God's sake, Nick, there's not been a single solitary second when I haven't been longing for him, hoping against hope every time the phone's rung, or a letter's arrived, it might somehow, by some miracle, be him. And every time, because it never bloody is, I want to howl like a baby . . .' And more of the same, poured out with an incandescent passion beside which the screen performance that had melted audiences into slobbering heaps of Kleenex faded to mere puppetry. Playing for real, un-scripted and unrehearsed, this woman could out-Garbo

Garbo. '. . . but I can't understand why. What went wrong. I mean . . .' Her voice faltered. 'I thought at one time, OK, maybe he never actually put it into words, but –'

'Honestly, Candia, what is all this?' demanded Roderick, butting into their tête-à-tête with a puzzled frown. 'You know you decided –'

'You and I,' said Nick, ignoring him, 'need to find somewhere quiet to talk.'

'Yes,' breathed Candia. 'Oh yes, I should bloody well think we do.'

Intent on Candia's face, Nick had only dimly registered the trill of a telephone bell nearby. But it was impossible to miss the sound of his own name.

'. . . Bevan, yes . . . For Pete's sake, how should I know what he's doing over here?' Max, a few feet away, was grimacing into the telephone. 'Honey, *language*. Your mom's turning in her grave . . . Well he didn't say Llewellyn, but he's certainly a Taff so I guess that's the one. Hell, how many Nick Bevans do you know?' Max smiled round at Nick, and then at Roderick. He seemed to be enjoying an excellent private joke. 'Whose damn party is it anyhow? Seems to be your beaux stacking the place out. And I warn you, Candia's getting pretty pally with . . . Well, sure she's here with me, couldn't you have guessed? . . . Cool it, honey, you're burning a hole in my ear. Look, here's Nick and Roddy Chad, glaring at one another like a pair of stags in rut. I wonder which you'd like to talk to first.' The smile widened. Definitely, alarmingly, mischievous. He beckoned to Nick. 'Seems like you're the lucky boy. Take it in the study, why don't you? Door across the passage. I'll put this one down.' At the same time, he picked up a tumbler from a passing waiter, filled it generously with Bourbon and tucked it into Nick's hand. '*Courage, mon brave*,' he whispered, and rolled off laughing.

Like a bloody pirate king, thought Nick, prodding me off down the plank. 'With you, um, in a minute,' he mouthed at Candia as he backed away.

After the crowded room, the hall was as hushed as a church. He opened the door opposite: bookshelves, desk, leather swivel chair the size of an astronaut's. He swallowed convulsively as he strode across and, wishing the condemned man'd had the wit to request a final cigarette, closed his fingers round the telephone receiver. Monday. She *could* have got his letter. It was ... dinnertime? Well, something like that in London now. Monday evening. He'd sent it airmail Friday, so ...

'Hi,' he croaked.

'What the *fuck* are you doing in my house?' shrieked an outraged voice.

Paradoxically the vibrating fury reassured him. No, more than that, it positively inspired him, blasting new and fiery life into a very frail spark of hope.

'As Goldilocks said,' he murmured, slipping into Daddy Bear's mighty desk chair and taking a slug of his whiskey. 'More or less. Look ...'

'No, *you* look, buster. I want you out of there in ten minutes.'

'What?'

'By the time I arrive I don't even want anyone to remember you ever were there in the first place.'

Nick choked on the Bourbon. 'You arrive? Here? Mary, where are you?'

'Nothing to do with you.'

'She's in New York,' said Max Hamilton, sticking his head round the door. 'Just checking you'd found the phone.' He vanished with a wave and a wink. A wink?

'New York?' gasped Nick.

'Where, let me tell you, I've wasted two fucking hours trying to locate Candia.'

'Two hours? Do me a favour. I've spent a whole weekend on the trail. And now I have. Found her. That – for your information – is why I'm here. And because your father insisted we come. Nice man.' There was no response to this. Just a few crackles from the phone line. 'Did you get my letter?' he ventured.

'What letter?'

'I had to send it to your office because –'

'I've not been near the place,' she snapped. 'It's where I *should* be now, but Andrew had the nerve to tell me I was cracking up and I knew it was Pa's seventieth, so . . .' This time the silence was as pregnant as the pause between lightning and thunder but, eventually, she sighed and concluded tamely enough: 'And I guess I promised you in my letter I'd do what I could about Candia. So I got on a plane.'

'Concorde?'

'What? I mean – sure.'

'Thought so. Probably cost a quarter of my annual earnings. Just thought I'd mention it.'

'Well, it was a waste of goddamn money, wasn't it?' she shouted, with a swift resurgence of fighting spirit. 'I might have guessed you couldn't leave this to me. You had to stick your interfering, sanctimonious nose in and –'

'I was just about to,' he agreed cordially. 'But Candia only arrived ten minutes ago and . . . Oh, sod Candia and John. They can sort themselves out. What about you and me? For heaven's sake, tell me where you are.'

'Since you ask, the lobby of the Wessex Park Hotel.'

'The *Wessex* . . .? What are you doing there?'

'Looking for Candia, I told you. She wasn't at the studios and she always stays here and . . . What's the big joke?'

'Jeez, I've only been walking past the joint twenty times a day,' Nick groaned. 'Can you believe it? A whole weekend looking for the woman, and she was two blocks away.'

'Your own fault,' she retorted ungraciously. 'If you'd left it to me –'

'If I'd left it to you,' he shouted, 'I wouldn't be here now, and I wouldn't be talking to you and, oh God, Mary, if you only knew how desperately, ever since I got your letter, I've wanted to talk to you. There's so many million things I've got to tell you . . .' So many, he didn't seem to be able to frame one of them coherently at this minute. He took a gulping breath. 'Look, thing is, I know I may be the world's cruddiest dresser, and a clumsy big-mouthed idiot . . .'

Rattle of coins. '*Fuck.*'

'. . . and bankrupt and unfamous,' he was gabbling, 'and, hell, anything else you want to throw at me, but' – the phone was making odd noises – 'don't hang up, please, because so help me, I love –'

But the line was dead. 'No,' roared Nick, slamming the receiver into the cradle and willing it to ring, snatching it up again at the first faint bleep. 'Mary?'

'Sorry, you still there? You were saying . . . ?'

'This is hopeless,' he wailed. 'Look, my stuff's still at our hotel. Just across the street from you. Darling, please, *please*, will you promise to stay where you are now, if I get in the car this minute and –'

'No way,' said Mary, and he felt as though he'd hit the ejector button. He was hurtling down through bottomless icy space. 'You stay right where you are, Nick Bevan. Just tell me your hotel. And your room number.'

'What?'

And suddenly he could hear – actually hear – her smile. That slow, steamy, come-back-to-bed smile: 'You mean you won't be needing a toothbrush?'

'Belvedere Tower, Room three hundred and – Lord, I can't even remember.' He began, helplessly, to laugh. 'Mary, oh sweetheart, forget the room number. We're all packed, ready to go, the bags are with the hall porter.'

'Already packed?' Her answering chuckle was jingling every nerve in his body. He could swear high-voltage lust was fizzing back and forth along the telephone line. 'So you had other plans for the next few days, eh?'

'Ditched every last one.' Was his hair really quivering on end? 'As of this instant.'

'Then . . .' Suddenly, her voice sharpened up an octave: 'Shit, that really was my last dime.'

'Give me a minute,' he squawked in panic. 'Speaking as one with experience of inveigling other people's property out of hotels, you'd better let me ring them first and –'

'Fine. I'll go and buy Pa a birthday present.' She laughed. 'After all, I'm turning up at his party. I don't want him cooking up smart ideas about ulterior motives.'

'I think it might be –' But the line was dead again. Nick knew he was grinning like a Cheshire cat and wanted to yowl like the randiest neighbourhood Tom. '– a bit late for that.'

After rummaging in his pocket for a crumpled brochure, he flattened it in front of him like a piece of music and stabbed in the hotel number with the panache of Ashkenazy at his favourite Steinway.

31

'Nick? Oh sorry, didn't realize you were on the phone.'

As Candia walked in, Nick had his feet propped on the desk and the idiot grin still plastered across his face. Across his voice too, it seemed, because the hotel management clearly thought they had a nutter on the line.

'This is Gotham City,' whispered Nick to Candia. 'And I'm the bloody joker. Oh, sorry, yes, of course . . .'

Only after he'd supplied credit card details and listed his weekend's phone calls ('Want my inside leg measurement while you're at it, love?') did they agree they would hand over his chattels to the Ms Hamilton who would be arriving shortly.

'You look pretty pleased with yourself,' observed Candia as he smacked the receiver back into place.

You bet your life he was. So pleased he wanted to spread the happiness around. A serious case of the Fairy-Godmother complex. It wasn't enough simply to tell Candia that John would walk across burning rivers to get to her, that slaying the odd dragon would give his brother-in-law (animal lover that he was) positive pleasure, he wanted to prove it to her. Set everything right. Now. This instant.

'OK, OK, I believe you,' protested Candia, laughing. 'Except . . .'

Except he had to explain about Sally. And the child. And by the time he'd done that, tears were dripping off Candia's chin. No mere cinematic sparklers these: great racking, coughing sobs, touching in their very ugliness. 'Why didn't he – why couldn't John tell me himself?'

'Frightened of fouling present happiness on the wreckage of the past, I guess. Which is exactly what he did do. Silly prat.'

Candia's chest heaved. 'He is not a prat,' she declared thickly. 'He's bloody wonderful.'

'If you say so,' said Nick, prepared to be generous. 'Blimey.'

Blotched, red-nosed and piggy-eyed, she was hugging him. 'And now – I've snivelled all over your nice shirt and I can't find a tissue, and I should have guessed all along . . . Oh Nick, I just want to talk to him.'

A would-be Fairy Godmother knows his cue. 'And so you shall, my dear.'

'Don't be daft,' she retorted, indistinctly because she was blowing her nose. 'You told me you don't even know where he is. Look . . .' She sniffed resolutely, unpeeled herself from his shoulder. 'It's OK. I can wait. The moment he gets back home, I'll –'

But Nick silenced her by announcing grandly that he knew a foolproof way of tracking John down to his second cousin once removed. 'I thought of it over the weekend.' (And had promptly decided he'd better think again.) 'I'll ring Caro,' he said. 'It's her cousin too.'

'Caro?'

'John's sister. My ex-wife. Currently honeymooning on a yacht somewhere in the Caribbean.'

Candia's eyes widened. 'You're going to ring your ex-wife? On her bloody *honeymoon*?'

'She'll be enchanted to hear from me,' said Nick. 'Anyway, I want to wish her happy. Deeply, deeply happy.'

'You have an, um, number for this yacht?'

'Watch me,' said Nick, and dialled his wife's London flat. Sure enough, Caroline's recorded voice intoned that, although she was away for a few days, anyone who urgently needed to speak to her could ring, via satellite . . . 'It's simply not in Caro's nature,' he explained, stabbing the numbers she had dictated into the telephone, 'to vanish without leaving a forwarding number. She hasn't got to where she is today by letting the small matter of a honeymoon interfere with her career.'

After an orchestra of pips and bleeps, a foreign-accented voice answered.

'Can I speak to Caroline Be –' Nick caught himself up just in time. What the devil was Daniel's surname? 'To Caroline?' There was a pause. Nick smiled and rather fancied he could hear wind soughing through the sails.

'Hello? Caroline Bevan speaking.'

'Crikey, haven't you changed your name yet?'

'Shit, yes of course I have. I meant . . . *Nick?* Nick, what on earth are you doing ringing me?'

'I just wanted to wish you well. With all my heart. I hope you and Daniel are blissfully, nay, *deliriously* happy together.'

'Are you drunk?'

'Caro!'

'Well . . . Thanks. I mean, thanks very much. Was, um, was that why you called?'

'And also,' continued Nick smoothly, 'I'm ringing to enquire whether you happen to have about you your cousin Henry's telephone number. Or, failing that, his address.' He turned and nodded smugly at Candia. 'She has both. Of course. Never travels without a complete filing system, my wife. My, ah, ex-wife. Oh, thanks, Caro, great.' He picked up his pencil again and scribbled down the number. 'What? Actually I'm playing Cupid, would you believe? You remember, ahem, about Candia Mayhew? Quite, yes, as per page whatever . . . miraculous, eh? No I bloody well don't want to talk about Mr Darcy.' He thrust his hand over the receiver and mouthed something at Candia about an old family joke, too fatuous to explain. Caroline, in the meantime, was informing him that he couldn't fool her. He was high as a helium baloon and if it was Mary Hamilton pulling his string then the best of luck to her.

He laughed, leaned back and kicked up his legs as he twirled luxuriously round in the desk chair. 'OK, well, someone else's phone and all that, so my love to the son and heir and enjoy the rest of your . . . *What?*' Nick bounced to a halt, sitting upright. 'I'm sorry, Caro, I don't think I'm quite following you.' He could feel sweat chilling his forehead. He was willing there to be some misunderstanding, some obvious slip in words.' Christopher is on the boat with you.'

'Sorry? I don't get the joke.' But she was laughing. 'I was quite touched, actually, the way he cancelled all this at the last minute, just because he thought you were sounding miserable.'

'Cancelled . . .? Caro, where is he?'

Her voice sharpened, sounding all at once several thousand miles closer. 'Don't play games, Nick, I'm not in the mood. He went up to Yorkshire early instead, as you –'

'But I'm not in Yorkshire,' yelled Nick. 'I'm halfway across Connecticut.'

'What? *Where?* I don't understand.'

'I told you . . . well, maybe I didn't tell you, I forget, doesn't matter anyhow. Point is, I'm here. In the States.'

'Oh my God,' screamed Caroline. 'Then where's Chris?'

Nick drew a lumpy breath and managed an apologetic smile at Candia who was staring at him. 'Don't worry,' he croaked. 'Small domestic cock-up. Nothing to do with you.' He took his hand off the mouthpiece. 'Look, Caro, we mustn't get this out of proportion. Chris isn't a child.'

'He's just seventeen. He can't even drive a car. We put him into a cab going to King's Cross on Friday afternoon. Even if he got himself on the train up to York, what then? John . . . hell, even John isn't there!'

Nick felt his unease prickle more sharply. 'You're sure Chris was heading for Maltbury?'

'That's what he said.'

'What he said to me – specifically said to me, on Friday morning no less – was that he was coming with you. You and Daniel.'

'Christ,' wailed Caroline. 'Do you think he's deliberately . . .? I mean, he kept on and on at me to let him go off on his own this holiday but –'

'He knows I'm in the States. Course he does, I remember giving him George's office number just so he could reach me if he needed to.'

She took a shuddering breath. 'I must get back to London. And when I find the little bastard I'm going to skin him alive.'

'I'm first in the queue with the hatchet,' muttered Nick. 'Anyway – anyway, this is crazy. You're on your honeymoon. If anyone's flying back to England, well, it's got to be me, hasn't it?'

He heard Caroline's sob of relief. 'Oh Nick, will you? And please, for God's sake, find him.'

'Sure,' said Nick. 'Sure. I'm leaving now.'

'Where will you go? Where will you start looking?'

'Fuck knows. But if needs be I'll take London apart brick by brick. Caro, Caro love, try not to worry. I'll ring you as soon as I've any news. We'll keep in touch.'

He put the phone down very carefully. Turned to Candia whose anxious gaze had never left his face.

'Look, Mary's on her way.' He glanced, despairingly, at his watch. 'But she won't – can't – be here for at least another couple of hours yet. I simply daren't wait. Explain to her, would you?'

32

New York time, it was past midnight when Nick landed at Heathrow Airport, having squeezed the cheapest available ticket inside the overstretched limit of his credit card. In England, he was blearily amazed to find himself walking to the long-stay car park under a crisp and cloudless early morning sky. Tuesday morning. He had adjusted his watch as instructed on the plane. Adjusting his brain was trickier. He suspected he shouldn't drive his car. Not because he had been drinking – he had shut his ears to the siren rattle of the drinks trolley – but because he had not managed to sleep either. He supposed this must be jet lag, stuffing his skull with cotton wool and dragging his limbs through treacle.

For the past twelve hours he had been ransacking his memory for a clue to his son's whereabouts. Even before quitting Max Hamilton's in a flurry of incoherent apologies, he had been convinced this was no simple misunderstanding. On Friday morning, Christopher had said he was going with his mother. Christopher had been lying. The boy had deliberately played one parent off against the other and give them the slip.

George had insisted Nick take the hire car, murmuring that there was no need for concern about him and Victoria. Not only were they swamped with promises of transport back to the city from their newly made friends but Max (such a delightful chap) Hamilton had actually offered them a lift to LA on the company jet, which just happened to be flying via the west coast to Hong Kong. Max, said George with a beatific smile, was arranging for their luggage to be collected and the flight to be held back at their convenience. Victoria remarked caustically that if she'd known the prospect of a private executive jet would cure George's flying phobia, she would naturally have tucked one in his Christmas stocking. She added that Nick must drive carefully and not worry himself silly. Boys would be boys. She had looked at her husband as she said this.

But just what kind of boy's trick was this? On the plane, ignoring the movie and already twitchy with coffee and cigarettes, Nick recalled Chris mentioning some project in London. Expenses paid. If that was all, why lie? If he'd simply wanted to remain in town with his crony Rupert, neither of his parents would have objected. Not as long as they knew Rupert's mother was prepared to put up with him. Rupert's mother . . .

By some magical stroke of fortune, Nick actually found a number and a Hampstead address, ringed in the margin of his diary with Christopher's name. He had stretched back in his seat for the first time, weak with relief. And yet, when he finally landed and entered the terminal building, that wasn't the first number he called. It was as though he was saving this, his most promising lead. First of all, as soon as Customs had scowled his crumpled, unshaven, luggage-less figure through, he rang the Black Lion, and woke Sarah.

'Who?' Her voice, thick with sleep, tightened fast when she understood what he was asking. But no, not only had Chris not turned up in the village, she could tell Nick for a fact he wasn't at Ernie's place either. Yes, she knew he'd stayed there at half-term, but as it happened she'd bumped into Ernie in York yesterday, and he'd asked her how the lad was getting on. Oh dear, poor old Nick. Was there anything she could do?

'Not to worry,' he said hastily. 'I've a number for a friend of his, here in London.'

So then he had rung Rupert's. And waited. And ...
nobody answered. Disappointment made his head swim and
his knees buckle. Not that he'd entirely been able to believe
Chris would simply be there in Hampstead – although, by
God, he'd hoped. But, short of that miracle, he'd long since
decided Rupert's family had to be the starting point of any
search. Christopher had left from their house, the morning of
his mother's wedding. They must have some clues. But no
one was picking up the phone. At seven o'clock in the
morning. Could they be on holiday ... and Chris with them?
Hardly. Nothing worth hiding from parents in that. Perhaps
it was just that they were all in bed and couldn't hear the
ringing. Perhaps – grasping at straws now – the line was out
of order. They'd all been at home a matter of days ago. Well,
he'd just have to drive to Hampstead and find out.

Nick strode into the car park, praying there was enough
sterling in his wallet to cover the parking charges. Maybe the
blast of fresh air sharpened his wits. The warmth of the plane
had been as soporific as a throbbing womb. Suddenly, standing beside his car and fumbling for his keys, he thought of
Sasha Floyd. For no reason. None at all. Christopher had only
hung around with her at half-term, had never so much as
mentioned her name since. Not as far as Nick could recall.
The idea was crazy.

Except ... The boy had talked to him about flight times,
right? Flying back. As though he meant it. Nick didn't
believe Chris could spout total lies so fluently. He'd been
vague about times and numbers. Deliberately vague? Would
the flight details have given his little game away? But if he
was flying back, then flying back from where? Until that
moment Nick had been fuelled more by bewildered exasperation than real anxiety. Now, sitting in his car in the airport
car park with jets roaring overhead, he was remembering the
story of Mary's young and gullible film editor. Lured away
on a less-than-innocent holiday to Thailand. Oh ... God.

Funny: he'd written often enough about fear. He was a professional merchant of terror, adept at twisting the screw page by page, chapter by chapter. He knew exactly how to conjure up hot, bubbling, pulse-racing, sweating panic . . .

Crap, he thought. All these years he'd been getting it totally wrong. This was real live terror, and it was cold. He felt lead-stomached, granite-limbed and devastatingly clear-headed. Clear-headed enough to recognize and even momentarily to analyse what he was feeling. And then to be shocked at himself for doing so.

At any rate, he was sufficiently in control to crush an impulse to hurtle back into the airport and book himself on the first plane to Bangkok. Madness. Even if he could find a way of paying for the ticket, searching London top to bottom would be a picnic compared to landing in Bangkok on the merest suspicion his son might be there, wandering the streets with a junkie.

A groundless suspicion. The ravings of a fear-cranked imagination. No, drive to Rupert's first, ask the neighbours for their whereabouts if necessary and, if all that failed he'd . . . he'd think of something else. But that was the sensible course. Had to be. He yanked out the choke, twisted the iginition key and revved hard. The car coughed and farted as though it had been sitting unused for a year, not a weekend. Besides, he'd promised Caro that's what he would do, that he would take London apart brick by brick if needs be. Caro, though, didn't know about Sasha. Sasha and her dangerous friends . . .

But even if – *if* – this outrageous, no, this totally fantastical conjecture could be right, then Christopher wasn't returning yet. Not for another week at least. The boy had definitely said he wouldn't be flying home until after his dad, and Nick was back a whole week early. What's more, remembered Nick wonderingly, Chris had actually talked about leaving his flight times with George's office. Fat chance, if he was set on slipping the parental leash. Nevertheless, Nick, pulling up at the barrier of the car park, glanced at his watch. By the time Miller and Hillard opened for business he could have been to Rupert's, made a string of phone calls and probably located the little bastard.

He accelerated away from the car park like a Grand Prix contender. Half a mile beyond the Heston services, there was a mighty and terrible thump under the car as the exhaust pipe fell off.

By the time Nick finally gave up stabbing the bell and hammering the brass lion's head on the door of Rupert's house – with not so much as a twitch of life in the ruched blinds of the neighbouring houses – it was mid-afternoon. The AA man had been helpful, the garage to which he was towed had replaced the exhaust system (with much tutting and sighing over the barnacled hull of the original) as fast as the mechanics were able, and Nick had written a cheque which would undoubtedly bounce unless he spoke sweetly and swiftly to his bank. But that, at the time, was no more than an irritating irrelevance.

He hadn't wasted the day, once he'd delivered the car into their oily hands. No point in taking the tube into London just for the hell of it. Besides, a weekend scouring New York for Candia Mayhew made him wary of plunging off on a search without a few hard clues. So instead he had inveigled a fortune in change out of a nearby newsagent and applied himself to the payphone in the grimy, petrol-scented waiting room of the Eezi-Fit Exhaust Centre. At ten on the dot, he'd rung Miller and Hillard. Anthony, who handled foreign rights, answered. Sorry, but he didn't know anything about Nick's son. Nick should talk to Daisy.

'I know that,' Nick had roared. 'Where is she?'

'Dental hospital. Trouble with her wisdoms. Back by early afternoon she promised, but you know the National Health Service these days . . .'

'Don't – don't for Christ's sake let her leave the office until I've talked to her. Please.'

And then Nick, for nerve-shredding hours, had gone on ringing everyone he could think of. Rupert's (still no answer); their school; other friends (numbers supplied by school); a great-aunt; even Pentagon Productions. Who had told him in no uncertain terms that they had no idea where Sasha Floyd was to be found, and promptly disconnected. Mainly, though, people were only too sympathetic and soothing. If just one more faceless voice told him not to worry Nick felt he might smash the phone. He was finding it increasingly hard to believe that Chris was in London at all. Or that, even if he were, he was hanging out with the innocent sort of friends Nick could track down with a couple of phone calls.

The change ran out and still the car wasn't – quite – ready. Tiredness plays cruel tricks. He found himself wondering, as he dozed on a cracked vinyl chair in the waiting room, whether he wasn't perhaps dreaming the whole scenario. He even began, insidiously, to believe that Chris might be waiting for him up in Yorkshire at the cottage. Why not? He'd told his mother that's where he was going. He had his own keys to the place. He'd probably taken a girl up for a few nights of barely legal passion away from two sets of parental eyes and ears, randy little bugger. That was it. Taxi from York and of course Sarah hadn't seen him. He'd be lying low. And he'd know Uncle John was safely out of the way . . .

Nick leapt to his feet, cursing his own stupidity, and punched in his own number. The connection took so long he actually thought the hissing silence meant the call had been answered.

'Chris?' he shouted. 'Chris, are you there?' But then the ringing tone had started. And it had rung, and rung, and gone on ringing.

Now, as he finally let the brass lion's head drop back on to Rupert's door he felt tears misting his eyes again, just as he had then. Frustration, rage, sheer exhaustion. Pull yourself together, he muttered. Bloody well *do* something.

So he walked round to the High Street, found a bank. Which promptly swallowed his cash card, leaving him with rather less than five pounds sterling and a handful of dollars. Defiantly, he bought himself another packet of cigarettes and a phonecard. Finally, almost beyond feeling, let alone hope, he found a phone box which worked and wearily called George's office again.

'Miller and Hillard, good afternoon?'

'Daisy? Oh Daisy, thank the Lord you're there now. It's Nick.'

'Hello, darling, how's you?' Daisy talked like a bad rep actress playing Eliza Doolittle before the Prof got his hands on her vowels. 'Catching the worms, are we?'

'Sorry?'

'Early birds and all that. Bloody breakfast time in Los Angeles, innit?'

'God knows, but it's past five in Hampstead, and . . . look, no time for explanations. Have there been any messages for me? From my son?'

'That Christopher? Course there is.' Nick felt his knees buckle and slumped against the glass wall of the phone booth as Daisy continued cheerfully: 'He's a right one, innee? Didn't you get it then?'

'Get what? I mean – no.'

'Honestly. He sent a fax. I faxed it straight on to your hotel, oh, yesterday afternoon this was, and they promised faithful they'd give it to you, told me you hadn't picked your bags up yet and –'

'I never went back to the hotel. Too complicated to explain. What did it say?'

'Real little globe-trotter, eh? Now did I throw it away or . . .'

'*What did it say?*'

But Daisy had evidently left the phone. Someone was praying. Nick was shocked to realize it was himself. Aloud. Jingling doggerel verse, *Gentle Jesus, meek and mild, send me back my little child* . . .

'Here we are,' announced Daisy at length. 'Cleaners haven't emptied the bins. As per usual. Makes you wonder what we pay them for. Want me to fax it to you, love?'

'I'm in a bloody public phone box. Sorry, didn't mean to shout . . . Please – please, just read it to me, will you?'

'"Dear Dad, Bit of a surprise. You will notice I'm not on the love boat with other parent . . ." Oh, I get it, sorry lovey, there's a letter heading at the top. Acker . . . Can't pronounce this, somethink-somethink Hotel, um, Bangkok. Very nice too.'

'Bangkok,' breathed Nick stupidly. 'He's in Bangkok.' All the hours he'd spent busily convincing himself it wasn't possible. That this was the stuff of books, not real life. That Christopher should actually be . . .

Daisy was still reading. 'Who's this? Sarah? Sandra?'

'*Sasha?*' The name exploded out of him in a howl of rage, so raw a woman gazing into a shop window nearby turned, then jerked her dog's lead and hurried away.

Daisy was giggling. 'Come again?'

Nick drew a shuddering breath. 'Sorry. Go back a bit, will you? Tell me again what he says.'

Christopher was about to pull off the decade's coup of investigative journalism. Nick would be proud of him. As Daisy read, he could picture every word in his son's scrawly handwriting and felt tears burning down his cheeks. Sasha – Dad remembered Sasha Floyd? – was lining up fantastic contacts for him out here, had got him the tape-recorder, would fix editing facilities back home, the lot.

'Bright boy,' commented Daisy, breaking off. 'How old did you say he was?'

'Please,' he whispered. 'Just go on reading it.'

Dead cert they would be able to flog it round the independent local radio circuit. Who were only interested, of course, in sex, rock 'n' roll andYOU KNOW WHAT.

'He's put that bit in capitals,' said Daisy. 'What's he on about?'

'Nothing,' he snapped. Sweet Jesus. Worse and worse. 'What else?'

Christopher would be flying home – and by the way, if his kind-hearted Dad felt inclined to support this pioneering piece of broadcast journalism by driving down and meeting him at the airport then that would be *much appreciated* . . .

'He's underlined that bit, too,' said Daisy. 'Cheeky bugger.'

'When? When's he flying home?'

'. . . "otherwise, I'll go back into London with Sasha and catch the next train up to York. Arriving Heathrow Tuesday . . ." Er, can't quite make this bit out . . .'

Nick found he couldn't breathe.

'. . . oh yeah, week on Tuesday. That's a week today, innit? That's right, he says the twenty-sixth. Ten to eight in the morning. He's got a nerve, expecting you to get down there that hour of day. D'you want the flight number and that?'

'Yes,' he gasped, weak with relief, for the respite, the week's grace, the chance to do something. When Daisy had said Tuesday, he had felt himself slipping over the edge. Tuesday was today. He was seeing his son – at this very moment – innocently opening a suitcase under the eyes of a regiment of customs officials on the other side of the world, being bundled off to some nameless gaol, the shadow of a noose on the wall . . . 'No,' he interrupted, as Daisy began to reel off letters and figures. 'Give me the number of the hotel first. The telephone number. Is there one?'

'Sure.'

Nick fumbled to find a pen. His hand was shaking so much it took him three attempts to write legibly.

'There's another message for you here, somewhere,' said Daisy. 'Aren't you a popular boy? It's –'

'Chris? He's phoned? Another fax?'

'Nah,' she said. 'That's all from your Christopher. This was somethink to do with the new book. Now where'd I put it?'

'Doesn't matter,' said Nick. 'Thanks, Daisy. Got to go.'

33

'What?' Caroline screamed. 'I can hardly hear you. Where the hell are you?'

'I told you, back at Heathrow, and –'

'Oh my God, I don't believe I'm hearing this.'

'Look, it's OK. I think.' Hope. Pray. 'Like I said, I've actually spoken to the hotel in Bangkok. He's paid up, checked out. Flying home, they said.'

'They *said?*'

'Swore he was going to the airport. And yes of course I've been on to the airport. For pity's sake, Caro, I've spent hours chasing between airline desks here and sodding telephone boxes. Far as I can make out, he was on a flight that left . . .' Nick squinted at his watch, tried hopelessly to calculate international time gaps. 'Well, it had left anyhow. Hours late, but before I finally managed to get through to the right desk in Bangkok. Point is, Christopher is actually on his way home.'

'With what in his luggage? Why did he change plans? Why should he suddenly leave like that a week early? He can hardly have been in the country forty-eight hours.'

'How should I know? Maybe – maybe he twigged. Got the hell out soon as he could.'

'Have you spoken to the police?'

'What, to tell them my son is flying back to this country and I suspect he may be carrying a load of heroin? Caro . . . Caro, are you still there?'

'If anything happens – I'll never forgive you.' Her voice was rising dangerously.

'You think I'd ever forgive myself? Love, this sort of talk won't get us anywhere.'

'What's taken you so fucking long? It's hours and hours since you found out where he was.'

'You ever tried tracking someone down halfway across the world on a public phone system? Feeding phonecards into machines like sardines to starving penguins? Because you weren't able to locate a single old friend at home in the Greater London Area who might be able to lend you a phone, or a tenner, and you've changed your last sodding dollar and –'

'My *God*, that's just typical. You're telling me you're broke at a time like this, when I'm tearing my hair –'

'Look,' bellowed Nick, and then steadied his voice with an effort. 'Look, the panic's off, OK? The flight Chris's on takes thirteen and a half hours. It's going to be a long night. Soon as I've got my hands on him, I'll let you know.'

There was a choking sob. 'Sorry. I'm sorry, Nick.'

'Hush. Don't worry.'

'What about money?'

'I said, don't worry. But this is my last phonecard and it's running out faster than water.' He sighed. 'Anyway I'm here now at the terminal, and I won't budge. OK?'

'Won't you? I mean – shouldn't you try and get some sleep? Book into a hotel?'

With what? thought Nick. Six quid and a rubber cheque book? Besides, weary as he was, at this moment he felt as capable of sleeping as of walking on the ceiling.

After he replaced the receiver he stared at it for a few seconds. So help him, he was beginning to hate telephones. What time would it be in Connecticut now? Six hours back: two o'clock? Didn't seem possible. Hardly more than twenty-four hours since he was spinning round in Max Hamilton's huge chair grinning down the phone at Mary. He called the Connecticut number. Felt like half a lifetime ago.

And now that same phone rang unanswered. Just like a million others. All day. All bloody weekend. What the hell. There wasn't enough credit left on the card to get to the end of a sentence. Mary would understand, surely.

The Thai Airways flight from Bangkok to Heathrow was delayed. Two hours late departing, a little more arriving. By the time the plane landed, it was ten o'clock on Wednesday morning. Nick had smoked two packets of cigarettes and drunk over-priced, under-caffeined coffee until his money finally ran out and he was way beyond calculating how many hours it was since he had last slept or eaten.

He had watched crowds flow in, thicken, and then ebb and vanish again out of the echoing cathedral of the terminal. He had heard the announcers' voices change shifts. He had been instructed that the airport's non-denominational chapel was open twenty-four hours a day, and he had even contemplated visiting it. He was painfully – paranoiacally – conscious of policemen: radioed, uniformed and non-uniformed, they were strolling, standing, scrutinizing, chatting, lurking in every damn corner.

Finally – *finally* – the flight arrival was announced. It seemed an eternity, though, before a trickle of crumpled, whey-faced travellers began to emerge from the back of the arrivals hall. The trickle swelled to a crowd. He scanned the faces desperately, almost beyond believing that Christopher's could be among them. Maybe Sasha had pulled the same trick. Skipped safely out of the country ahead of him. Dumped him on the plane after hers.

Nick's hands were clenching and unclenching, the nails biting into the flesh. If it was her waif-figure that emerged from this crowd, well, God help him, he couldn't be responsible for his actions. He felt perfectly capable of murder. And the crowd was thinning. With ... no glimpse of either of them.

Then all at once, he heard a voice next to him.

'Strewth, Dad. What a fuss about nothing.'

Episode Four

From the *Daily Post*, Londoner Column, Thursday 21 July:

... also spotted in Heathrow airport yesterday afternoon was Candia Mayhew, fresh from New York. Sources tell me the bubbly British actress, 29, has been making a guest appearance in an American television sit-com. In fact, she wasn't expected to fly back until next month, but Ms Mayhew, looking not so much jet-lagged as jet-propelled, declares she's thrilled to return to dear old Blighty.

Why? Well, Candia wasn't giving away any secrets, but your correspondent suspects it might just have something to do with the blond Adonis taking charge of her luggage trolley. Six foot two, eyes of blue and very nice too ...

34

'I tell you, man, I take this very badly. Very badly indeed.'

Nick could barely will his eyes to squeeze open and he felt as though glue was binding his head to the pillow. *His* pillow? His pillow. The recognition that he was indeed at home, in his own bed, his own cottage, with Christopher safely in tow, swamped him afresh in relief so sweet it actually hurt. The telephone had not woken him. Christopher had, and unceremoniously stuffed the receiver into his hand.

A strange voice was still buzzing away like an enraged wasp: 'In my book, a verbal agreement is binding as any piece of paper . . .' An enraged *Welsh* wasp.

'Sorry?' Nick croaked. 'Look, I'm sorry. I'm half asleep.'

'At half past eleven in the bloody morning?'

'It's a long story. Uh . . . Sir Geraint?'

'Yes?'

'I meant, it is you?'

'Are you drunk?'

'Actually no. Just brain dead. Look, was there something?'

The pitch of the voice at the end of the telephone upped half an octave and several decibels. Was there something? *Was* there something? 'As far as I'm concerned,' roared Sir Geraint, 'we had secured a two-year option on your book, um . . .'

'*Snow Black*?' offered Nick, with a bleary flicker of interest. 'Terrific.'

'Terrific is it? So why, tell me, is your agent now informing my commissioning editor's assistant that the rights have been bought by one Mary Hamilton?'

The name operated on Nick like a bucket of cold water. 'Mary?' he gasped.

'Mary bought it?' he had bellowed yesterday morning at Heathrow when Christopher, looking spruce, relaxed and ever so slightly intoxicated, had informed him that this was how he'd come to travel first class. (Which frankly, Dad, was the only way to travel on these long-haul jobbies.) She'd bought him the ticket, hadn't she? At which point, Christopher had elbowed past Nick (with a muttered aside that he stank like an old ashtray) whistling and beckoning furiously.

There was a driver in the middle of the concourse. No, a chauffeur. Peaked cap, grey uniform, the full leather-gloved works, and he was holding up a large white card with the words CHRISTOPHER BEVAN printed on it.

'Shouldn't think we'll be needing you now, thanks all the same,' Chris was saying, 'since my dad's unexpectedly shown up. Although . . .' He glanced back at Nick, 'I'm not sure he's in a condition to drive us anywhere much. Here, Dad,' he hissed urgently. 'Got a fiver?'

'I haven't got five pence,' snapped Nick.

With a weary sigh, Christopher extracted a handful of change from his own pocket and handed it over to the chauffeur, who, with a little salute, tucked the card back under his arm and departed.

'D'you suppose it was a Roller?' enquired Christopher watching him with interest. 'Wouldn't be surprised, knowing her.'

Minutes earlier, Nick would have sworn that he was capable only of falling on his son's neck and weeping tears of rejoicing. Instead, he was fighting a lively urge to punch him on the nose.

'What was Mary Hamilton doing in Bangkok? Buying you air-tickets? And – and ordering you chauffeur-driven cars?'

Christopher fixed aggrieved eyes on him. 'You tell me, Dad. There I was just quietly getting into bed in my hotel room and in she rolls like the fucking KGB. Told me it was all her fault I was there. I mean, I tried to point out I *wanted* to be there, but she wasn't having it. Claimed she was acting on your behalf, and I was to come with her pronto. She wouldn't even let me pack my case, can you believe it? Handed me this crappy carrier bag and said to put my passport and anything valuable in it and next thing I know we were in a cab on the way to the airport. Driving like Nigel Mansell all the way. No kidding, Dad, she bloody well kidnapped me.'

'A hi-jacking, that's what I call it,' roared Sir Geraint Pryce-Evans in his ear. 'Daylight bloody robbery.'

'Look,' said Nick thickly, sitting up in bed and scowling at the phone. 'I knew nothing about this, right? And what I'm hearing, I don't like.'

'I will not be held to ransom. Our offer stands at what it was. If that woman wants to throw six-figure sums at you, then all I can say is, I will not be stooping to compete.'

'Six-figure sums?' bellowed Nick. 'Who the hell does she think she is?'

'Who does she think she is?' Christopher had said. While the stream of travellers swirled round and past them as though they were a couple of statues. 'Jack-booting in, and on your so-called behalf.'

'We're . . . friends.'

'You don't say,' murmured Christopher, miming a yawn.

'I'm in no mood for sarcasm,' said Nick dangerously. 'Jesus, what was she *doing* in Bangkok?'

'That's what I'm asking you.'

'How'd she know you were even there? Where to find you?'

'Oh I can tell you that,' said Christopher. 'From my own flaming fax, would you believe?'

'The hotel,' exclaimed Nick. 'My hotel, in New York. She was picking my bags up. They'd have given her the fax.'

'Apparently. And her comments on my spelling were pretty uncalled-for. I told her I didn't intend it for worldwide circulation and she shouldn't be reading private correspondence. Anyway,' said Christopher, 'she had. Nosy cow. Told me she tried to ring you at . . . well, wherever you were at, but you'd pissed off, so off she went.'

'But why?' wailed Nick. 'Why set off after you herself?'

'Search me. Except, like I told you, she kept saying it was all her fault. And she wasn't going to let it happen again, blah, blah . . .'

Sasha, thought Nick dazedly. Mary blames herself for not turning her over to the police. Even so, to hurtle across the world because my son . . .

'Know how she got from New York to Bangkok?' Chris was still talking. 'Private jet. No, seriously. Commandeered her Dad's company runabout which just happened to be revving up on a handy runway. You'll be all right there, squire. God, what with her and Daniel, I reckon I should be in line for a car on my eighteenth. I'm beginning to see there are perks to being the victim of a broken marriage.'

Nick stuck his chin out. 'And what makes you think you're acquiring Mary as a stepmother?'

'Do me a favour. I suppose she's just your tiddly-winks partner? Come on, then. We can't stand here all day.'

'Hold on a minute.' Nick grabbed his arm. 'Christopher, what the *fuck* were you doing, sloping off to Bangkok – Bangkok of all places – without telling us? With a heroin addict for company. Or didn't you know Sasha was a user?'

'Course I did. That was what I was making the programme all about. How else would she be promising me all the contacts?'

The words might be defiant but Chris was scuffing the heel of one foot with the toe of the other. Suddenly Nick could see the five-year-old who had shredded ten pages of sweated-over copy into a nest for his hamster. He blinked a couple of times. 'You great lumbering idiot.'

Chris scowled. 'I'm not stupid, Dad.'

'Oh no?'

'I'd have been fine. If you'd just left me to get on with it.'

Sepia-tinted memories of a little boy faded. 'Get on with what exactly? Next you'll be telling me drug-smuggling's as safe as train-spotting for a little holiday pastime.'

'You don't seriously believe I was planning to smuggle the stuff back?'

'Of course I didn't. I –'

'And like I tried to tell your friend Mary, there was no way any of Sasha's dodgy chums was going to plant anything on me.' Christopher met his gaze squarely. 'I'd have been careful. Was bloody careful. I just wanted to pick up some interviews, right? Like they said at Radio Dales – OK, stop snarling, like *Sasha* said – you've got to look for the big issues round your own age group. Well, this was drugs, the inside story, Bangkok to Brixton. Sasha reckoned the ILR stations would jump at it, and her production company was funding the trip so –'

'Sasha's company?' snapped Nick. 'Or her dealer? Giving a whole new angle to the concept of a *package* holiday.'

'Very funny.'

'Who's laughing? Maybe they thought it was safer using a seventeen-year-old. You're probably not old enough to be hanged. Just to rot away there for a few decades if you happened to get caught.'

The boy paled slightly. 'Look, Dad. I can see you're a bit upset –'

'Upset?' bellowed Nick and his voice echoed round the hall. A blue-shirted policeman glanced in their direction. He gulped and resumed in a whisper: 'A bit upset? Now I've heard it all. Come on, we've got to go and phone your mother. Oh my God, the phonecard's dead. How many ten pences will it take to reach a radio phone in the fucking Caribbean?'

'Keep your hair on, it's all right. Mary was ringing her from Bangkok. I gave her the number.'

'Mary? Christ, yes, where is she?' Nick looked round wildly, as though expecting her to materialize.

Christopher shrugged. 'She said she was going to find Sasha before she left. Does she know her family or something? Anyway, that's why she fixed the car for me this end. Tell you what, Dad, it makes you realize what it means being seriously – and I mean *seriously* rich. One phone call, bip, bip, bip, from halfway round the world and you get Parker there rolling up with the Lady Penelope mobile.'

Nick covered his face with one hand and groaned.

Christopher looked at him with a touch of concern. 'Actually, I'm sorry we didn't take it. You don't look fit to drive anywhere. Shall we go and book in a hotel?'

'Sure, if you want to get arrested for credit-card fraud,' said Nick bitterly. 'At this moment, I am in possession of exactly three pence, and the cash machine has swallowed my card.'

'No prob,' said his son, calmly producing a wad of traveller's cheques.

'Where the hell did you get those?'

'Mary, natch. She gave me the dosh just in case the car she'd fixed didn't . . . Dad? Dad, where are you going?'

'To the car park,' said Nick, defiantly. 'Call me stupid, call me an old-fashioned chauvinist, call me anything you like, but having had my son rescued at a cost of private jets and God knows how many million pounds it will no doubt take me the next ten years to pay off, I cannot – will not – use Mary's money to pay outrageous hotel prices to –'

'You're off your head.'

'Probably,' said Nick. 'But I'm driving us home.'

'Got enough petrol?'

'If necessary,' said Nick grimly, 'I will rob a filling station.'

'I will not,' he declared now to Geraint Pryce-Evans, 'be bought.'

'I'm sorry?'

'You heard me. Mary bloody Hamilton can offer what she likes for the rights, but it's my book, and I am not accepting charity.'

'Did you say charity?'

'I am what I am. Cruddy jeans and all, and if that's not good enough for her then —'

'Well now, I believe I'm beginning to see the light.' Sir Geraint's tone was outraged, the preacher ancestry quivering in every rolling syllable. 'Am I to understand this is not simply a professional relationship between you and Miss Hamilton? That our agreement was tossed aside like so much scrap paper because, in truth —'

'No! I mean, no, it wasn't.'

'But nevertheless you and Mary —'

'Me and Mary nothing,' snapped Nick.

Sir Geraint gave a little cough. 'Very wise, if I may say so.'

Nick glared at the phone. 'What?'

'Take an older man's advice, boy, and steer clear. Formidable female. A ball-breaker if ever there was one.'

'How *dare* you?'

'I beg your pardon?'

Nick clutched his head. 'Oh, forget it. Look – look, I've said you can have the book. Can we talk about this some other time?'

'Whenever you like, my boy.' Satisfaction resonated fatly down the phone line. 'You go and catch up on your beauty sleep.'

'As a matter of fact,' said Nick with dignity, 'I am getting out of bed. And I am going down to my local pub. And once there, I intend to get very, very drunk.'

35

It is a truth, well known in the village of Maltbury, that in the quiet hour before the Black Lion opens to the public, the proprietor is generally to be found in the saloon bar with his feet up, enjoying a half-pint of Best and a contemplative cigarette as he peruses his newspaper. That particular Thursday lunchtime was no exception.

'. . . *spotted in Heathrow airport yesterday afternoon,*' Bernard was reading, if not actually aloud, then at least by shaping the words with his lips, '*was Candia Mayhew. Sources tell me . . .* Et cetera, et cetera . . . *blond Adonis . . . Six foot two, eyes of blue . . .?*'

Bernard lumbered to his feet. 'Sarah!' he yelled. 'Blooming heck, shift your arse through here, woman, and get a load of this.'

Sarah allowed her customary few minutes to elapse before answering the summons, by which time Bernard had read the short column in the corner of the gossip page several times.

'It's our John,' he chortled. 'Look at the picture. No mistaking them shoulders. By gum, I knew the lad had it in him. Our John, God bless him.'

Sarah's half-moon reading spectacles gave her a headmistressly air, '. . . *eyes of blue and very nice too. No prizes for scenting love in the air at this airport.*' She took off the glasses and tucked them inside the bib of her apron again. 'Well, isn't that good news?'

268

And, indeed, although she was surprised, Sarah was disposed to be happy for John. The lovers, she observed judiciously, had taken a fair old time uncrossing their stars, but for all that she dared say it was a consummation to be wished. If anyone deserved their two penn'orth of bliss then John Hope-Simmonds surely did. Which was what made Nick Bevan's reaction all the more curious.

A few minutes later he shambled in. Unshaven, grey-gilled and red-eyed, he looked – as Bernard muttered in her ear – like he'd forgotten what mirrors were for. But at least he'd got young Christopher in tow who, in contrast with his Dad, was looking fresh as paint, the young monkey.

'You found him then,' Sarah cried. 'Thank God.'

' 'Tisn't God I've got to thank,' grunted Nick enigmatically.

Poor soul, she thought. Whatever was the matter with him? To cheer him up, she thrust the paper under his nose. And all he said was: 'Good, she phoned him then. Give us a large Scotch, would you, Bernard. In fact, make it a triple. And have you got a spare fag?'

Christopher, meanwhile, was pulling faces behind his back, tapping his forehead, sticking out his arms and . . . miming an aeroplane? Sarah and Bernard watched him, bemused. But when Nick turned round, the boy immediately lapsed into an inane grin and asked for a Coca Cola. 'I'm only bailed from house arrest,' he explained, 'on a promise of good behaviour.'

'Too right,' growled Nick, and clapped his emptied glass down on the bar like a cowboy in the Last Chance Saloon. 'Thanks, Bernie, I'll have another. It'll, um, it'll have to be on the slate. I'm fresh out of cash.'

'Have it on me . . .' Christopher began, but was silenced by a glare from his father.

'By heck, you're going it a bit, aren't you?' said Bernard, but shut up when Sarah suddenly kicked his shin.

'Nick's wife,' she hissed, pretending to rearrange the glasses behind her husband's head. 'Remember? She was getting herself wed at the weekend. Poor lamb. It's obviously hit him worse than he was letting on.'

'Ah,' said Bernard, nodding sagely before strolling over to Nick again with a well-filled glass. 'On the house, lad.'

Sarah smiled maternally at him. 'Would you like something to eat, love?'

'Yes,' said Christopher promptly. 'He would. He hasn't eaten for –'

'I've given up food,' said Nick. 'Impedes the progress of the alcohol through the system. Ah. That's better.'

'Dad,' protested Christopher, 'you look half-cut already.'

'Good.'

Suddenly the bar door was flung open.

'Blimey O'Reilly,' cried Bernard. 'Talk of the devil. Come in, come in the pair of you.'

Love shone from John Hope-Simmonds and Candia Mayhew bright as the halo round a pair of painted saints. Even Sarah could be heard to sigh – although only by a very sharp ear – as they laughed, called for champagne, and proceeded to hug everyone within reach. 'You dark horse,' Sarah tutted as John planted a smacking kiss on her cheek. 'Saved us all a lot of worrying if you could have sorted yourself sooner.'

John, undeceived by her severity, grinned. 'I wouldn't have sorted anything if it hadn't been for this man,' he said, turning and clapping his brother-in-law on the shoulder. 'Nick. What can I say?'

'No need to say anything,' mumbled Nick, managing a smile so forlorn it must have wrung Sarah's heart had her eye not been distracted by another figure flashing past the window. John and Candia had not arrived alone.

'What's her friend called?' she hissed to her husband. 'The big bossy madam?'

'How should I know?'

'Come on, Mary,' Candia was shouting. 'Champers on the way, and Nick's here.'

Nick's head shot up. 'Mary?' And he sounded very odd indeed. '*Mary?*'

Indeed, Mary Hamilton appeared in the doorway.

'Hey-up,' muttered the landlord. 'Who's rattled her cage?'

'Why, sure I'm here, Nick,' she drawled. If this was the Last Chance Saloon, then she was leaning against the door jamb like a visiting gunslinger who knows this bar ain't big enough for the two of them. 'Or should I say, Llew?'

Nick blinked a couple of times. '*Llew?*'

'You don't mean to say it isn't in your script that I turn up now? I should tell you,' she continued, striding into the room, kicking the door shut behind her and ignoring everyone but him, 'I've talked to your ex-wife. I rang to assure her I'd put her son safely on the plane and we had a really interesting conversation.'

'Caro?' he said faintly. 'You – you had a chat with . . . What about?'

'Oh, this and that. Like your recent unpublished writings. And don't forget I'm an authority on this particular scenario. Although frankly I think you were a bit tough on your son, sending him off to Thailand. I mean, Lydia Bennet only got herself ravished, and I'd imagine Chris would've been more than happy to stick with the original plotline there. From what I hear, Sasha's quite a hot number in that department.'

'Plot?' gasped Nick. 'Script? Mary, you can't seriously believe I ever planned –'

'What's she talking about?' interrupted Christopher. 'I say, Mary, did you find her then? Sasha, I mean? Because I felt a real scumbag just leaving –'

'Found her, paid her bill, delivered her personally back to her poor bloody parents,' snapped Mary and returned immediately to Nick. 'And so now we've finally hit the last chapter, eh? Mr Darcy sorts everything out, trots back to Hertfordshire, Lizzy falls into his big strong arms and Bob's your fucking uncle. That right?'

'Oh shit,' croaked Nick, burying his head in his hands.

Sarah, visibly swelling with indignation, prodded Bernard. He glanced at her, then cleared his throat and stepped forward. 'Now hang on a minute, madam,' he said. 'Our Nick's got troubles enough without –'

'Jet lag,' chipped in Christopher helpfully. 'As I've been trying to explain. Got to make allowances for the old man, he's been on the go for days. Only just woken up.'

Nick, peeping out between two fingers, nodded hopefully.

'I've travelled right round the bloody globe,' retorted Mary. 'Snatching naps in airline seats, so jet lagged I didn't know whether it was day, night or Christmas Eve.'

Nick dropped his hands. 'Well I couldn't sleep on the plane at all,' he said, not to be outdone. 'Fact, I didn't close my eyes at all for thirty-six days – I mean, hours – forty-eight . . . Oh hell, for *ages*, anyhow.'

'Nick Bevan, are you drunk?' she demanded in tones of outrage.

'And what's more,' he declared, rising to his feet and swaying alarmingly, 'I will not be bought.'

'*Bought?*'

'You may go jetting off to Thailand like . . .' He hiccuped. 'Like – like fucking Superwoman in pursuit of my son, and I'm not saying I'm grateful. I mean, not grateful. I mean, I am. Very grateful. Although personally I think a chauffeur-driven Roller was just a tidgy-widgy bit over the top but . . . What was I going to say?'

'Dad,' protested Christopher.

'Shut up, Christopher,' snapped Mary. 'Well, Nick? What *were* you going to say?'

'Money,' he pronounced loftily, 'is not everything. But I

haven't got any. At the moment. And that, let me tell you, is fine by me.'

'Fine by me too.'

'So I'm afraid . . . It is?'

'What's money go to do with anything?'

'The point is: you've got it. And a brilliant career and private jets and . . . and everything.'

'For Christ's sake,' she cried. 'I've spent my whole adult life fighting to stand on my own two feet and my own salary. And if because, just for once, I borrowed Dad's company plane –'

'Not that,' said Nick doggedly. ''Snot that at all. I'm talking about my book. If it's good enough, it will sell, right? If I'm good enough, I can earn my own living. I don't need you dishing up six-figure handouts just so – just so I can buy myself decent trousers.'

'He'll wreck everything,' muttered Christopher, closing his eyes in despair. 'What's the old fool on about?'

'Book?' snarled Mary. 'I haven't so much as bought a book of yours off an airport bookstand.'

'Well you wouldn't,' roared Nick. 'I'm not famous enough for airport bookstands. Well, most airport bookstands. And I'm not famous enough for six-figure television rights, either. So you can stuff your offer –'

'Look, I say . . .' Candia had to raise her voice to be heard. 'Nick?'

'Sweetheart, I wouldn't,' said John, grabbing her arm.

'I haven't made any offer,' said Mary flatly. 'Six figures. Six dollars. Six pence.'

'Excuse me,' said Nick. 'Sir Geraint let the cat out of the bag. Rang me up to tell me how George'd gone behind his back and flogged the rights to Mary Hamilton and . . .' His voice trailed off. 'But George's still in the States.' He shook his head with the baffled air of a boxer who's taken one punch too many. 'I left him at your dad's . . . Mary, have you – have you ever met my agent? By any chance?'

To the astonishment of everyone, this innocent question operated like a match on the proverbial blue paper. 'The bastard,' screamed Mary, a five-foot-eleven firework of spitting, incandescent fury. 'I knew he was up to something. I'll kill him. I swear it. This time I really will kill him.'

Nick gaped at her. As, indeed, did everyone else in the bar. 'Um, who? I'm – not following.'

'Nor me neither,' whispered Bernard. 'Sarah, love? What's going on?'

Sarah's face was tight with anxiety. 'God alone knows. But I don't like the sound of it.'

'Aye,' said Bernard, and tightened his belt purposefully. 'Aye, that's what I reckon and all.'

'My father,' Mary was yelling. 'My interfering all-powerful Big Daddy, who always thinks he knows what's best for me, can sort things out for me, do bloody everything for me. And so he goes shovelling money on to you just because –'

'Hang on a minute,' croaked Nick. 'You can't mean Geraint got the wrong . . . It couldn't have been *Max* Hamilton?'

'That's what I've been trying to tell you,' declared Candia exasperatedly. 'No, John, shush, I know all about this. I was there when Nick's agent was doing the deal.'

Nick turned to gape at her instead. 'Deal? George?'

'Well, he'd certainly given Max some book of yours, and I know they were fixing to talk soon because –'

'How dare he?' Mary rounded on Nick again. 'Just because Pa thinks you might be good for me.'

'Max actually said that, did he?' Nick began to smile, but thought better of it. 'What d'ya mean, just because I might be good for you? I don't suppose it crossed your mind your father might think my book was any good? Good for him, even? Well let me tell you, sunshine –'

'Right,' bellowed Bernard, thrusting himself into the fray, jaw stuck out. 'Right, I think I've heard just about enough.'

'What?' shouted Mary and Nick in perfect unison.

There was a second of stunned silence. Then John began to laugh.

'Darling!' exclaimed Candia, shocked. 'This isn't . . . funny.' But her mouth was already twitching. The next minute she was burying her head in John's shoulder, rocking with mirth. Even Christopher was grinning shame-facedly. Bernard, however, remained grim as a statue, with Mary and Nick glaring at one another across him.

'Either kiss and make up,' he pronounced in a voice which had emptied many a rowdy bar of a Saturday night, 'or it's on yer bikes, the pair of . . . Ow! Watch it Nick, that were my foot. Hey, you two! Hey, look, it was only a turn of speech, kiss and make up, I didn't say you was to have a blooming orgy. This is a public bar, Nick, Maggie, whatever you're called, behave yourselves, will you?'

'Go away, Bernard,' muttered Nick.

Mary squinted at the landlord out of the corner of one eye. 'Who's directing this scene anyway?'

'I can only tell you,' said Nick, indistinctly, 'that I didn't write it. Oh Mary.'

'And about time too,' sighed Candia, beaming mistily at John.

'Attaboy,' breathed Christopher, emptying the remains of his Coca Cola into a potted plant and holding out his glass to Bernard. 'Champagne all the way for me from now on.'

'Well I'll be buggered,' gasped Bernard. But his wonderment was only temporary. 'Course I saw which way the wind was blowing. Sarah? Sarah, didn't I say all along this was the girl for our Nick?'

Sarah, however, took no notice. She was screwing her apron into a ball as she leaned forward, her face uncharacteristically dark with worry. 'Nick?'

'Sarah, come here,' he said, releasing Mary and stretching out his arm.

'Nick, it's only, I mean' – she lowered her voice to a

troubled whisper – 'this, *she* . . . it can't be what you wanted? Can it?'

'What do you think?' he said.

Elizabeth Bennet put the case rather more eloquently. *It is settled between us*, she declared, *that we are to be the happiest couple in the world.* And even Nicholas Llewellyn Bevan, sophisticated master of suspense, has no objection to the slushiest of happy endings. Strictly in real life of course.

So, as credits begin to roll and a thousand strings weep, we may feel free to peep into a future which stretches cloudlessly into the blue ever after. Can this be Bernard we spy, hugely cummerbunded, emerging from a limousine? He's attending the royal premiere of *The Liquorice Fields* and a ripely pregnant Candia waddles down the red carpet after him on John's arm. We can certainly be confident that the movie will be acclaimed universally save, perhaps, in the Bristol University student magazine, whose newly arrived media correspondent, one Christopher Bevan, will already be a by-word for iconoclastic savagery. And we can even imagine Sarah, reading his column with wry amusement, as she sips aromatic coffee on the balcony of a certain docklands flat where she is a frequent and welcome visitor . . .

Perhaps. At that moment, however, Sarah, who was gaping at Nick's undeniably, indeed, scorchingly happy smile, was rapidly having to adjust her ideas along with her apron.

'Well, that's all right then,' she murmured as he hugged her. 'I suppose. Oh get away with you, you soft ha'porth, you've made me spill my drink. Anyone else wanting to slobber all over me,' she added, raising her voice, 'can find me in the kitchen. I've a party in the Public waiting this twenty minutes for pâté and toast.'

'A toast!' cried Bernard, mishearing her and seizing his glass and his chance. He climbed on to a crate of stout which rattled ominously under his weight.

'Oh crikey,' breathed Nick.

'This is nothing,' whispered Mary laconically. 'Just wait until we tell Big Daddy.'

'Raise your glasses now, Candia, Mandy . . .'

'*Mary*,' snapped Nick, and turned back to her. 'Your father'll be pleased?'

'Ecstatic.'

'I made that big an impression, huh?'

'Last hope of perpetuating the line, you jerk. No, only joking, honestly . . .'

'These boys,' declared Bernard, with just the suspicion of a catch in his voice, 'are like family to me. Straight up. So, on this auspicious occasion, it's my pleasure to welcome you girls into the family . . .'

'Mary,' whispered Nick, 'was that a proposal of marriage?'

'Course it was,' said Candia. 'Shut up, you two. Bernard's trying to make a speech.'

'. . . pleasure and, dammit all, *pride*,' roared Bernard doggedly. 'And I think I can say – without prejudice, mark you – that you couldn't have found yourself a better pair than these two lads.'

'Quite,' cried Nick, and hissed in Mary's ear. 'I accept, you lucky girl. Can I have it in writing before you change your mind?'

Mary smiled down her long nose. 'Write it yourself, buddy,' she drawled. 'If you haven't already.'

End Credits

All the personages in this story are, you may be sure, figments of fiction. But (as is insisted at tearful length in any film awards ceremony), heartfelt thanks are due to the very real people behind the scenes who have been most generous with their time and wisdom.

Script Editing	*Richenda Todd*
Screen Writing Consultant	*Geoff Newton*
Unit Transport & Travel	*Roger Rees*
Company Lawyers	*Peter White*
	Tina Hartley
Dialogue Coach	*Carolyn Mays*
Radio Co-ordination	*Ivan Howlett & colleagues at*
	BBC Radio Suffolk
	Jane Sampson
Satellite Communications	*Roger Murray*
Liquorice Consultant	*Angela Hind*
Press Officer	*Alf Gregory*
Welsh Language Subtitles	*Teleri Bevan*
Unit Catering	*Beverley Wilkinson*
Best Boy	*Ian Carmichael*
Grip	*What on earth's a Grip anyhow?*